Welcome to Harmony

Titles by Jodi Thomas

Welcome to Harmony

JODI THOMAS

**Doubleday Large Print
Home Library Edition**

BERKLEY BOOKS, NEW YORK

This Large Print Edition, prepared especially for Double-day Large Print Home Library, contains the complete, unabridged text of the original Publisher's Edition.

THE BERKLEY PUBLISHING GROUP
Published by the Penguin Group
Penguin Group (USA) Inc.
375 Hudson Street, New York,
New York 10014, USA
Penguin Group (Canada), 90 Eglinton Avenue East, Suite 700, Toronto, Ontario M4P 2Y3, Canada (a division of Pearson Penguin Canada Inc.)
Penguin Books Ltd., 80 Strand, London WC2R 0RL, England
Penguin Group Ireland, 25 St. Stephen's Green, Dublin 2, Ireland (a division of Penguin Books Ltd.)
Penguin Group (Australia), 250 Camberwell Road, Camberwell, Victoria 3124, Australia (a division of Pearson Australia Group Pty. Ltd.)
Penguin Books India Pvt. Ltd., 11 Community Centre, Panchsheel Park, New Delhi—110 017, India
Penguin Group (NZ), 67 Apollo Drive, Rosedale, North Shore 0632, New Zealand (a division of Pearson New Zealand Ltd.)
Penguin Books (South Africa) (Pty.) Ltd., 24 Sturdee Avenue, Rosebank, Johannesburg 2196, South Africa

Penguin Books Ltd., Registered Offices: 80 Strand, London WC2R 0RL, England

For information, address: The Berkley Publishing Group, a division of Penguin Group (USA) Inc., 375 Hudson Street, New York, New York 10014.

ISBN: 978-1-61664-458-1

BERKLEY®
Berkley Books are published by
The Berkley Publishing Group,
a division of Penguin Group (USA) Inc.,
375 Hudson Street, New York, New York 10014.
BERKLEY® is a registered trademark of Penguin Group
(USA) Inc.
The "B" design is a trademark of Penguin Group (USA)
Inc.

PRINTED IN THE UNITED STATES OF AMERICA

**This Large Print Book carries the
Seal of Approval of N.A.V.H.**

Prologue

JANUARY 2006

A SLIVER OF A CRESCENT MOON ROSE OVER THE farmhouse Stella and Bob McNabb leased five miles outside Harmony, Texas. Stella sat up in bed as if she'd heard a cannon.

Bob tugged off his headphones, flipped on the reading light, and waited. He hadn't been asleep, but Stella always insisted they go to bed together, so most nights he plugged in to a ball game on the radio and listened while she wiggled herself to sleep.

"I've had a vision," she announced. "A terrible vision, all black smoke and fire."

In the forty years they'd been married, she'd had a hundred visions and as far as he knew none of them had come true. "Now, Stella, just because you play the fortune-teller at the 4-H fair once a year doesn't make you psychic. The vision's probably tied to the three enchiladas you had for supper."

She glared at him, and he couldn't help but think she was one woman who definitely looked better with makeup on. Lots of makeup.

"But I saw it, Bob. Some strange kind of storm's coming. A big one. The kind of storm that shatters lives."

He patted her hand. "Don't you worry about a storm. We could use the rain."

She turned away from him and wiggled back down into the covers. "I got Gypsy blood in me on my mother's side and I know things. We better get ready, 'cause trouble's coming."

"All right, hon, I'll stay awake and worry. You go back to sleep." He put on his headphones and stared out the open window at the cloudless sky, knowing nothing much ever happened in Harmony, Texas. Odds were, nothing ever would.

Chapter 1

FEBRUARY 2006

AS THE OLD FORD PICKUP STOPPED AT THE FIRST street-light past the city limit sign, Reagan jumped off the back. Harmony, Texas, population 14,003.

She doubted the driver even noticed her departure. At the truck stop in Oklahoma City he'd only looked at the pint of whiskey she offered him in exchange for the ride.

That was the way Reagan preferred it. In the sixteen years of her life, any time someone had bothered to watch her closely, trouble followed. No one could track her this time. By morning the farmer would have a hangover and little memory of her.

For once, no one would look for her—thanks to a runaway who'd taken her bed at the shelter. Even if the impostor was discovered, foster care wouldn't search too long or hard for her. In fact, if she guessed right, they'd mark Reagan Moore off their rolls by noon as if she were resting in Resurrection Memorial Cemetery in northwest Oklahoma City. The druggie who'd climbed in to sleep in Reagan's bed had found a place to rest, and Reagan had found a way to disappear.

Flinging her backpack over one shoulder, Reagan slipped into the shadows. Harmony had been her goal for almost a year and, finally, she was here. It didn't matter if the place measured up to her dreams—nothing ever had—but at least she'd made it. She'd accomplished what she set out to do. She found the little town in the middle of nowhere. Reagan couldn't help but smile.

Six months ago she decided this place was her hometown, so she had to at least see the small farming community. No one would ever know this was her first time to set foot in town. For her, and for them, she was simply and finally coming home.

Walking in the shadows, she took in the place like an art student taking in the Louvre. Brick streets. Storefronts without bars that pull down at night. A movie theater at the far end of Main with lights blinking. Traffic moving as slow as if passing time and in no hurry to get anywhere. She felt like she'd stepped into an enchanted world.

This street was called Old Main, she remembered from an article she'd read. New Main was at the other end of town, where tire stores, a shopping mall of four one-story stores, and five small restaurants had been built. But here, on Old Main, was the way she always imagined the town to be.

The jukebox music from a diner, almost a half block away, drew her like a pied piper toward the center of town. A painting of a midnight sky and a full moon ran the awning. Above the shade were the words BLUE MOON DINER. Reagan felt as if she'd stumbled blindly into a picture-book story. She'd heard the words but never seen the drawings, and now they were coming alive around her.

The place was ten years past needing a coat of paint, but the light glowed golden from windows in need of washing just as old Miss Beverly at the Shady Rest Home had said it would.

The old lady would always say, when she talked of the diner, "You ain't been to Harmony until you've eaten at the Blue Moon."

Reagan walked inside feeling like a preacher who'd studied heaven all his life and finally set foot in it. The diner even smelled like she thought it would. A mixture of grease, baked apples, and burned toast.

A year ago she'd been cleaning rooms in a nursing home in Oklahoma City for eight bucks a room when she'd found a newspaper, the *Harmony Herald*'s Centennial Edition. Reagan had read every article, what happened in the past, what was happening in the fall of 2005, what folks hoped would happen in the future. Somehow, the town filled a place inside her. A place that had always been empty.

Home.

"What can I get you?" The waitress startled her as Reagan stuffed her backpack under the table. "We ain't got much pie left, but if it's fries and drinks, we're still open."

Reagan looked at the menu written on the wall. "Fries," she said, "and a water."

"Chili or cheese?"

Reagan stared at the chubby middle-aged waitress who looked like she'd already had a long day. Her apron was spotted, her eyes tired, but her smile was real.

"You want chili or cheese on them fries? It doesn't cost extra after ten." The waitress tapped her pencil on her pad in rhythm to an Elvis tune.

"Both," Reagan answered, thinking the doughnut she'd had for breakfast had been far too many hours ago.

The woman winked. "You got it."

Reagan leaned back in the booth and took a deep breath. "Finally," she whispered as if she could wish it true. "I just know this time I'm home."

She'd cleaned that nursing home room for a week before she'd met Miss Beverly Truman and began to stay after work to read the old woman her mail. Beverly must have been pen pals with half the town.

After they'd read all the gossip, they'd talk about Harmony. Miss Beverly might forget where she put her teeth, but she remembered every detail about the town where she'd lived most of her life.

Reagan closed her eyes as if filling in a blank on an invisible test: The night waitress at the Blue Moon Diner was named Edith. Miss Beverly always said she had a good heart and a husband who wasn't worth the iron in his blood.

She pulled her tattered manila folder from her pack and spread it out on the table. Someone had handed it to her years ago when she'd been moved from one foster home to another. It had a big label on the front with her name and nothing else. Like no address had ever belonged to her long enough to stick to paper.

She'd hidden the folder away while in transport and kept it. One envelope held all that was her. Birth certificate listing father as unknown, a copy of her mother's death certificate, a school picture from the fourth grade, and an award she'd won once in an art class. Tugging out a pencil, she scratched out her last name and wrote *Truman* in its place, then, with a bold hand added *Harmony, Texas* under her new name.

"I put the chili in a bowl so it wouldn't get your fries soggy." The waitress was back.

Reagan slid the envelope aside. "Thanks, Edith."

The woman seemed in no hurry to leave. "You from around here?"

"Yes." Reagan ate, chewing down the lies along with the fries. "But I've been gone a long time."

Edith studied her for a few minutes. "You must be one of the Randall kids that used to live north of here. Their youngest girl would be about your age."

"No," Reagan said just before she shoved another spoonful in her mouth. "This is great chili."

The waitress was on a quest and refused to be distracted by the compliment. "You Willa May Turner's granddaughter? I heard you might be coming to live with your grandparents."

Reagan shook her head. "As far as I know, I don't have a single living relative here now. Not one that would claim me, anyway."

The woman smiled. "You never know. Everybody's related in this town. We laugh and say if the gene pool gets any shallower in these parts we'll have to declare a drought."

Reagan swallowed down water and began her new life with another lie. "I'm Beverly Truman's granddaughter."

"I thought I saw Truman blood in you. Don't know where you got that red hair, but your nose is shaped just like every Truman I ever knew. Old Jeremiah Truman still lives on the homestead place a few miles out on Lone Oak Road. He's as mean as Beverly is nice; it's no wonder no woman in the county would marry him. We all miss Beverly, but we don't blame her for moving a state away just so she wouldn't have to live with him and clean around his collections."

Edith slid into the booth across from her. "How is your grandmother? We used to buy all our cream pies from her. Folks would come in here after the movies just for a slice of Miss Beverly's coconut pie. Cut our profits in half when she moved."

Reagan chose her words carefully, thinking of how Beverly would have answered. "I haven't heard lately; she may have passed on to be with the Lord." In the year she'd known the old woman, Reagan had never seen a visitor and, when she died, Reagan was the only one who cried. She guessed that made her more a relative than anyone else.

Edith leaned over and patted Reagan's

hand. "We all have to make that journey, child, and you can bet your sweet grandmother made it on the express flight if she passed. Both her grown children and her husband going before her must have left her in a powerful hurry."

Before the waitress could start asking questions Reagan didn't have the answers to, the front door bumped open and the number of customers in the diner doubled when one man entered. He looked like he could have been a model for western wear except for the anger in his eyes. Tall, broad shouldered, and furious.

Reagan took one look and fought the urge to slide under the table.

The waitress just smiled at him as if he were cute as a newborn pit bull.

"Edith!" he yelled from the doorway. "Get a thermos of coffee ready. I'll be back for it." He plowed his hand through jet-black hair and shoved his hat down hard as if about to face a storm.

The Blue Moon Diner door slammed closed and he was gone.

"Who was that?" Reagan asked, figuring this would be the first name on her list of people to avoid.

Edith laughed. "That's Hank Matheson. He's headed across the street to Buffalo Bar and Grill to break up a fight." The waitress laughed. "It's Saturday night and Alex McAllen is either passed out drunk or starting a brawl. One of the bartenders calls Hank every time to come get her before she gets in too much trouble."

"Why don't they just call the police?"

Edith giggled. "You *have* been gone a long time. Alexandra McAllen has been the sheriff for three years. Barely had time to accept her master's in criminal justice down at Sam Houston State before she pinned on the badge."

Reagan smiled and quoted a line from the Harmony paper she kept. "Three families settled in to work at the Ely Trading Post in 1887: the Trumans, the Mathesons, and the McAllens. When old Harmon Ely died, he left a third of his land to each family and together they founded Harmony."

"Good." Edith smiled. "You do know your history. Most folks driving by think we was named Harmony after a mood, but in truth, folks just got tired of calling the town Harmon Ely and shortened it to one word. Kind of a private joke for locals, being the old man was as mean as a two-headed snake on a hot rock."

Edith stood and moved around a long counter to make the thermos. "If you know that much, you also know the three families have never gotten along."

"But Hank's helping Alex, and she's a McAllen."

Edith wobbled her head so far from side to side she almost tapped her shoulders. "Yeah, and she'll hate him for saving her in the morning. Once she got so mad he rescued her that she tried to get him fired as the town's volunteer fire chief. When that didn't work, because it's impossible to fire someone who's not paid in the first place, she blacked his eye with a wild punch."

"And he still goes into that bar on a Saturday night to save her?"

Edith screwed on the top of the thermos. "I guess he figures it's the best way to irritate her."

A scream and a string of swear words could be heard from outside.

"That'll be Alex." Edith rushed to the door.

Reagan watched through the window as the waitress hurried out with the thermos to give to Hank. He was shoving a woman, fighting and kicking, into the passenger side of a Dodge Ram.

He slammed the door and climbed in on the driver's side.

When he opened the window to accept the thermos from Edith, the wild woman he'd trapped managed to open the door and was halfway out before Hank jerked her back.

Edith didn't seem concerned. She just nodded at Hank and hurried back toward the diner.

Two feet inside, she ordered, "Truman, if you want a ride out to your great-uncle Jeremiah's place, Hank said hop in and he'll take you. He's headed that way anyway."

It took Reagan a moment to figure out who Edith was yelling at. Then she remembered. She was a Truman. She'd been one for at least ten minutes now.

"Great," she said, and pulled her pack out from under the table. She couldn't stay here; it would look strange. Maybe she'd just hop out of the truck and find somewhere to sleep until morning. Down the road seemed as good as any place to go.

Edith walked her out and held her pack

as she climbed into the bed of Hank's huge pickup truck. Reagan settled in between saddles and serious-looking riding gear.

She noticed that Alex, looking tall and blond, sat perfectly still in the passenger seat, but Hank was swearing that he'd handcuff the sheriff if she tried to get out again. Reagan wasn't sure either of them even noticed her hitching a ride.

She leaned toward Edith. "Doesn't anyone think they're a little strange?"

Edith frowned and looked at them, then shook her head. "He's the only one brave enough to stand up to her when she's had a few, and she's the best sheriff we've had in forty years. Besides—"

Hank threw the truck into drive and roared down the road before Edith finished.

Reagan leaned back on one of the saddles and tried to figure out the couple yelling at each other just beyond the back window. Somewhere in an old paper she remembered reading that a McAllen had died in the line of duty. A highway patrolman maybe, or a marshal. Or maybe, she guessed, the last sheriff of Harmony.

By the time Hank turned off on the

farm-to-market road, he had to be going eighty. He hit the first pothole so hard Reagan almost bounced out of the truck bed. Three minutes later he was braking and she was rolling around in the back like the last pumpkin on the way to market.

He was out of the cab before she could settle enough to sit up.

"Sorry, kid," he said as he offered her a hand down. "Alex is threatening to throw up. I can't waste any time."

Reagan grabbed the strap of her pack and let him lift her down. He couldn't be much over thirty, but the worried tone in his voice made him seem older. When she put her hand on his shoulder climbing out, he felt solid as rock.

"It's all right. I understand. Thanks for the ride." She thanked her stars that Jeremiah's house wasn't farther from town.

"Will you be all right from here on?" Hank asked. "The old man's house is a hundred yards up that dirt road. I'd turn in there, but he's left holes wide enough to swallow the truck."

"I'll be fine." Reagan fought to keep her voice from shaking. The shady lane he pointed to looked like it could easily make it onto the "Top Ten Most Likely Places to Get Murdered" list.

Hank reached into a toolbox and pulled out a flashlight. "You can leave this at the diner or the fire station next time you're in town." He hesitated, then added, "Good luck with the old man."

Reagan took the flashlight. She didn't want to go on down the road, but she wasn't about to climb into the bed of Hank's truck again. One more mile and she would have had brain damage for sure.

They both heard someone vomiting.

Hank groaned and climbed back into the vehicle. He was gone before Reagan could figure out how to turn on the light.

Chapter 2

HANK DIDN'T SAY A WORD AS ALEXANDRA THREW up into his best Stetson while he drove across the bridge and onto McAllen land.

She lived in a cabin on the north rim of a small canyon when she wasn't sleeping at the office. McAllen land wasn't fit to farm, but when her big brother, Warren, had been alive, he'd run cattle. Alex and her kid brother, Noah, pretty much let the cattle run wild now. She was too busy in town, and Noah still had a few years of high school before he could even think about being a rancher.

The cabin that Alex now called home

had been used as a line shack years before and converted to livable by her big
brother. No one who hadn't been to the
place could have found it in the daylight,
much less in the dark, and of course, she
hadn't bothered to leave a light on.

Hank pulled up to the long porch and left
his brights on. Carrying her through the
unlocked door, he flipped on the living
room switch with his elbow. In mud-covered
boots, he stomped straight to the bathroom.
Without a word, he dumped her in the tub
and turned on the cold water, then walked
out to clean up the cab of his truck before
the smell of vomit sank into the upholstery.

By the time he'd finished and walked
back inside, Alex was wrapped in a robe
on the couch, her face resting atop her
knees. Her beautiful blond hair now hung
like wet roots about her head.

"Want a fire? I could bring in some wood.
It's getting cold."

She didn't answer.

"You can't keep doing this, Alex." He'd
sworn he wouldn't argue or preach at her
again, but she made him so angry. "What
if that trucker had taken you out of Buffalo's?" Half the drunks in the place

wouldn't have noticed if she'd been screaming and the other half wouldn't have chal-
lenged the guy.

"I wasn't going with him. I was just having fun. I would have stopped it without
you."

"Another drink and you might not have
been able to stop it."

"I could have." She sounded tired. "And
if I hadn't or couldn't, what difference would
it have made? I was off duty. I wasn't the
sheriff. I was just a woman looking to get
picked up. Last I heard, that wasn't a crime."
She glared at him. "Or any of your business, for that matter."

He fought down words he knew he'd
regret. "You want a cup of coffee?" he asked
after a moment.

"No," she said. "I'm going to bed." She
walked to the bedroom door. "Alone, thanks
to you, Hank."

He glared at her.

She turned and added, "How long does
Warren have to be dead before you stop
being my brother's best friend and let me
live my own life?"

"*Screw up* your own life, you mean."

"Whatever." She waved a hand. "I don't

care what you think anymore. I do my job all week. I should be able to do whatever I want on my own time."

He didn't argue. Grabbing a blanket, he headed for the couch.

"You're spending the night again, aren't you? Guarding over me so I don't break out and go back to town."

"Something like that." He tugged off one boot and tossed it toward the doormat.

"Well, you'd better be gone by morning or I swear I'll arrest you for breaking and entering." She slammed the bedroom door so hard it echoed off the rafters.

Hank barely noticed. It had been the way she ended every conversation they'd had since her brother died. Warren had been her hero, her big brother, the only father she claimed, but Warren had also been Hank's best friend. Alex couldn't seem to look at him without remembering Warren, and he couldn't look at her without remembering his promise to a friend.

When Warren died, something had shattered in Alex. She'd turned all her energy, all her talents, all her soul into doing her job better than anyone else ever had. Except for one tiny part of her time. Her

Saturday nights, she'd turned into her own brand of hell. The wound to her heart hadn't healed, but festered with time.

And Hank had fallen right into the fire with her. He didn't allow himself one drink, one solid night's sleep on the weekends. Somehow when Warren died, Hank had become Alex's guardian. He'd butted into her life, where he knew he wasn't welcome, and they'd been slugging it out with neither one of them having any idea of how to stop.

Hank sank down and spoke to the closed door. "The next time you want to sleep with an idiot, Alex, all you've got to do is open that door. There's one waiting right here on your couch."

Chapter 3

REAGAN WALKED INTO THE BEAM OF LIGHT FROM the borrowed flashlight, feeling like Indiana Jones. Huge old evergreens permanently bent by the wind blackened most of the path. An ancient house, with half the windows boarded up, waited at the end like a troublesome shadow in a horror film.

Not one light flickered from the direction of the house. Old Jeremiah was probably dead, she thought. Probably had been for weeks, but he was so mean no one bothered to come check.

Miss Beverly never talked about her brother, other than to say he would drive a

saint to swear. He'd served in World War II
and brought his army ways home with him
when he returned. Beverly said once that
he hated farming but, as far as she knew,
he'd never tried anything else after the war.
"Some folks," she'd said, "had rather stick
with what they can complain about than
wander off into something new that they
might enjoy."

When Beverly Truman's divorced son
had died of lung cancer, she'd decided she'd
rather move up near Oklahoma City, where
she knew no one, than have to move back
in with her brother, Jeremiah.

Reagan remembered that Beverly had
mentioned once that Jeremiah collected
something, but she couldn't remember
what. Probably skeletal remains of teen-
agers.

When she got out of the line of trees,
Reagan was surprised by the yard around
the house. It seemed orderly, the kind of
stiff, planned arrangements of an institu-
tion, not a home. She spotted several
chairs and tables turned in different directions, all facing away from the house, and
a hammock stretched across an opening
between two trees. Both ends of the porch

drooped, making the place appear to frown. Rusty wind chimes clanked in the midnight breeze.

The hammock looked as safe a place to sleep as any. She wasn't about to knock on the door and wake up the old man. A blanket she found in the hammock smelled of rain, but nothing else. Reagan wrapped it around her and crawled in with her pack cuddled against her. She'd figure out what to do in the morning. Right now, she needed sleep.

Closing her eyes, she whispered, "Harmony, I'm home."

Dreams drifted in her thoughts as they always did. She was walking through a house trying to find her room, but every night, every dream, it was a different house. Some big, some small, some with secret turns and hiding places, but in one way they were all the same. None seemed to have a room for her.

She'd just cuddled into a corner somewhere in her dream when a bright light woke her. Reagan opened one eye and watched the sun spread across an open field that shone between the tree branches. The ground looked pink, then violet, then golden. The sunrise was so bright it spar-kled white and, for a moment, the light turned the earth to a shining lake of silver.

Reagan smiled. It was the most beauti-ful thing she'd ever seen.

She heard a clank and turned to see an old man sitting in a chair five feet away. He'd put down his cup and lifted a metal coffeepot that looked like it had been used on open fires since the Civil War and never cleaned.

"You want some coffee before you start explaining what you're doing on my land, kid?"

His hands were big, and tiny scars flashed white against his tanned skin. He could have been eighty or a hundred. Once some people get so old, they kind of fossil-ize.

"Yes, I'd like some coffee . . . please." She almost tumbled out of the hammock trying to sit up.

When her feet were planted firmly on the ground, she walked close enough to him to take the cup and took a seat in the other metal lawn chair facing the sunrise. It was so rusty she couldn't make out what the original color had been.

The sun was a ball now, sitting on the horizon, and the morning pushed all shadows away.

The old man watched the dawn and didn't seem too interested in her. He also didn't seem worried or afraid she might try to rob him. Maybe the seventy-pound German shepherd at his side accounted for some of that. The dog watched her as if he thought she might be a take-out breakfast.

"You got the Truman nose," Reagan finally said.

"I've been told that before. It's the only nose I got and I'm a Truman, so ain't no surprise to me that I got a Truman nose. You come all the way out here to tell me that?"

"No," she answered, wondering what she could tell him. "I hadn't planned to come out at all. I was just talking to Edith at the diner and she asked some guy named Hank to give me a lift out here. I guess she thought because my name is Truman that I might be welcome."

"Well, you ain't," Jeremiah said. "I welcome company about the same as I do black mold."

"I figured that." Reagan really hadn't expected the world to change just because she made up a hometown and a last name, and a dead grandmother. "I guess I was just wishing."

"What were you wishing for?" he asked, not sounding like he cared much what the answer was.

"Oh, I don't wish *for* things. I gave up on that years ago. Never got me anywhere." She drank a long draw on her coffee and added, "If I do anything, it's reverse wishing."

He raised a bushy eyebrow on a face so wrinkled a mosquito would have trouble finding a landing spot.

"You know," she said, just to talk. She'd never see him again after a few minutes, so she might as well tell him her thoughts. "People are always reverse wishing around me and they don't even know it. Like them saying, 'I wish you'd never been born,' or 'I wish I didn't have to take care of you,' or 'I wish you'd move on and leave me in peace.' That's the only kind of wishing that I've ever seen work. So I don't wish for good things to happen, I just wish the bad things would leave me alone for a while."

"And if you were doing this reverse wishing, kid, what would you wish for?"

She couldn't look at him. His eyes were so hard and cold they could have been frozen marbles. She'd be better off to go back to the diner and ask Edith for a job. Maybe she could even find a place to rent a room somewhere and tell everyone she was eighteen. Only problem with that was she was a sixteen-year-old who could pass for twelve. Half the people she met couldn't even tell if she was a boy or a girl.

"I'd wish, if I were reverse wishing, that I didn't have to leave this place."

He was silent for so long, she thought he'd surely died on the spot. Then he said, "You can stay for breakfast, and then I'll take you back to town. Looks like it might rain today, and I wouldn't want you falling in a mud hole on my land and suing me."

Reagan looked at the cloudless sky and decided the old man had floaters in his eyes. Miss Beverly had floaters. She was always swearing there were bugs in her oatmeal.

Jeremiah stood slowly, as if testing to make sure his legs still worked, then walked toward the house. "We're having eggs." He didn't turn around. "Damn chickens keep laying them faster than I can eat them."

She watched him, not believing he'd invited her to breakfast. Somewhere an ounce of Miss Beverly's goodness must have been in him. She ran and caught up to him just as he stepped in the side door.

She wasn't sure what she'd expected, but a spotless kitchen with long countertops and linoleum almost scrubbed off the floor hadn't been on her list. Everything, from the walls to the appliances, was in black and white. She felt like she'd stepped into an old, old movie.

Jeremiah rolled up his sleeves. "You think you can make yourself useful by squeezing the oranges while I cook?"

"Sure," Reagan answered as she reached for the top orange in a white mixing bowl.

"Wash your hands first, kid."

After she did that, he had to show her how to cut the fruit and grind them over this strange bowl with a bump in it. "I didn't know you could do this to make the juice," she said, loving how easily the center of the bowl ground out orange juice.

"Where'd you think orange juice comes from?" he asked.

"The store," she answered.

He turned his back to her, and she wanted to believe that he was smiling. More likely, he was thinking she was the dumbest kid ever born.

They didn't talk as they ate eggs and toast made with homemade bread. He'd dotted it with butter, then sprinkled sugar and cinnamon over it before sliding it into the bottom of the oven. The sugary mixture had bubbled and crusted over the bread. She decided it had to be maybe a hundred times better than toast made in the toaster.

"You in school?" he finally asked.

"I was," she answered between bites. "I dropped out. If I wait a year I can take the GED test and it'll be just like I'm a high school graduate."

"Smart, are you?" He didn't sound like he believed she was.

"Smart enough." She took a breath and dove in. "If I could stay around here, I could help you to earn my keep. I wouldn't be any trouble, and I don't eat much."

He glanced at the empty plate he'd shoveled five eggs onto a few minutes ago. "I can see that."

"I could clean and I could learn stuff that needs to be done." She fought to keep her voice from shaking, thinking of all the times in her life she'd begged to stay when someone was telling her to go. She knew all the excuses. *There's not enough room. You're getting too old. It's time to move along before you get too attached to one place.*

She straightened. She'd be fine without him. She'd find somewhere in town to stay.

He frowned at her. "What's your name?"

"Reagan Truman."

He scratched his beard. "Got saddled with two presidents, did you?"

She forced herself to show no reaction.

"Well," he finally said as he stood, "I guess you could stay for a while. There's a ton of work to do on the orchard before spring. I always have more work than I have time to do, and spring may come early this year. I can't pay you much, but I'll give you room and board for two hours' work on weekdays and pay you for up to eight hours' work on Saturday."

"I can work more."

"I wasn't finished. I got one rule, other

than if you mess up the kitchen, you clean it."

"All right, what else?"

"You go to school every day. Folks who think they've learned everything they need to know are usually dumber than chickens."

"But . . ."

He turned his back on her and moved to the sink. "That's my terms. Take them or leave them. I don't much care. If you're going, don't slam the door. If you're staying, bring that plate over here and wash it."

Reagan didn't know whether to laugh or cry. He was letting her stay, even offering to feed her, but she'd have to go to school and she hated school. "I could work all day every day." It would be easier than being the outsider with tattered clothes. The child no one talked to. The student in the back of the room trying to be invisible all day.

"No." He snapped out the words like a drill sergeant. "It's not open for discussion. My house. My rules."

She had a hint of why his sister might have left. Only Miss Beverly must have had money to move to Oklahoma and get a room at the nursing home. Reagan had four dollars in her pocket. "All right. I'll take your offer and am grateful to have it." To her surprise, she meant it. She'd somehow survive school if she could stay in Harmony, and this seemed the only way.

"How dumb are chickens, anyway?" she asked as she washed her plate.

"They'll stand in the rain watching until they drown." He almost smiled. "And believe me, kid, you don't want to be that dumb."

Chapter 4

TYLER WRIGHT HATED SUNDAYS ALMOST AS much as he hated Halloween.

Folks probably thought since Sunday was the only day he didn't do funerals that he'd like the time off, but they'd be wrong. As the town's only funeral director, he never had a day off. More often than not he'd have to drive somewhere and pick up a newly departed, or get ready for a service on Monday morning. On weekends when he didn't have a corpse waiting in the morgue, there was always a mound of paperwork he never seemed to finish.

"Morning, Tyler," someone said from behind him.

Tyler moved up the line toward the counter before he turned around and smiled. On Sundays the only place to get a good cup of coffee was at the shop in the bookstore, and Tyler loved any kind of brew he didn't have to make himself. The problem, of course, was that he'd run into people if he went out. There was always someone who'd been a member of the family from a funeral he'd done last week or ten years ago. They'd know him, sometimes even hug him. After all, he'd done them a great service during their time of grief. He'd been there, he'd handled things, he'd been their rock in stormy seas.

Only problem was, Tyler never remembered them. He was one of those cursed people in the world who didn't remember names or faces. They'd be bawling on his shoulder, telling him how hard it had been since the death of their loved one, and he'd be trying to place them.

"Morning, Mr. Wright," a pretty teenager said as she took his coffee order.

"Morning," he answered with a smile while he tried to remember where he'd seen her before. The great-granddaughter of someone he'd laid to rest about six months ago, he decided, or maybe she sang in the Baptist choir. They were always pulling the whole choir in for a Baptist funeral.

"You want two blueberry muffins with that, like usual?" she asked.

Great, he thought. *She remembers my order and I couldn't swear in court that I'd ever seen her before.* With a lucky glance, he noticed her name tag. "Yes, thanks, Gracie."

She handed him the muffins and Tyler tried to find a chair that faced the wall. Otherwise, he'd be talking to every third person who walked by. There weren't more than a dozen people in town that he could relax enough around to enjoy talking to, and it looked like none of them came in for Sunday-morning coffee.

Why don't these folks go to church, he wondered, then the coffee shop would be empty and he could enjoy his breakfast and *New York Times* without having to talk to anyone. Tyler rarely went to church. He'd usually filled his quota of visits by Friday every week.

He slipped out the side door planning

to eat in his car, as he did almost every Sunday.

"Something is wrong with me," he said aloud as he wiggled beneath the steering wheel. Whoever heard of a funeral director afraid of people? He didn't like idle talk with folks dead or alive.

Tyler almost spilled his coffee laughing as his employee Calvin came to mind. That man usually talked to the customer all the way from the embalming to the dressing as if he were a shoe salesman trying to get the fit right.

Taking a bite of one of the muffins, Tyler decided his problem was he didn't know how to have a real conversation with most people. All he ever talked about was death. *I'd kill myself, but then I'd feel bad about someone else having to drive to Harmony to take care of my body.* Tyler smiled and thought, with his luck, Calvin would do the job and talk to him until they closed the lid.

A lady with two little boys walked in front of his car and waved at him.

Tyler smiled and waved back. There were even too many people in the parking lot these days. Starting his car, he headed

WELCOME TO HARMONY   39

for the Wright Funeral Home, an impressive white stucco building on West Street.

He was the son of a son of an undertaker. He'd known how to act and what to say to people crying over a body since he crawled out of the crib. His ancestors had moved to Harmony after Harmon Ely died, slicing the town up and giving it to the residents since Ely had no kin. His great-grandfather had been penniless after the Civil War and missed old Ely's funeral by a matter of weeks. In so doing, he also missed out on any split of land.

Tyler thought about how his family hadn't missed a funeral since. Great-Grandfather came to Texas looking for a fresh start. They would have starved if he hadn't hung a sign in front of their shack that read: WILL UNDERTAKE ANY WORK OFFERED.

The offers were made for several kinds of labor, but the job no one else wanted to do was to dig graves and prepare bodies for burial. Tyler's ancestor took on the responsibility. Within a year he'd learned to build a coffin overnight and embalm a body in the kitchen before the women started preparing the funeral meal.

As the town grew, so did the Wright family. In thirty years, two sons worked with their father. They not only made caskets for the dead of Harmony, but shipped them all over the state. They'd built a funeral home as grand as any business in town. Tyler's father, the only male heir, took over the reins of the funeral home while his three sisters married and moved away. He'd planned to have a big family, but he'd waited until almost fifty to marry. Tyler was his only child. So for Tyler there was no one else to take over. Four generations had built up a business, a trust, a life in Harmony.

Tyler had no doubt that all before him would haunt him if he sold out and left, but still, he imagined living in a beach house down on the gulf. He dreamed of talking to a woman who forgot to ask what he did for a living, but at forty years old and fifty pounds overweight, he doubted the dream would ever come true. He longed to have a conversation that wasn't related to dying.

He pulled his Cadillac into his space outside the three-story building. The first floor consisted of offices, a chapel, and state-rooms for viewing. The basement housed the embalming room and storage. The second and third floors were the only home he'd ever known: a five-bedroom rambling apartment, where he lived alone.

Tyler unlocked the door to his office and sighed as he stepped inside. He might as well get some of the paperwork done; then he wouldn't feel so bad about spending the afternoon and evening with his hobby. If he went upstairs before dinnertime, his seventy-year-old housekeeper would glare at him as if she were sorry he hadn't died of a heart attack while out.

Alone in the huge oak-paneled room his grandfather had built, Tyler sat in his desk chair, turned on the computer, and did what he did every morning. He checked his e-mail.

He began deleting. Thank-you notes from families. Advertisements. He'd moved through twenty before one caught his attention.

The subject line read: *Hi from Quartz Mountain.*

He knew no one from Quartz Mountain. He'd stopped at a lodge there almost a year ago. He'd been on his way to pick up a body in Elk City and decided to take some time and wander the back roads.

Both his employees had offered to go, but he looked forward to the drive, only the ice on the back roads had forced him to pull over and a lodge tucked away in the hills around the lake had been his only choice.

The stay at the lodge had been uneventful, except for the dinner he'd shared in a darkened bar with a woman also traveling. They'd been about the same age, early forties and all business in a room full of fishermen and vacationers. They'd sat in a shadowy corner near the view of the water and talked of the Native American artwork lining the walls of the lodge and of their childhood vacations spent on lakes. Tyler remembered shaking her hand and introducing himself, but he didn't remember her name. Her e-mail address was simply a jumble of numbers and letters offering no clue.

Her eyes though, he'd never forget . . . warm hazel like a cloudy day in late summer.

He clicked on the e-mail.

Stayed at the lodge again and thought of you. Since I remembered your last name, the clerk gave me your e-mail. Just wanted to say hello.

Tyler smiled and wrote: *How is my hazel-eyed dinner guest?* He watched wondering how long it would be before she answered.

When the screen blinked, he jumped in surprise.

Fine, she wrote. *Do you remember the art?*

Leaning back in his chair, he described a few of the wonderful pieces that had drawn him that night. She answered back with details on some of the artists she'd learned on her latest visit. The lodge was gearing up for a big weekend and the halls were full.

He told her of the tribes he'd looked up in southwestern Oklahoma just because of one painting that had seemed so alive it could have stepped from the frame.

He wasn't sure how it happened, but they e-mailed back and forth for a half hour.

Finally, she wrote: *Have to work. Loved talking to you. Let's do it again. Kate.*

He stared at the screen. Kate. Her name was Kate. Glancing over at his forgotten coffee and muffin, he smiled. If he had a few more conversations that were this interesting, he'd be below two hundred pounds in no time.

Three hours later he wrote Kate back.

How about taking a break and having lunch with me?

Staring at the computer, he waited until she blinked back. *Give me five to get my salad.*

Pulling a Coke and a couple of candy bars from the break room, he waited. When she came back, he lied and told her he was also eating a green salad.

They talked about food and the weather and how much they both wished they were on a beach. Neither asked any personal questions. She'd told him a great deal without writing a word. She was working on Sunday and in no hurry to go home. He knew without asking that she lived alone.

When she finally wrote: *Have to go.*

He asked: *Tomorrow?*

She answered: *You bet. Is nine too late? I've got a hell of a day, but visiting with you would be a nice way to end it.*

I'll be waiting.

Tyler turned off his computer and grinned. He'd talked to someone, really talked . . . well, almost talked . . . and they hadn't mentioned death once.

Chapter 5

REAGAN HATED HAVING TO GO TO SCHOOL. She'd enjoyed Sunday working in the orchard with Jeremiah. He didn't talk much. He just showed her what he needed her to do, and she did it. In a strange way she liked taking care of the trees, mothering the saplings and trimming up broken branches.

Old Jeremiah gave out and had to sit a while about mid-afternoon, but told her he thought she should learn to drive. She picked up leaves and threw them in the back of a cart he called his little truck. She felt like she was really driving for the first time, even though her truck was the size of a golf cart with a pickup bed welded on the back.

When she circled by him to ask what to do with the dead branches, he was sound asleep. By the time he woke up, she had another load of limbs stacked and ready to transport.

They'd stopped at sunset and had a supper of ham sandwiches and fried potatoes, then he'd showed her a room with all the furnishings covered in sheets.

"This used to be my sister's room. If she comes back, we'll have to find another place for you."

She didn't have the guts to tell him Beverly was dead. He'd ask too many questions.

They took the sheets off everything and he gave her a fresh stack of linens to make up her bed, then closed the door without a word.

The place should have made Reagan feel creepy with all the old pictures and old furniture, but everything reminded her of Miss Beverly and nothing about the old woman had been creepy. Reagan pretended she'd come to visit Miss Beverly and been welcomed.

She slept without waking all night. At dawn she awoke to Jeremiah pounding on her door.

"If you're going to have time to eat before you leave for school, you'd better hurry up."

She pulled back on her same clothes she'd worn working the day before and ran downstairs. In the shadows of boarded windows, she saw the other rooms. All were covered with sheets as if no one lived except in the kitchen. A light shone beneath a closed door down a dark hallway. She guessed that must be Jeremiah's bedroom, but didn't ask as she moved to the counter in the kitchen and began making juice.

"I don't want to go to school," she complained as he shoved oatmeal and toast in front of her.

"I don't care," he answered.

"I don't have any of my papers to transfer in."

"I'll take you. They'll let you in."

She wasn't so sure. "If they don't, can I come back here? There's still a ton of work to be done out in the apple trees."

He didn't answer. By the time she finished

washing up her breakfast dishes, he and the dog were waiting outside in an old green pickup.

A few minutes later, he walked into the school and told the assistant principal that Reagan Truman was enrolling. No one questioned him. In fact, half the people in the office looked afraid of him, making her wonder just how mean Jeremiah Truman was.

She shrugged. He was good to her. That was all that mattered. She didn't care if the volume on him was broken. Reagan almost laughed. She'd been tossed around so long that anyone who didn't hit her was considered a saint. Jeremiah had fed her, given her a place to sleep, and driven her to school. So what if he didn't talk to her? He was high on her list of friendly.

When they passed her paperwork to fill out, he walked to the exit without saying a word to her, then turned at the door and bellowed, "You got a bus that goes down Lone Oak Road after school?"

"Of course," the assistant principal answered.

"Then see that she's on it."

Reagan wrote her name without looking up when the door slammed.

The assistant principal glanced down at the paper. "Reagan Truman," he read aloud. "You related to that old man?"

She nodded. "He's my great-uncle."

"Sorry about that," he answered.

Reagan raised her head and glared at him. "Don't you ever say anything about Uncle Jeremiah. Not ever."

The assistant principal looked surprised and more than a little angry, then took a breath and answered, "You're right. I was out of line. You got a right to stand up for your kin. Welcome to Harmony High."

If anyone else had anything to say about Jeremiah Truman, they kept their mouth closed. Reagan had a feeling they were thinking that she was definitely related to the old man.

Chapter 6

TUESDAY MORNING AT SEVEN FIFTEEN, HANK Matheson walked into the diner with his four-year-old niece on his shoulder. Two days a week he drove her into town for pre-school, and on Tuesdays that always meant breakfast out.

He removed his straw hat as he shoved the door closed with his foot. He missed the felt Stetson, but Alex had ruined it. He had no idea when he'd have time to drive over to Lubbock for a new one. It was too early in the year for straw to feel right.

"Let me hang it up," Saralynn squealed.

He leaned forward so she could reach

the rack, his hands firmly on the metal braces around her legs. "Thanks, Princess."

"You're welcome, Horse. Now gallop on."

"Morning, Saralynn. Hank," Edith said as they passed her. "Hope you can find a seat this morning. Place is hopping."

"I'm a princess today, Edith, and this is my horse."

Edith's quick one-second smile told Hank she didn't have time to bother with the kid's fantasies this morning. Last week Saralynn had been a frog and would only croak. "Find a seat, I'll get to you when I can. The morning waitress quit on Cass as he unlocked the door. Said she'd thought about it and decided she was a night person. When he told her he'd see if I'd be interested in trading shifts, she also decided she wasn't a waitress person. If he don't find someone soon he'll be serving the meals as well as cooking."

Hank moved down the row between booths. Cass lost several waitresses a year. Some said the only reason Edith stayed around was because she worked nights and didn't have to put up with him much. Others thought Cass might be easier to get along with than Edith's husband waiting for her at home.

The place was packed. He saw one empty seat in a front corner booth that held only two. Trouble was, Ronelle Logan was in the other chair. No one in town ever sat at the same table with Ronelle. She wouldn't have allowed it if they tried. Ronelle worked at the post office sorting mail. If you wanted your mail, you left her alone, so Hank kept moving down one of the center aisles.

Hank noticed that the only other open seat was half of a booth in the middle of the room. The other half was taken up by the local undertaker. Hank moved through the crowd, relieved to find a seat across from someone who wouldn't talk his ear off.

"Morning, Tyler. Mind if the princess and I join you?"

He carefully lifted his little passenger down. Hank would have sat her next to him, but Saralynn pointed to the space next to Tyler.

The chubby man grinned. "I'd love to have royalty join me for breakfast."

"I'm Princess Saralynn," the thin child

said. "And you are Sir Wright, my most trusted knight."

"Great." Hank gently moved her legs beneath the table without bumping anything. The slightest bump would cause a bruise on her legs. "I get to be the horse and you're knighted."

"Can't win them all, Chief." Tyler Wright laughed.

Hank nodded while he tried to think of something to say to Wright. "How's business?"

Tyler looked up from his paper. "Business is slow. Only one pending."

"Anyone I know?"

Tyler shook his head. "You know what they say, the young leave this town for the big city and the dead return to be buried with their kin. This newly departed had been gone from Harmony for sixty years. Half his kin don't remember him."

"Well, it's only Tuesday. Maybe business will pick up." Hank smiled. He liked the undertaker. He considered Tyler Wright a friend. They'd shared breakfast at the Blue Moon more times than either of them could count.

His chubby friend asked Saralynn, "How's your mother?"

"Fair," Saralynn said as if she were grown and not four. "She's stopped crying and started painting."

Hank studied his menu. He didn't like talking about his newly divorced sister, but he guessed everyone in town knew she'd moved back to the ranch. She'd re-painted her old bedroom for Saralynn and turned the attic into a studio loft, where no one was allowed. In the four months she'd been back she'd done six paintings, all of men dying horrible deaths.

"Glad to hear she has a hobby." Tyler pulled a quarter from his vest pocket. "I've been saving this for you, Princess Saralynn." He handed it to her. "It's the new one."

Saralynn smiled. "Thanks. I'm going to collect them all." She turned it over in her hand. "Do you collect anything, Sir Knight? I could help you."

Tyler shrugged. "I like old maps. I'm kind of a cartophile."

"Really." Hank was taken aback. He'd known Tyler all his life and never thought to ask if he had a hobby.

Saralynn lost interest in the conversation

and began playing with her quarter. Tiny hands slid it from one hand to the other.

Tyler looked embarrassed. "Yeah. I got maps of this area that go all the way back to the cattle drives. Sometimes I drive out trying to see how much of the original roads are still around."

Hank wanted to know more, but Edith was back. "What'll it be?" She pointed her pen at Saralynn. "The usual for you, one pancake with blueberry eyes and a banana smile."

"Yes." Saralynn straightened. "And oats for my horse."

"That's right, the usual for your uncle."

She turned to Tyler. "And you, Sir Knight?"

"I'll just have coffee for now." He folded his paper.

A few minutes later, Edith slid a diet special of two egg whites, dry toast, a cup of blueberries, and oatmeal across to Hank. He ordered the same meal every Tuesday.

"There you go, Hank, try to enjoy it." She turned to Tyler. "Did you decide what you'll be having, Mr. Wright? We got biscuits and gravy with sausage in it for the special this morning."

"No thanks." Tyler closed his eyes as if

forcing himself to forget the offer. "I think I'll have what Hank's having."

Edith stared at him as if she saw proof of alien occupation. "All right. Anything else?"

"No," Tyler answered.

As the waitress walked away shaking her head, Hank was smart enough not to comment. He wouldn't ask. One of the things he liked about sitting with Tyler was neither got too personal with questions. That and Tyler always remembered that Saralynn collected state quarters. Anyone who was nice to his niece was all right as far as Hank was concerned, even if he did have a strange hobby.

Tyler straightened the gap in his shirt. "I'm thinking of taking off a few pounds."

"Oh." Hank put jelly on his bread, then took a moment to clean syrup off the princess's face.

"Yeah. I know it won't be easy," Tyler added as he winked at the little girl pouring more syrup on her smiling pancake. "I'm invited to every family meal after the funerals, and everyone knows there's no better food than funeral food."

Hank nodded. "If you decide to work out some, you're welcome to come down to the fire station. We got some pretty good exercise equipment." He didn't add that he'd bought most of it and moved it to the station, hoping the other men would use it. Some of the volunteers were barely fitting into their uniforms.

"I might do that," Tyler said. "Thanks for the offer."

Hank drank his coffee, thinking that Tyler wouldn't exactly fit in with the firemen. Willie, just a kid whose parents made him move out the day he turned eighteen; Brad, bunking there because he was in the middle of a divorce; and Andy, who stayed around because he didn't want to go home alone. Twenty other men made up the volunteer fire department, but they came when needed and then left.

Edith set a box down on the end of the table. "Sheriff brought this by and said to give it to you when you came in."

Hank looked at the box. He didn't have to open it. He knew what it was.

Saralynn lifted the lid with sticky fingers. "Look, a hat, just like the one you have, Uncle Hank."

"Had," Hank answered without offering any further explanation. The town had enough to talk about without him telling everyone within hearing distance what happened between him and Alex in private this weekend.

Edith leaned her head over as she studied the Stetson. "What I can't figure out is how she guessed your size."

"It's not the first she's bought," he answered, wishing they'd move on to something other than the Stetson.

Tyler helped him out with the first thought that crossed his mind. "They say it may rain this weekend. We might get some relief from this dry spell. If it comes with a cold front, I wouldn't be surprised if we don't see a late snow."

Edith looked bored and moved on down the line of booths.

Saralynn picked up her napkin. When it stuck to her fingers, she began waving the paper square, letting it dip into her plate of syrup and dribble about.

Both men decided not to notice.

"I wouldn't mind rain," Hank said to Tyler. "Fire danger signs have been up so long they're starting to look wind-worn." The grass had browned enough to burn fast and hot if sparked. "A grass fire could cost dearly in lives and property." His volunteer forces hadn't been trained properly to fight the hundred-acre fire two years ago that had taken one life, and they weren't trained now.

Hank wondered if Tyler, too, could still smell the odor of burned flesh. Hank and his men had fought the fire, but when one man suffered a heart attack and fell into the flames, it had been Tyler and his crew who'd tended, with loving care, to the blackened remains.

Edith walked by and took the napkin away from Saralynn with a stern look at both men.

"Don't look at me," Hank snapped. "I'm just the horse."

Tyler straightened. "And I would never question a princess." He placed his paper over the sticky table, hiding the evidence.

Edith looked at the mess. "I expect royalty tips double?"

Both men nodded. As soon as the waitress moved on, Tyler moved his paper away so the princess could continue her syrup painting.

"Did you hear old man Truman's great-niece is in town?" he asked Hank.

"I thought she might be since I dropped

a kid out by his place a few nights ago. Couldn't imagine anyone going out to the place unless they were kin."

"They say she's grumpy as Truman, but that couldn't be possible." Tyler laughed. "The last time I asked Jeremiah how he was doing, he accused me of trying to drum up business."

Edith passed Tyler his plate and all conversation stopped while they ate.

A few minutes later, Alex McAllen walked in dressed in her tan uniform. She looked all business with her hair tied up and her gun belt around her waist. She looked around, her eyes narrowing when she spotted him. She headed over.

Official trouble, he thought, wrapped in a body he couldn't keep out of his dreams lately. One of these days he'd voice his thoughts and Alex would probably get so mad she'd shoot him, putting them both out of their misery.

"Move over," she ordered, looking like she might flash her badge if he didn't make room for her.

Hank did so without comment, but Tyler smiled a welcome. "We'd love to have you join us, Sheriff," he said motioning for Edith to bring another cup. "I'm having breakfast with Princess Saralynn."

Alex winked at the tiny girl. "Morning, Princess. Morning, Tyler."

She didn't look at Hank. He might as well have been the horse in the room.

"I just have a second. Phil called in a few minutes ago from his patrol south of town to tell me there's a cow in that grave you dug last night."

"Great," Tyler mumbled as he scooted out the far side of the booth. "I've got until two to get it out before the graveside service. Won't be many at the service, but they're bound to notice a cow in the grave."

Hank bumped her leg with his, forcing Alex to look at him as he laughed. "Whose cow is it?" The cemetery was bordered by McAllen land. It had to be one of the half-wild cattle that ran over her land.

She turned her sky-blue eyes directly at him and said sweetly, "Yours."

He frowned, but didn't move his leg away. Neither did she. He couldn't tell if she liked his touch or was just calling his bluff. "How's that possible? My field's five miles from the cemetery."

"One of your men was hauling a dozen

head in this morning and it appears he forgot to latch the trailer gate. There are Matheson cattle scattered out for half a mile along the cemetery road."

"Any hurt?"

"Phil said they're all standing, except the one who fell in the open grave." She slid from the booth and smiled. "I wanted to be the one to tell you."

He stood. "I'll just bet you did." He grabbed the new hat without saying another word and lifted Saralynn out of the booth and onto his shoulder.

"I want to go see the cow," Saralynn yelled as she tried to clap her sticky hands.

As everyone at her table left, the sheriff called out, "You're welcome!"

Hank stormed to his truck trying to figure out which he disliked more, Alex drunk or Alex sober. He waved as Tyler pulled out. "I'll meet you there."

He had no idea how to get a cow out of a six-foot hole, but they had until two to figure it out.

Chapter 7

Two days, Reagan thought, two days and no one had said anything to her. She'd seen them watching her. Knew they talked about her. But not one person at Harmony High had been mean to her.

She walked out the side door of the cafeteria and found a bench to eat the apple she'd brought with her for lunch. She'd thought of asking Jeremiah for lunch money, but her pride wouldn't let her. He already fed her breakfast and dinner.

A dry wind blew from the west. The warmth of it surprised her because she'd felt like the temperature had been almost freezing at dawn. She watched dirt from the field next to the school whirl in a tiny dust devil. The baby tornado widened and rose, blending with the wind. Reagan shifted, not wanting to be pelted when the dirt blew over her.

A tall, thin shadow crossed the ground in front of her. She looked up.

"Hi." A boy, so thin he looked stretched, folded to the ground in front of her like some kind of double-jointed metal chair. He pulled a bottle of juice from his pocket. "Mind if I join you?"

Reagan ignored him. She'd seen him before. How could she have missed him? The guy was a head taller than almost everyone in the sophomore class. He had a bad complexion, a farmer's tan, and a lopsided smile. All he needed was an L painted on his forehead and he'd be the complete package.

"It's nice out here." He looked around and lowered his hat against the dust. "I can see why you'd like leaving all the noise behind." He took off his battered cowboy hat and propped a corner of his backpack against it so it wouldn't blow away.

She stared at him. "Maybe I just want to be alone."

Stretching out one booted foot, he nodded as if agreeing with her.

"Completely alone," she added, hoping he'd get the point.

After a long draw on his drink, he asked, "What's your name?"

"What do you care?"

He laughed. "I care because if you're about to walk into traffic or fall off a cliff, I could yell at you." He gulped down more juice.

She glanced at the road in front of the school. "Don't have much traffic around here, and I've yet to see a cliff."

He tossed his empty juice bottle in the trash next to her bench, then stood in front of her as if waiting for her to look up at him.

Reagan refused. He could stand there like a pole all day.

"I'm Noah McAllen, but most folks call me Preacher," he said finally, in a low voice flavored with determination.

Great, Reagan thought. The only thing worse than being picked on by a bully was being recruited by the school religious nut. Despite her resolve, she looked up at him.

"You got the most unusual color of hair." He frowned. "No offense, but it kind of reminds me of the color of the mud down at the Salt Fork of the Red River. Kind of red and brown at the same time."

She thought of snapping something back at him, but she wasn't sure he meant it as an insult.

"Look, Preacher, I don't need saving, I'm not interested in dating, and I'd just as soon not be your friend, so why don't you go peddle 'Let's be friends' somewhere else."

A grin spread across a face that could almost grow a beard. "They call me Preacher because I seem to get religion when I ride bulls. I'm the junior state rodeo champ. Not to hurt your feelings, but I don't want to date anyone—but I wouldn't mind having a friend."

"Why?"

He shrugged. "Maybe just to have someone to talk to that's been outside the city limits."

"I'm not good company." She'd spent far more time in her life arguing than talking. "I'm not easy to talk to."

He shook his head. "That don't matter.

If I liked easy, I'd go out for football or track."

She hid a smile as she took a bite of apple. "Reagan," she said as she chewed. "Reagan Truman."

He nodded, and she was pretty sure he'd already known her name. "Trumans and McAllens don't get along in this town, but I guess I could make an exception. After all, you may be the last survivor in that clan, and McAllens grow like weeds." He offered her his hand. "Friends."

She stared at him for a long moment before she shook.

Leaning down to pick up his hat and backpack, he added, "Don't worry about the way I look. In a few years, when my face clears up and I get a little more muscle around these bones, I'm going to be a hunk. Then, Reagan Truman, we'll talk about dating."

Reagan laughed.

He raised an eyebrow. "Don't you believe me, Rea?"

"Sure," she answered. "The way I see it, you've got nowhere to go but up in the looks department and, as far the dating, I'll pass on that."

He fell backward as if shot, then lifted his head and smiled at her.

Just for a second, underneath the pimples and patches of facial hair, she saw it. A glimpse of what he'd be. Noah McAllen was right. In a few years he'd break half the hearts in Harmony. He wouldn't even notice by that time that she wouldn't be one of them.

He put on his tattered cowboy hat. "See you, Rea."

"See you, Preacher."

Chapter 8

THURSDAY, 8:30 A.M.

SHERIFF ALEXANDRA MCALLEN CLIPPED A CELL phone onto her belt and moved toward her cruiser. She'd rather arrest a drunk or pat down a drug offender than have to play the Grim Reaper. But there was no way she could pass off this duty to one of her deputies.

She had to drive out to Jeremiah Truman's place and tell him his sister was dead. It was her job but a hell of a way to start the day.

As she backed out of the parking lot, it occurred to her that the old man might have a heart attack and die on the spot at the news. He had to be close to ninety by now; he'd been old all her life.

She swung around to the fire station. Maybe she could talk one of the firemen into going with her. It made more sense than going alone. Most of the men who volunteered at the station had more training in emergency care than she did; Hank had seen to that over the years.

Alex smiled. At least she wouldn't have to worry about Hank being at the firehouse. He always worked his ranch during the week. If he did come into the station, it was usually before dawn to work out or at night for a meeting.

She told herself she could care less about his habits, but it was hard to miss his huge Dodge pickup when it was parked directly across from her office. She pulled into the empty spot marked as his and ran up the steps.

"Morning, Sheriff," Willie Davis yelled from beside the fire truck's engine.

Willie was the youngest volunteer fireman. He was rail thin and had hair that always seemed a month past needing a cut.

Willie had quit school two years ago, but Hank hadn't let him start training until he was eighteen. Then, he couldn't get enough of the station. If Hank had allowed it, Willie would have moved in permanently.

"You missed a spot." She pointed at the dirty bumper.

He sloshed his bucket back a few steps and frowned. "You're right."

Alex didn't step closer, fearing he'd accidentally turn the water hose toward her. "Anyone else around?" Willie would be little help on her mission. At the rate he was learning, he'd be in training for another ten years.

"Hank's in the office. He had to drop his truck off for an oil change, so he said he'd catch up on paperwork till the work was done. You want me to go get him?"

She backed away. "No. Never mind. I don't want to bother him."

Hank stepped out of the office before she could get out of sight. "What do you need, Sheriff?" he asked as if they barely knew each other.

"Nothing really."

He kept staring at her with those dark eyes she swore were more black than brown. He had chameleon eyes, she decided, changing with his moods.

She knew he'd never believe she'd dropped by to visit, so she decided the truth would be the best way not to look like a fool. "I was just headed out to Truman's place to give him some bad news, and I thought there might be one of your men around who'd come along in case the old man takes it hard." She started backing out the door. "But I see everyone is busy."

"I'll go with you." He grabbed his jacket and hat. "Willie, load up one of the medical aid kits in the back of the sheriff's car."

Alex wanted to argue that he didn't need to come, but she wouldn't risk a life just because she hated the thought of being with Hank. They were both professionals. They could ride a few miles out of town and back without yelling or hitting one another. After all, this was Thursday morning, not Saturday night.

Heading out to her car, she tried not to think about what happened at ten every Saturday night. Her life felt like some kind of reverse fairy tale. When the clock struck ten, her mind filled with the memory of her brother lying spread out on the center stripe of a two-lane road. He'd bled so much a river of red had run off the asphalt and into the dirt.

It had been three years ago. She'd just returned to Harmony that night, a week away from graduation and wanting to celebrate. Alex had been waiting in her brother's office for him to get off work when the call came in that he was in trouble. She'd ridden out with one of the patrolmen, thinking her brother must have had a flat or dead battery.

But his patrol car was still running, its lights on bright, shining across his body. She'd watched from the shadows as Hank Matheson and two medics fought for her brother's life . . . Hank had kept fighting even after the others stopped. Finally, he'd held his best friend, her brother, and cried as he said good-bye.

And she'd watched and said nothing . . . done nothing.

Silently, Hank now climbed into her cruiser. Alex pushed her memories aside as she threw the car into reverse before he closed the door.

They were almost out of town before he

asked, "What's the bad news for old Jeremiah Truman?"

"Beverly Truman died almost a week ago.
It took a few days to find anyone to call who
knew her next of kin, and then the morgue
in Oklahoma City couldn't get in touch with
Jeremiah. Apparently he doesn't have a
phone. They overnighted him a letter three
days ago, but I wouldn't be surprised if the
old guy never bothered to open it."

"So they called you?"

"Right." She glanced over at Hank, who
was frowning as usual. "How do you think
he'll take the news that his last relative has
died?"

"I don't know. He's had two heart at-
tacks that I know of. My aunt checks on
him now and then since we're neighbors,
but every time she does, she comes back
mad and claiming the old guy doesn't have
a heart. Last time she took him her Christmas sponge cake, he declared it to be far
more sponge than cake, and you know
how Aunt Pat feels about her prizewinning
cakes." Hank grinned. "Aunt Pat says it's
hell being a good Methodist with old Truman for a neighbor."

Alex smiled, finding it hard to imagine

Miss Pat ever saying *hell*. The old woman and her sister were in church every time the door was unlocked.

Hank was silent for a minute, then added, "You were right to come get me. The old man may take it hard. He's not the last Truman, though. His great-niece is living with him."

Alex turned off the main road. "What niece?"

"The one we—" Hank stopped. "Never mind, you wouldn't remember. Edith said the girl is Beverly's granddaughter. I don't know where she came from, but she's been out there since Saturday night."

Alex kept her eyes on the road. "How old is she?"

"About fifteen or sixteen, I guess. She'd be in school right now."

"I'll go there next. She may want to come home." Alex turned off Lone Oak Road and into the long tunnel of evergreens that led up to the house. The road was neglected, with steep drop-offs in places where pavement should have been, and trees blocked the sun. "Overgrown," she said to herself as she looked at the tumbleweeds and trash caught in the low branches.

"Fire hazard," Hank added. "One spark and these trees would burn all the way to the house. Half of them are more brown than green."

They pulled to a stop. Hank followed her up to the front door.

Nobody answered when she knocked.

"His truck is here." Hank pointed at an old pickup parked beside the house. "He's probably in the orchard."

"If he were around the house, that dog of his would be barking." Alex looked around. "Last time the old canine chased me all the way back to my car. I don't know if he has enough teeth left to bite anyone, but I didn't want to take a chance."

Alex walked back to her car and reached in. She honked twice and waited. "When I got the news," she said quietly to Hank, who had joined her by the car, "I called Tyler Wright and woke him up. He said he'd take care of the details. The body's already been embalmed so it could be shipped, but Tyler said he'd go get it. He said Miss Beverly would want it that way."

From a distance, they heard the puttering sound of the cart Jeremiah drove around his place. The dog was riding shotgun, growling louder than the motor.

Alex stood straight, waiting, dreading her duty. After more than a hundred years, the three of them represented the original families of Harmony: the McAllens, the Mathesons, and the Trumans. How strange it seemed that two of the families had multiplied many times over but the Trumans were almost all gone.

Beverly had been Jeremiah's only sister. She'd had two children, both already buried in the Harmony Cemetery. The son divorced without children. No one had ever heard of the daughter marrying, though she'd been gone from Harmony for twenty years before she died. She could have had ten husbands and a dozen kids from the time she left until Beverly brought her home to be buried. Apparently she'd had at least the one. Strange that Beverly never mentioned Reagan. Maybe she hadn't approved of her daughter's choices or known about children left abandoned along the way. Maybe her daughter wanted nothing to do with Beverly or the town she grew up in and had kept secrets. Most people leave out details they don't like about their family but it seemed odd that Beverly Truman left out a granddaughter.

The cart came into view from between the trees. The old man leaned over the steering wheel, his body so thin she swore she could see the outline of his bones from a hundred yards away.

Sucking in a breath, she steeled herself for what she had to do. Hank's hand pressed lightly against the middle of her back. "Breathe," he said in a none-too-friendly order.

She pushed his hand away. "I hate doing this."

"I know," he whispered.

"What're you two doing here?" Jeremiah yelled when he was ten feet away. "It's too far away from Halloween for you to be coming dressed up like civil servants."

Alex waited until he came to a stop. Just as he'd always been old to her, she'd probably always be a kid to him, she thought. "Good morning, Mr. Truman."

He unfolded from the cart without offering his hand in greeting. "What do you need? I'm betting you didn't come out to pass the time and since I don't smell smoke,

Matheson, it must be the sheriff making an official visit."

"You're right," Hank said. "Why don't we step into the shade on the porch?"

Jeremiah tugged off his hat and let stringy white hair blow in the breeze. "Bad news don't taste better in the shade. I'll take it in the sun, thanks anyway."

Alex cleared her throat and did her job. Efficiently, cleanly, without emotion.

Jeremiah stood in front of them and took the news of the death of his sister with no change of expression. His hard face must have frozen into a frown years ago. Only a nod told Alex he'd even heard her words.

Hank had moved close enough to Truman to be able to catch the old man if he collapsed.

When Alex finished talking, Jeremiah looked out at the orchard and said nothing.

"Would you like me to drive you to town so you can talk to Tyler Wright later about the arrangements?" she finally asked.

"No," he responded. "He'll know more what Beverly would want than I would. Tell him to just do it and send me the bill." He dropped his hat, but didn't seem to notice.

Hank picked it up and tried to hand it to the old man, but Jeremiah just looked at his feet. Hank placed the hat in the back of the cart.

"What about your niece?" Alex wished the old guy would at least look at her. "Hank said she moved in with you last week. I could go get her from school so you wouldn't be alone out here."

"My niece?" Truman huffed as if he'd forgotten he ever had a niece.

"Mr. Truman," Hank said politely. "You remember her. Reagan."

Truman looked at Hank as if he'd just noticed the man was there. "Of course I remember Reagan. She's been helping me for almost a week. Good worker, that one, even if she can down more eggs than a lumberjack."

"I'll go get her." Alex glanced at Hank.

He seemed to read her mind. "I'll stay here until you get back, Sheriff."

Truman grumbled that he didn't need a babysitter, but Alex ignored him. If Truman could forget he had a niece, he didn't need to be left alone.

In her car, she circled back down the

tree-lined road to the pavement and headed toward town.

Five minutes later, she walked into the high school office and asked to see Reagan Truman.

Chapter 9

REAGAN WATCHED A STUDENT OFFICE AIDE deliver a note to the worst history teacher in the world. The teacher paused in his dull lecture to read the note and then look directly at her.

She was in trouble. She knew it.

"Reagan Truman," he snapped. "You're wanted in the office."

As she gathered up her books, Reagan heard the aide whisper to one of her friends in the front row, "By the sheriff."

The urge to run bubbled in Reagan's blood. Big trouble. She tried to think of something she'd done lately. She had been in school only four days . . . not long enough even to have skipped a class. She did steal that pint of whiskey she'd paid for her ride from Oklahoma City to Harmony with . . . but surely the law wouldn't track her across the state line for that.

As she walked past Noah McAllen, he winked at her. "Maybe you won the lottery, Rea."

She tried to smile. "I didn't buy a ticket, Preacher."

"Tell me about it at lunch," he offered.

"If I'm still on the loose."

He laughed. Apparently he thought she was kidding.

Just outside the door, the tall woman sheriff was waiting. She was too pretty to be a warden in a B movie, but she was all business just the same. Even if Reagan had thought of an escape plan, she wouldn't have had time. Sheriff McAllen looked totally sober today and perfectly capable of arresting her.

"Reagan Truman?"

"That's me." She thought of adding *Almost*, but saw no need to confess to any new crimes. Besides, swapping out her last name didn't seem like a major crime.

"Mind if we take a walk outside?" the sheriff asked, but Reagan knew it wasn't really a question.

Reagan followed the sheriff out the door. This made sense. By the time the law finished listing her crimes, they'd be at the police car and the sheriff could toss her in the back.

"I got some bad news," the sheriff said. Reagan started, not from the words, but from the sheriff's arm around her shoulders.

"I just came from your uncle's house."

"Did he die?" Reagan pulled away from the sheriff. "Don't tell me he died." If he died, she might as well cut herself up in little pieces and market herself on the Internet as a bite of bad luck.

McAllen mistook panic for caring. "No, honey, he didn't die. He's fine, but I'm real sorry to tell you your grandmother did pass away."

Reagan hid her face in her hands, needing time to figure out her imaginary family tree. Her made-up great-uncle was still alive; good. Her made-up grandmother was dead. No news there. Only the town must just be finding out about Beverly Truman.

If the sheriff had told Jeremiah, and now was here calling him her uncle, the old man must know she'd lied to everyone about being his niece. Reagan decided she'd been nuts to think he wouldn't find out, but she had hoped it would be later, not this soon.

The arm of the law came around her again. "I'm so sorry," Sheriff McAllen whispered. "Go ahead and cry if you feel like it, Reagan."

Cry! She wanted to scream nonstop. The old man was just starting to like her . . . well enough to grunt at her over breakfast, at least. He hadn't even paid her yet and she'd worked almost a week. Now, he'd probably have her arrested for impersonating a Truman. One hope flashed through her thoughts: Jeremiah hadn't told the sheriff she wasn't his niece. Maybe he was waiting to expose her in front of others, or maybe, just maybe he also wanted to believe in the lie.

Reagan didn't look at the sheriff as they drove back to his place. McAllen was saying all the things she figured a sheriff would say. Reagan tried to think of where she could go next. Oklahoma City wasn't an option, and when Jeremiah told the sheriff she wasn't his niece, staying here wouldn't be possible, either. Reagan knew that clinging to the hope he'd go along with her lie now was about as likely as trying to convince herself he liked having her around.

She had two dollars in her pocket and nowhere to go from here.

They got to the farm so fast she swore they must have teleported. Reagan kept her head down as she followed the sheriff up the steps where Jeremiah and the fire chief who'd given her a ride out last week were waiting. There was no telling if Truman was furious. He looked angry on good days.

Hank Matheson nodded at her in greeting, but didn't speak as Reagan passed him and faced the old man. If Hank planned to complain about her not returning his flashlight, he'd have to get in line. A wholesale load of trouble was already headed her direction.

"I'd like to talk to my niece alone." Jeremiah looked over Reagan's head at the sheriff and Hank. "You two can take the cart and go see how the apple trees are doing.

Hank, I expect your aunt Pat will want some this year as always. I put in a gate in the fence between your land and mine. She's getting too old to climb over the fence and check on the trees." He waved them on with one bony hand. "You tell her I'm taking good care, and both of you stay out of the mud where I'm irrigating."

Reagan fought down an unexpected smile. Jeremiah was treating the sheriff and the fire chief like they were ten years old.

Jeremiah motioned her into the house as the cart pulled away toward the apple trees. For a second she thought about calling them back, but something inside her knew she had to face the old man alone. She owed him that much. He had a right to have his say after what she'd done.

He went to the first room to the left of the front door. It looked like an old parlor Reagan had seen once in a movie set. She'd never set foot in it and, from the layer of dust, she guessed he hadn't either in years.

He ordered her to open the shutters. "We got some things to straighten out, girl. We might as well do it in the light."

"Yes, sir," Reagan said, giving him a mock salute. If she was going to get kicked out, she'd go her own way.

"Don't get smart with me," he said as he pulled the cover off an old rolltop desk. "We ain't got time."

He sat in an office swivel chair while Reagan fought with the shutters for several minutes. When the room finally flooded with sunlight, she took a seat on the nearest window bench and waited. About the time she decided he must have slipped into a coma, Jeremiah reached for something.

Reagan stared as he retrieved a roll of bills tied with a rubber band from one of the pigeonhole drawers.

He looked up at her and, for the first time, she saw sadness in his eyes. The kind of sadness that made her heart hurt to look at it. She dropped the attitude and leaned closer, recognizing grief so deep he couldn't speak of it.

No word she could have said would have helped.

Finally, he took a deep breath and cleared his throat. The mask of anger returned to all of his face except his eyes. "I have no desire to go to town and have folks hugging on me just because Beverly died. It won't bring her back. She was a silly woman who should have stayed here with her family."

"She wasn't silly," Reagan corrected. "I think she just liked her privacy."

He glared at her. "So you did know her. That much at least isn't a lie."

"I cleaned her room at the nursing home where I worked after school and read the paper to her. Sometimes I even read her letters to her. We'd talk about Harmony."

"She tell you why she left?"

Reagan shook her head. Miss Beverly had been sad, but not lonely. There's a difference. Even though all her friends were miles away and she only talked to them in letters, Reagan got the feeling she wanted it that way. Beverly had told her once she had a hundred books she'd planned all her life to read. If Reagan had thought about it at all, she probably figured that was why Beverly stayed at a quiet place like the home.

Jeremiah huffed. "She said it was because she couldn't live with the memories of her husband and kids in town and she didn't want to live with me out here."

"I guess you two weren't close."

He was silent for a few moments. "I was in the army by the time she started school. When I came home, she was grown and married. We were never close. A part of me still thinks of her as that little girl I'd swing around. We never had much to say to each other after I came home from the war, but she was my sister and I want to do right by her."

He shoved the money toward Reagan. "You go into town with the sheriff. Buy a new dress for Beverly, a nice one, and order a big bunch of flowers to set on top of the casket. Beverly would like that. Just tell the store to make sure Tyler Wright gets them as soon as possible."

Reagan almost swallowed her gum. "All right," she managed.

He wasn't finished. "While you're there, you might as well get yourself some clothes. Something nice for the funeral and whatever you need for school. I'm tired of looking at those you got on. I've seen refugees fresh off the boat who dress better than you do."

"But . . ." Reagan couldn't argue with his opinion of the clothes. They were hand-me-downs from the thrift store. But the money . . . She'd never held this much money in her hand in her entire life.

"If everybody in town thinks you're my niece, you might as well look like you're not living on the streets." He stared at her. "When the funeral's over, I'll go into town and set up a few accounts for you so you can charge what you need at the drug-store and that Lady Bug store that claims to have everything females need. I'll not tolerate excess, but I am aware a girl needs certain things."

"You're not kicking me out?"

"You got somewhere else you want to go?"

"No." She almost added, nowhere that she *could* go, but she figured he already knew that if she was staying here.

"Spend what you need and put any left over back in this drawer along with the re-ceipts." He pointed at the square little drawer in the middle of the desk. "If you want to air out this room, you can. It's yours to use if you need it." He cleared his throat. "Beverly always liked to read in this room when she was a kid."

Reagan twisted the roll of money in her

hand. No one had ever trusted her with a dime. "Thanks for letting me stay . . . Uncle Jeremiah."

She waited for an explosion, but none came.

He moved to the front door. She followed and they watched a battered old pickup pull up behind the sheriff's car. "I'm the last Truman," he whispered, more to himself than her. "If you want to pretend to be family for a while, I don't mind."

Reagan shifted beside him, guessing he wouldn't welcome a hug. "If I go to town with the sheriff, how do I get home?"

"It ain't that far. I've walked it many a time," he said. "But, if you want, I'll drive over about five and pick you up near the post office. We could go to the funeral home and pay our respects. I imagine Beverly will be waiting there by then."

They walked onto the porch just as Noah "Preacher" McAllen reached the first step. The old dog, who barked at everything, including fireflies, was licking Noah's left hand in welcome.

"Who are you?" Jeremiah demanded. "Folks are wearing out my road today."

Preacher removed his hat. "Noah

McAllen," he said. "And if you don't mind me saying, there's not much of a road to wear out, sir."

Jeremiah snorted, and Reagan wondered if that was his idea of a laugh.

"I heard about your sister dying, Mr. Truman, and I'm real sorry," Noah said. "I want you to know if there's anything I can do to help . . ."

Jeremiah frowned. "News travels fast."

Noah smiled. "Cell phones. I called my sister when I heard she'd pulled Rea out of class, and she told me. I came straight over to see what I can do."

The old man stared, taking measure of the kid before him. "You could drive her to town. She'll be making the arrangements. I've got work here that can't wait."

Reagan shoved the money into her pocket, and Noah barely had time to say good-bye before she pulled him toward the truck.

Once they were on the road, an awkward silence rested between them. Preacher looked like he was worried about her breaking into tears. Reagan couldn't tell him that she'd known Miss Beverly was dead for almost a week.

Finally, she broke the silence. "How come old Dog didn't bite you? He still looks at me like I'm a burglar half the time."

Noah shrugged. "I'm good with dogs and babies."

"Try again."

He smiled. "I tossed him the last of yesterday's lunch I'd left in the truck. He ate it, bag and all."

Chapter 10

HANK GRABBED TWO OF THE WALKING STICKS IN the back of the cart and handed one to Alexandra.

She followed along behind him, glad to be away from the scene at the house. "Does your aunt Pat really climb over the fence and steal apples?"

"Yep, and I drive the getaway car. She says they make the best pies in the county. She also considers it her duty to check on the trees now and then to make sure Jeremiah is taking care of things."

Alex pulled on one of the branches,

feeling it give in her hand even though it looked dead with winter.

"Now if you'd like to join the thieving come spring," Hank said, "you have to do it right, so listen to the rules. Only get the ones on the ground. Aunt Pat says then it's not stealing, it's retrieving."

Alex laughed at the thought of Hank's eighty-year-old aunt stealing apples. "You know I could arrest her for it whether she's picking or lifting."

"Go ahead," he said as if he meant it. "One less woman at my ranch would suit me fine. I got my mom, two widowed great-aunts, two divorced sisters, and a four-year-old fairy princess. I haven't said a word at the dinner table in five years."

Alex raised an eyebrow. She almost felt sorry for him. No wonder he spent so much time at the fire station. The old family ranch had been his unofficially since he turned eighteen, but his mother had always lived there. When Hank's two great-aunts retired from teaching school years ago, they moved in. Then Hank's sisters came home a few months ago, both broken from divorces. She couldn't imagine how Hank handled them all. Two old women, two divorced women, a mother who thought of herself as an artist, and a four-year-old niece too ill to walk.

When Alex looked up, he was smiling. She'd almost forgotten what he looked like when he smiled.

"Arrest them all," he said. "I could use the silence. Aunt Pat may steal them, but Aunt Fat eats them."

Alex laughed. Hank had always called his two great-aunts Pat and Fat, even though his aunt Fat was thin. She'd known the two old ladies all her life and had no idea what their first names were. When they'd taught they'd both been called Miss Matheson.

"How long have you been helping your aunt in these robberies?" She pointed a finger at him.

"All my life." He held the old walking stick up as if on guard. "Plan on arresting me, too?"

"No. It'd just be a waste of time. Your aunt would recruit another mule to haul her loot. I might as well wait until I catch you all red-handed."

She swung her stick in challenge. He blocked. She swung again, and the fight was on. They moved into the shadows of the trees where the air was still and cold. Something seemed different here. As if they'd stepped out of the real world and into the Sherwood Forest of their childhood dreams.

The aroma of freshly watered soil circled around them. She wondered if Hank felt it, too, but she didn't ask for fear of breaking the spell.

When he raised his hands in surrender, she laughed, remembering how it had always been Hank who let her win when they were children and never her brother Warren.

She looked at him, wondering if he, too, was remembering how the three of them had played in the trees as children. But Hank's eyes were smiling. They were two outlaws now. Old man Truman had chased them off so many times, he'd learned their names.

When they set the sticks in the bed of the cart, he grinned. "Thanks for the memory, Little John."

"You're welcome, Robin," she returned. "But next time, I want to be Sundance and you can be Butch." She rubbed the mud off her boot on the dried grass. "We go for the gold on a train."

He touched two fingers to his hat. "You bet."

They climbed into the cart and drove back to the farmhouse. By the time they'd said good-bye to Jeremiah and were in her car, they were no longer outlaws—just two responsible people doing their jobs.

Chapter 11

TYLER WRIGHT LEFT A NOTE FOR WILLAMINA and drove out before dawn. He wanted to get to Oklahoma City and back before two. That was when he liked to send his first e-mail to Kate, his hazel-eyed pen pal. She usually didn't answer until close to five, but it didn't matter; he got a kick out of waiting, checking, anticipating.

When she did e-mail back it had been the same answer for four days. Yes, she'd have dinner with him. He'd fill his plate and stare at the screen while he ate.

He took the back roads so he could speed, knowing that on the way back, he'd stay on the main highway out of respect for dear Miss Beverly. She'd dropped by his office about a month after her husband died and made plans for her own funeral. She had little left besides her Social Security, but she wanted to pay for her funeral so no one would be out anything.

Tyler doubted that her brother, Jeremiah, had any money. He was land rich and money poor, like most folks around. Beverly had said she didn't want to bother anyone. She'd cried when she told him that her husband had borrowed money from almost everyone in town and never offered to pay any of it back. Her husband had thought of it as a game, but she'd been ashamed for years. Ashamed enough to change back to her maiden name after forty years of marriage. She'd paid for her funeral, then given Tyler a slip of paper with all the people in town she owed. She asked him to keep it until Jeremiah died and then ask whoever handled the family farm if they'd pay each one back with her half from the sale of the land.

Frowning, Tyler doubted the slip of paper would hold up in any court. Jeremiah wouldn't sell any of the land, not even to pay his brother-in-law's debts, and now that he'd outlived Beverly, he owned all the land.

As Tyler drove, the sun was coming up. He was forty years younger than old Jeremiah, but in a way they were the same. When they died, so did the family line. When Tyler had been younger, he'd always thought there was plenty of time ahead in which to have children. He had a business to run and his hobby to keep him busy. He was too young to marry in his twenties, not ready in his thirties, and now in his forties he could not think of a single woman he would want to date. Or, to be fair, who would want to date him.

Tyler would never sell the funeral home, not for any amount of money. If he did, he'd have no home, no roots. But he had thought he'd have a wife and children living with him by now.

Three years ago he'd had a blind date with someone's cousin who was visiting Harmony after her divorce. They'd gone out a few times for dinner and managed to keep a conversation going, but when he'd reached for her hand, she'd pulled back. When he walked her to the door, she explained that she couldn't stand the thought of touching a hand that had touched dead people all day.

He hadn't bothered to explain the thousand things about his job that didn't involve touching dead people.

Tyler smiled suddenly. Tonight, when he visited with Kate, he'd ask her what she thought of blind dates. Everything they talked about was interesting. They'd discussed a dozen topics, and she'd never hesitated to tell him her opinion. She loved Mexican food, hated lines at the grocery store, loved her country, hated subways in every town in the world, fought against gun control, and had campaigned for women's rights since she could walk.

He had a feeling Kate was a woman no one would ever talk into anything, but no discussion would ever be dull. He even liked the little codes she had for her favorite swear words.

A little after ten, Tyler picked up Beverly Truman's body, then drove three blocks and pulled around the drive-through at Sonic for a foot-long chili-cheese dog and tater tots, and headed back to Harmony. He'd be home in time to send his e-mail.

Chapter 12

"ARE YOU SURE YOUR UNCLE TOLD YOU TO spend all this money?" Noah asked for the third time.

"All I need, he said." They'd already stopped by the flower shop and were now searching through racks at the Lady Bug for a dress for Miss Beverly. Reagan took her mission as seriously as if it were life or death. Jeremiah trusted her, and she'd decided she would not let him down.

Noah pulled out T-shirts that said things like BORN TO BE WILD and TAKE ME TO YOUR LEADER. "How about buying something like this, Rea?" he asked, holding it up to her as if trying to guess her size.

Reagan closed her eyes and repeated her orders from her new uncle. "Flowers for the casket, a dress for her, and clothes for me." She shoved the T-shirt away. "Nothing else. I can't waste money."

Noah scratched his head. "I don't see anything in this place that looks like dead old lady clothes." He picked up a sundress with tiny pink flamingos on it.

The sales clerk hovering around them must have heard him. "You're looking for a dress for someone who's passed on?"

He nodded and explained everything to this woman Reagan had never seen before. Then to Reagan's surprise, the lady told them to go to the funeral home. The woman was missing a sale, but was still trying to help them out.

So they drove over to the funeral home, where they found boxed clothes for the dead.

Reagan dug through the boxes while Noah wandered around. "This is great," she said. "I never dreamed they had this kind of thing. Every one of these looks like

Miss Beverly. She's probably been buying her clothes here for years."

Noah leaned out from behind an open coffin. "You mean your grandmother?"

"Yes," she said without meeting his eyes. "I didn't really know her." She tried to think of something that wasn't a lie. "The people where she lived just called her Miss Beverly, so I guess that's the way I think of her."

Reagan picked out a pretty blue dress with a white lace collar. She handed it to the woman, who'd followed them from the front desk, who smiled and promised Miss Beverly would be ready for viewing in a few hours. She was so nice Reagan almost wanted to stay around and visit. Almost.

Noah stopped at the Burger Barrel and bought Reagan lunch. She saved half for Jeremiah's old dog. It was time they made friends.

Then Noah drove her to the mall. The center of the mall had two cookie places, a deserted hot dog stand, and a McDonald's with a huge sign that read: LIMITED MENU. The only mall rats were a dozen walkers over eighty.

"How does this place stay in business?" Reagan whispered.

Noah grinned. "You should see it on a slow day."

They went shopping for her clothes. Noah took the work seriously, making fun of half the things she tried on, wiggling his eyebrows when he thought something was wrong, and smiling with all his teeth showing when she tried on western clothes.

In the end, she bought three pairs of jeans, six shirts, one dress, and a cowboy hat she thought looked ridiculous. He promised her it looked cute, and she almost believed him.

"Now you got the hat," he said as they walked out of the store, "you got to come watch me ride this weekend."

"All right. If you'll come to the funeral."

He stopped on the steps and faced her. "Of course I'll come. We're friends, Rea. That's what friends do for each other."

She wondered if he could tell that all this friends stuff was new to her. "I've never been to a funeral," she admitted. "I'm not sure what to do."

"Rea, I don't think anyone really knows what to do at a funeral. I usually just keep my eyes looking down and hug everyone who wants to hug me. Some folks think they have to do that to all the family left behind to suffer the loss."

"You've had family die?"

"Sure, my big brother, Warren, three years ago. I cried all the way through the funeral. I couldn't tell you one thing anyone said."

"How'd he die?"

"He was killed on duty. He was a highway patrolman on his way to becoming a Texas Ranger. A man ran a roadblock and when Warren caught up to him, the guy shot him in the face when he walked up to the car. Strange thing was, the man was only wanted for outstanding speeding tickets. Warren wouldn't have even taken him in that night. He killed my brother for nothing."

"That's really sad."

He straightened as if pushing sadness aside. "You want to hug me?" he asked with a smile that didn't quite reach his eyes.

"No," she answered and smiled back.

"Times like this are like muddy water, Rea, you just got to keep moving through it until you get to the other side."

SHE HAD NO IDEA HOW TRUE HIS WORDS WERE, but she thought of them several times over the next two days. People brought food to the house and hugged her. They went to the funeral home and everyone there hugged her. Jeremiah had a graveside service and it looked like half the town came and most of them hugged her.

Reagan was all hugged out by the time she got home. Jeremiah must have felt the same, for he went back to his room without a word or a bite to eat and she didn't see him again the rest of the evening.

She went to her room and closed the door. *My room*, Reagan thought. Beverly would never be back to claim it. She could paint the walls or move things around. But she decided, for right now anyway, she'd leave it the same. In a funny way, Reagan thought Miss Beverly would smile if she knew Reagan was sleeping there.

Jeremiah was cooking breakfast in his work clothes when she came downstairs the next morning. All the flowers folks had brought to the house were gone, along with the cards and cakes. He must have thought it was time to get back to normal.

She silently agreed, having no idea what normal was, but it had to be better than the mud of funeral days.

Chapter 13

ALEXANDRA MCALLEN LEANED AGAINST HER patrol car and wiped the sweat from her throat. The morning was warm and her bulletproof vest always made it seem hotter. She'd been standing in the sun for a half hour trying to solve the latest crime in Harmony.

"I'm telling you, Sheriff," Dallas Logan said, not for the first time. "Every night it's not raining or cloudy some fool shoots this light out and I've had enough of it. You got to do something."

The overweight woman huffed, raising her breasts as if she'd use them as battering rams to get something done. At five feet nothing, she might not be intimidating, but she tried to talk everyone she met to death. "I've made a list of who I think it might be. All you got to do is go house to house investigating and you'll find someone who owns a rifle."

Dallas shifted from foot to foot as if playing some kind of senior citizen dodgeball. "You might have to cast a wide net, Sheriff McAllen. Last week, Stella McNabb came to the canasta game at my house and commented twice about how the glare of artificial light didn't seem natural in the night. You ask me, there's something wrong with her. I've seen it in folks who've never lived in town." Dallas wiggled her finger. "They frown at things you and me accept. I know for a fact Stella's never used the ATM. Now tell me that ain't strange. Might be worth a look to check her husband's car for a gun."

Alex guessed everyone within a hundred miles owned a rifle. "I think we'll just replace the bulb."

The round little woman huffed. "That's what you did last week and the week before that."

Alex thought about saying, *You win, Mrs. Logan, I'll round up everyone for five blocks around and interrogate them for hours without food or water. We'll get to the bottom of this crime if I have to jail half the town.*

"I had to fight to get this light here, you know. It wasn't easy. Ronelle and I went down to the courthouse a dozen times before we finally got them to put it up. This corner was far too dark. All kinds of worthless people could walk right up and look into our windows at night and we'd never know."

Somehow, Alex doubted Ronelle had held up her half of the fight at the courthouse. She'd said good morning to the girl every day since she'd been sheriff, and the postal worker had yet to answer back. If Alex started investigating broken bulbs, the next thing she'd have to do would be to search down the criminal who was working all the crossword puzzles in magazines before they were stuffed into mailboxes. Alex had a pretty good idea who was behind the post office crime, but until someone filed an official complaint, she wouldn't say a word to Ronelle.

Dallas Logan was still complaining about every neighbor around her when Hank Matheson and Willie Davis drove up with a ladder from the firehouse.

They got out and replaced the bulb without a word.

"Well, it's about time," Mrs. Logan said when they were finished.

Alex mouthed a thank-you to Hank.

He smiled. "The city boys were busy with a water leak, so I thought we'd pitch in."

Dallas Logan waddled back to her house mumbling to herself.

Alex watched Willie sweep up the glass, forcing herself not to look at Hank. They hadn't seen each other since the day in the orchard almost a week before.

Hank broke the silence. "Someone said your little brother won a buckle at the rodeo Saturday night."

"Yeah, my dad drove over from Amarillo to watch. We're all real proud of Noah, but I'm not surprised he takes to bull riding; Dad started putting him on sheep when he was four, calves by the time he was seven. I swear, I can still hear the echoes of Mom and Dad's fights over him trying to breed rodeo into his sons' blood. It didn't take with Warren, but Noah claims he was born to ride rough stock."

"Can't blame your dad," Hank said. "He was the best bull rider in the country when he was younger. I remember he took Warren and me with him to the rodeo in San Antonio once. He'd been retired for years by then, but every cowboy in the place paid their respects."

She couldn't argue with that. Her father had always been bigger than life. He had won his first national title before he turned twenty. When he'd finally given it up, everyone in town probably saw the restlessness in him. He'd started a cattle trucking company based out of Amarillo and was gone most nights. Warren took over taking care of the ranch and helping raise Noah while she went away to college. Their dad was always there, somewhere in the background . . . far in the background, but never around when they needed help with homework or just wanted to talk.

When Warren died, their dad lost what little interest he had in the ranch and moved full time to Amarillo. The fighting she'd grown up hearing between her parents now had settled into a polite-stranger kind of talk. They'd never gone to court to end the marriage, but any love they'd ever known had been beaten to death by words long ago.

"Your father stayed over Saturday night, right?" Hank's words broke into her thoughts.

She knew it wasn't a question. Hank was figuring out why he hadn't gotten a call Saturday night to come get her from one of the bars. He figured she'd already had a babysitter for the night—her dad.

Right there on that street corner in the middle of town, she wanted to scream at him that she didn't need him sitting up worrying about her every Saturday night. She didn't have to drink away the memory of what happened to Warren.

"How is Adam McAllen these days?" Hank said, hiding all emotion in his face.

"My dad's fine. Made out of granite, you know."

"All finished," Willie announced, unaware that the sheriff and Hank were doing more than passing the time while he worked. "Who you think keeps doing this, Sheriff?"

"Someone who hates the streetlight, I guess," she answered.

"I know how they feel." Willie folded the ladder. "I used to have a light shining right in my window every night. I finally put up drapes."

Alex turned slowly in a full circle. The street was like most in town, a mixture of different sizes and conditions of homes. Dozens of windows faced the light. It could have been anyone.

Hank helped Willie load the ladder, then turned back to Alex. He frowned before he blurted out, "Any chance you got time to have lunch? My sister flew to Fort Worth to try and sell her paintings of men dying terrible deaths. My mother and aunts went along to go shopping. I've got Saralynn for the day, and she's decided she's a sheriff. I'm sure she'd like to talk to a colleague."

Alex laughed. "Where's your other sister? The one who doesn't paint dying men. Couldn't she watch the kid?"

Hank looked like a criminal about to confess. Miserable. Lost.

"Liz is going to a time management course put on by the library at noon. She thinks it'll help me. I'm sure I'll get the notes and a full lecture tonight."

"You?" Alex bit down a giggle. Hank

Matheson did more than most five men in this town. He managed a ranch, ran the fire department, worked out every morning before dawn, corralled all the women in his life, and bullied her on Saturday night.

"Yeah, Liz thinks if I'd manage my time better, I'd have some hours left to date."

"Do you want to date?"

"No," he said. "I just want to have lunch with my niece and let you answer all her questions."

Hank had never been a man she thought she'd feel sorry for, but she took pity on him now. "Twelve thirty, Mexican Plaza?"

"Sounds great." He touched two fingers to the brim of the Stetson she'd bought him and turned away.

Chapter 14

HANK MATHESON HAD JUST CHECKED THE weather report when he noticed his sister Liz pull up in front of the station with Saralynn. He wasn't surprised. Even if she hadn't found a seminar to go to, two hours was about the maximum time Liz could handle babysitting. Thankfully, with all the women in the house, she wasn't asked to keep her niece often.

Liz claimed she didn't have a mothering bone in her body. Hank wasn't sure, but he had a feeling that might have been the reason her five-year marriage ended.

Unlike Claire, Saralynn's mother, who complained constantly about her ex-husband, Liz never said a word about her marriage other than it didn't work out.

"I'm running late!" Liz yelled as she opened the passenger door and unstrapped Saralynn from the car seat.

Hank rushed out in time to lift his niece carefully from the car. The leg braces she always wore clanked against the metal buckle on her child seat. "Maybe after the class you'll be able to manage your time better, Liz?"

"Don't be funny," she said, pulling out the child's bag of books and toys. "Claire called as I was loading the car and told me to make sure I gave the kid her medicine." She shoved the lunch bag of pills that always traveled with the four-year-old. "You'll have to do it. I don't have time to read which pill when."

He held his niece and both bags as Liz jumped back in her sports car and roared toward the First United Methodist Church.

"Good-bye," Saralynn whispered, and made a wave that wasn't answered.

"She just forgot to say good-bye to us,"

Hank said as he turned into the station. "We'll make her say hello twice when she gets back."

"No," Saralynn answered. "Someone stole her manners. It's a crime I'll have to investigate." She had a plastic star pinned to her pink jumper and one of his old toy guns strapped around her waist.

"I got a surprise for you." He looked down at his niece, loving the imagination that made up for all she couldn't do. "We're having lunch with another sheriff. I thought you girls could compare notes on how to fight the bad guys."

Saralynn kissed his cheek. "I love you, Deputy Hank."

"I love you, too, Sheriff," he whispered.

An hour from now, the two sheriffs would be sharing stories along with chips at the Mexican Plaza. Hank couldn't stop smiling.

The restaurant was on the south end of town, a round building set far enough off the road that only locals could find it. At one time it had been called the Mexican Hat, but the owner got tired of the wind ripping off the awning that almost made the place look like a sombrero, so he put a fountain in the center of the place, painted every wall a different color, and called it a plaza.

Despite his plan not to, Hank showed up early.

Saralynn ordered the extra-extra-mild hot sauce, which tasted like ketchup to Hank, and watched the fish in the fountain until Alex arrived. All the tables by the fountain were small, made for two, but the owner made room for three chairs just because Saralynn was the first four-year-old sheriff he'd ever met.

Hank stood when Alex sat down across from him. This was as close as they'd come in three years to being friendly, and he didn't want to do anything to shatter the peace between them. He didn't mind that she barely looked at him. She was smiling at Saralynn and giving the girl her full attention.

When she had the child laughing, Alex dipped a chip into Saralynn's special hot sauce and ate it. She looked at Hank and made a face. He slid his bowl of sauce toward her. She dipped again, and this time smiled, waving her hand in front of her mouth. He passed her his glass of water and motioned for the waiter to bring more.

As they ate, Alex talked to Saralynn about the trials of being a sheriff, and Saralynn agreed as if she knew each one personally. Hank ate his chile rellenos and listened.

About the time the second basket of sopapillas was delivered, his knee bumped Alex's leg under the table.

He'd opened his mouth to say sorry, when he realized she'd stretched her long leg out toward him. He bumped it again and heard the slight catch in her voice. She didn't look at him. In fact, she seemed absorbed in the story Saralynn was telling her about how often trolls steal things and hide them in mismatched socks forever circling in the dryer.

He let his leg rest against hers.

She didn't move.

She was playing with him, he thought. He decided to play back. This lunch meeting was about to get far more interesting.

As the girls talked, Hank leaned forward, moved his hand beneath the little table, and slid his fingers along Alex's leg. Her muscles tightened beneath his touch.

He heard her breathing grow shallow, but she didn't move away. Didn't look at him.

He shifted in the chair and slid his leg next to hers. All she'd have to do was move a fraction of an inch and they wouldn't be touching. But she didn't. He could feel the heat of her through his jeans. What they were doing made no sense. They couldn't say three sentences to each other without getting into an argument. She'd threatened to kill him a dozen times and tried to a few.

But something drew her to him. Something she probably didn't understand any better than he did. He liked the feel of her next to him, and he guessed she also did. He bumped her leg lightly, and she bumped his leg back.

He smiled, wishing she'd look at him. He had a feeling those stormy blue eyes of hers might be filled with something besides anger.

Alex's phone sounded and she moved her leg away. She took the call, then stood. "I have to leave, Sheriff Saralynn, but I've enjoyed having lunch with you."

"Me, too," Saralynn said. "Are you leaving because there's been a bank robbery?"

"No," Alex brushed her hand over the

girl's cheek. "State investigators up from Austin want to talk to me about an old case that may come up for retrial soon. I didn't expect them until two. They're early."

Hank stood, studying her. "Maybe we can do this again."

Alex continued to look at Saralynn, who was busy feeding the fish the rest of her sopapilla.

"I don't think so," she said, and finally looked at Hank.

The old sadness was back. She was looking at him, but she was remembering her big brother. If Saralynn hadn't been there, he might have said something he would regret. Warren had been dead for three years. They'd both seen his body on the road that night. They'd both grieved. It was time Warren's memory stopped haunting them both.

She was gone before he could come up with a response.

AFTER LUNCH, HANK WENT BACK TO THE FIRE station. The wind had kicked up to about thirty miles an hour. With the lack of rain, he was starting to worry. The land was ripe for a fire. It was only a matter of time, and he had to get everything ready while he prayed nothing would happen. He made a mental note to call Bob McNabb. The guy was far too old to be active as a volunteer, but he knew more about grass fires than anyone around.

Saralynn sat in the only comfortable chair in his office, her braced legs covered with one of the extra blankets from the station, while he worked at his desk. After worrying over a training schedule for a while, he looked up and smiled at the sight of her concentration on her coloring book. The tip of her tongue stuck out of the corner of her mouth. She was so cute, she had to be an angel.

"I love you, kid."

She looked up. "I love you, too, Uncle Hank. Mom says you're the only good man left on the planet."

He grinned. "I'm sure you'll find another one, better than me, one day. Then you'll get married."

She shook her head. "I'm going to live with you and Grandma and Momma and Great-Aunt Fat and Great-Aunt Pat and Liz all my life."

"Liz is your aunt, too, you know."

She nodded. "I know, but she told me to call her just *Liz* because *Aunt Liz* dulls her down." Saralynn frowned. "Have any idea what she means, Uncle Hank?"

He hadn't understood either of his sisters since they were born. When they hit puberty and got their periods about the same time each month, it was like living with a serial killer and a suicidal manic. His mother used to say they'd grow out of it, but they were now twenty-seven and twenty-eight. He saw no sign of it yet.

Saralynn went back to her coloring, and he went back to his paperwork and tried not to think of how good it had felt to slide his hand along Alex's leg. He wouldn't mind doing it sometime when she wasn't wearing trousers. And a gun, he thought.

A few minutes later he looked out the window and saw his mother's battered old Suburban pull up. The green truck was like a fixture in town. If she kept it much longer someone would stick a historical marker sign on the thing. Everyone knew where she and the old aunts were by where the van was parked.

Hank watched Claire, his redheaded, fiery sister, climb out of the Suburban and run toward the fire station. She hit his office door laughing.

She hugged Saralynn wildly and shouted, "They loved my paintings, baby! They loved Mommy's work."

"They did?" Hank and Saralynn said at the same time. Hank couldn't imagine anyone even giving them more than a blink of a glance. He'd seen one with a man spread out on a linen dining table. He'd been sliced apart about every inch down from his head to his toes. Claire had named the painting *Last Guest for Dinner*. He'd seen another one of a man's head with every tool he could think of implanted in his skull. She'd titled that one *The Perfect Tool*.

"Yes, they loved me." Claire circled around the room, dancing with an invisible partner. "They want me to do a show this spring. Imagine. My own show in Fort Worth. The walls of a gallery completely covered with my work."

Hank hoped the gallery didn't serve food at the opening. "That's great, Sis," he said. "I'm proud of you."

She lifted Saralynn. "We're celebrating tonight," she said to Hank. "Be home for supper by seven if you can."

"I wouldn't miss it." He picked up Saralynn's books and medicine bag and followed Claire out to the truck.

His two old aunts were on the third seat completely surrounded by shopping bags. "I see the hunt was successful." He grinned at them.

They both giggled. "We found Victoria's Secret," Aunt Fat whispered. "We went a little crazy, I'm afraid."

For a moment he pictured his bowling-ball shaped Aunt Pat walking the runway wearing one of the Victoria's Secret outfits of lace and feathers, or his aunt Fat in her thin frame wearing only underwear. The image made him want to grab the fire hose and screw it into his ear to blast the thought from his mind.

He closed the truck door and jogged back to his office in time to catch his phone before the answering machine picked up.

Chapter 15

REAGAN STOOD IN THE SPOTLESS KITCHEN AND stared at Jeremiah. "It's not a date," she said, fighting down a scream.

"You're going out. He's picking you up." Jeremiah cut himself another slice of coconut pie. "If it walks like a duck and talks like a duck . . ."

She leaned closer and pointed her finger at his nose. "Don't start that duck logic with me again."

He shoved her finger away with his fork. "You're full of spitfire and vinegar, girl. I can't believe any boy'd want to take you out. You sure he's right in the head? If he's riding rough stock like his old man used to, he's probably got mush for brains. I don't think it'd be wise to date some fellow like that."

"It's not a date and if I'm hard to get along with, it only proves I'm related to you. As for brains, I'm not too sure. Maybe I'm the one with brain damage, going to a rodeo when I don't even know anything about it."

Old Jeremiah snorted. "Don't change the subject. You got brains. I ain't worried about that. Which reminds me, don't think for one minute I don't know you made this pie in hopes of sweetening me up."

"Did it work? I used an old recipe from the box that looked like it was in Beverly's handwriting."

"No, it didn't work, but I will admit you make a fine pie." He carried the dessert to the table where his coffee waited. "And you can tell that boy who you're not having a date with that he'd better get you home early 'cause we got a full day of work tomorrow."

Reagan grabbed her hat. "I'll be ready to work at eight."

He stared at her. "You got money in your pocket? Never go nowhere without enough to get you home."

"I got money and I know my way home." She hurried out the door, almost choking on her last words. If he could call it her home, she could, too.

They'd work hard tomorrow and he'd complain about everything, but it didn't matter. For the first week she'd been at the most dilapidated place on Lone Oak Road, she'd counted the days, wondering how long it would be before he kicked her out. The second week, she'd been afraid to breathe. He'd known the truth about her, or at least some of it, and she thought any minute he'd tell everyone she'd lied about being a Truman. Then the state would come in and take her away even if she didn't want to go . . . even if he wanted her to stay.

Now, they'd made it two weeks. He was still griping about the chickens laying too many eggs, but he hadn't said a word about the things she'd bought in town. She'd been careful not to spend too much, but wondered if the old man had any idea how great it felt to have her own shampoo and soap and a hair dryer she didn't have to share. She had a dozen hangers in her closet with new clothes no one else had ever worn.

It couldn't last. Nothing lasted. But when it ended, she'd have something good to remember. She could look back and think of Harmony and the old house as home. And she'd feel, even if it were only for a little while, that she was with family.

Noah's truck bounced down the dirt road. "Ready?" he yelled when he saw her jump off the porch.

"Ready." She ran toward the truck as he leaned over and opened her door.

He never came to a complete stop as he circled the yard and headed back up the dirt road. "Hang on, Rea," he grinned at her. "We've got to make the forty miles to Bailee in thirty minutes."

"Does this thing go that fast?" She was so excited, she had to fight down squealing. She'd hung out with boys before. Not dates really, just group things where no one paired off until late. This was different. It might not be exactly a date, but it was the closest thing she'd ever had.

Deep down in her gut she wondered about what he'd do when it got late. From the few times she'd been around boys, she'd learned fast that they were like werewolves, changing into something different after midnight. She glanced at Noah, wondering if he would, too, and hating the thought that he might.

"Don't worry about this truck." He patted the steering wheel. "We'll make it. I thought we'd get to Bailee early and stop in town for a hamburger, but looks like I'll have to buy you dinner at the chuck wagon."

"You don't have to buy me dinner. I brought money."

He pulled onto the farm-to-market road and gunned the engine. "If you're with me, Rea, I pay. We may only be eating burritos out of the back of a truck, but I pay. That's the way it is."

She thought of telling him he was living in the past, but she didn't want to start the almost-date out with an argument. "But you have no idea how much I can eat."

He glanced at her. "I got twenty dollars in my pocket. If you eat more than that I'll borrow money from you and feed you, then I'll pay you back come Monday."

"Fair enough."

"I like that new shirt, Rea. It's not western, but it'll do."

She smiled her thanks. She'd been wearing T-shirts and jeans to school, but she wanted something different tonight. She'd found the plain blue shirt on sale in the boys' department. Tucked in, with a white T-shirt underneath, she didn't think it looked bad.

They talked about school until they reached the small rodeo grounds just outside Bailee. Noah left her at the stands while he ran to register, and then they bought dinner at the food wagon parked beside the stands.

When men on horses began lining up at the far end of the arena, he stood, tugged off his coat, and dropped it over her shoulders. "Keep this on," he said.

"But I'm not cold."

"No one will bother you if you're wearing it. I'll be back after I ride."

There was something in his eyes she hadn't seen before. A warning. Looking around, she saw no one sinister, but she didn't argue with Noah. This wasn't the streets of the city. She doubted there were a hundred people in the stands, and they appeared to be high school kids or parents. Noah was gone before she could ask what it was she was supposed to be worried about.

The coat did feel good; it still had the warmth of him inside. Reagan pushed her hands through the arms and shoved up the sleeves. The patches on the jacket marked Noah as part of the rodeo team, and his giving it to her seemed to make her a part of the team. Almost.

As the sun set, she leaned back against the bleachers and watched her first rodeo. There was a way of life here, a whole sub-culture she'd never imagined. She watched it all, fascinated. There was almost a dance about it, the way the horses stomped in the soft dirt, the flash of fringe on the chaps, the flow of riders and ropes.

Noah rode saddle broncs first. He fell off almost before he was out of the chute. But the announcer yelled that they should all give "Preacher" a hand, and Reagan clapped as loud as she could as she watched him dust off his bottom and collect his hat from the dirt.

When they switched to team roping, her heart slowed down a little. She'd never been interested in any sport, but this was different. This was one-on-one with the challenge, and the men were helping and rooting for one another. Again and again she saw them pick up another rider's gear or jump off the gate to guard a downed cowboy from the wild spins of a bull. One man in baggy pants and a red shirt looked like a clown, but the announcer kept calling him the bullfighter. It didn't take long before she realized he was there not to entertain the crowd, but to help out when needed.

A body plopped down beside her on the bench, and Reagan knew it wasn't Noah before she turned her head.

"You here all by yourself?" a voice whispered so close she fought the urge to swat it away like a buzzing fly.

"No." Reagan turned to look at the overweight boy about her age who was sitting next to her. He wasn't dressed western but wore baggy pants and a black T-shirt with holes in it.

"I'm Brandon Biggs," he said, as if she cared. "I looked around and I noticed only one girl I didn't know. So this is your lucky night. I'm going to sit with you."

He seemed to notice the jacket she wore for the first time. "Who's that belong to? It's not yours, for sure. Way too big."

She didn't want to talk to this guy.

Reagan had met creeps like him in every place she'd lived. He thought he ran the world. "It belongs to Preacher McAllen and I really wish you'd leave."

Brandon laughed. "It's a free country. I can sit here if I want to. Besides, I know who Preacher is. Saw him almost ride."

"Leave, or I'll leave."

She stood and moved one step sideways before he caught her hand.

"Don't go away. Preacher and me are tight. He wouldn't mind us hanging out." Brandon wiggled his eyebrows. "Besides, pestering you is far more interesting than this dumb old rodeo."

"But *I* mind. I'd rather sit somewhere else because I *am* interested in the rodeo." She didn't want to attract attention. "Let go of my arm."

Brandon opened his mouth to say something, then looked past her and seemed to think better of it. He pulled his hand away and huffed. "Prickly little girl, aren't you? I was just trying to be friendly."

When she tried to move around him, he shifted his leg so she'd have to brush it to get past him on the narrow space.

Reagan *brushed* his leg hard with the

heel of her shoe, a few inches below his shin.

He smiled for a second before her heel dug in, sliding down his leg, scraping skin as if it were the top layer of tree bark.

From the expression on his face it was obvious he was bleeding beneath his black jeans.

Pulling away, he let her pass, then yelled for some kid walking by to wait up. He limped down the steps, shoving people aside as he moved.

She expected to see Noah standing behind her, but when Reagan turned, no one was there. It was as if Brandon had been frightened by a ghost. No one was even looking at her.

Then she saw them. Blue jackets, just like the one over her shoulders, had moved in around her. Not so close that she'd noticed them, but close enough to make a point. She sat down as the barrel races started, aware of the blue jackets slowly moving away. Reagan had a feeling that if Brandon or someone like him returned, they'd be back.

It was a strange feeling, being protected. She'd thought she was alone watching while Preacher rode, but all along they must have been watching over her.

A few minutes later, Noah climbed the bleachers two at a time and plopped down next to her. He looped his arm lightly over her shoulders. "How'd you like my ride, Rea?"

"What ride? You fell off."

He laughed. "I stayed on four seconds. I was halfway there. Wait until I ride the bull. I'll make the buzzer."

"Before you fall off?"

He nodded. "Before I fall off."

She poked him in the ribs. "So this falling off is part of it, win or lose. Noah, doesn't that seem strange to you? Seems like if you make the time, they should train the bulls to stop at the bell and let you get off."

"I'll put that in the suggestion box." He laughed.

Thirty minutes later, he lasted five seconds on the bull before he was bucked off and rolled in the dirt and mud. She clapped, figuring he was making progress.

As the last few events wound down, the wind seemed to kick up as if pushing the crowd toward their cars. Families bundled up the kids and headed for home.

One of the blue jackets behind her walked past, his girlfriend right behind him with her hand on his shoulder to steady her.

"Wanta go down by the chutes?" the boy asked Reagan. "You can meet up with Preacher there."

His girlfriend nodded once, as if to reassure her.

"Sure," Reagan said, not wanting to be the last one left in the stands.

She found Noah behind the fence. He was dusting the dirt from his jeans. When he straightened, the light reflected off something wet on his shirt.

"What's that?" Reagan moved closer, touching the sticky liquid.

"Bull snot," he said.

"Oh." She wiped her finger on her jeans.

"It'll dry"—he slapped at his leg—"but this shit I fell in is all over me."

"Nice ride," she managed, trying not to think about what he was covered in.

"Yeah, I almost made the time."

She was beginning to think maybe he did have mush for brains. He didn't seem the least upset that he'd failed at everything he'd tried tonight.

He offered her the hand he'd been using to dust off his jeans. "Want to go to the dance?"

She swallowed and took his hand. "Sure." If it didn't bother him that he was covered in snot and shit, she guessed it didn't bother her. "But I don't know how to dance."

"Me neither."

They listened to the music and watched the dancers for an hour, and then he drove her home, explaining all the rules of the rodeo. She asked questions more because it was fun to listen to him talk, all excited and happy, about something he obviously loved.

When he pulled into the yard, she saw Jeremiah sitting on the front porch.

"Your uncle waited up," Noah whispered as he accepted his jacket back.

"He's probably asleep in the chair."

"He was worried about you," Noah added.

Reagan doubted that, but she said, "I'd better go in before this pickup turns into a pumpkin."

Noah grinned. "You had fun?"

"I did." She thought of telling him that this was very nearly the best night of her life. She'd laughed more than she had in months, and she'd felt protected. For her, both were too new to be taken for granted.

"You want to go with me again next week?"

"Don't your folks come?"

"No, my mom's never cared for rodeo. My dad lives in Amarillo and only comes over to one now and then. My sister is usually too busy being sheriff to worry about me. It was kind of nice having someone in the stands watching me almost make the ride."

"I'd like to come." She thought of being hesitant, playing it cool, but she couldn't. "Only I bring the food next week." She'd seen a few picnic baskets and buckets of chicken. She wasn't sure she could face another burrito that tasted like it had been made from the oldest bull.

"Fair enough," he said as she opened the door. "See you Monday at school, Rea."

"See you," she answered, and hopped out of the cab. "Thanks for not turning into a werewolf."

"What—"

She slammed the door and ran toward the house.

Chapter 16

HANK ROLLED OUT OF BED AND PULLED ON A worn pair of Levi's as he walked across the room to answer his cell.

"Chief." Willie's voice was high with excitement. "We're pulling out now. You said to call you no matter how small the fire if we took the truck out."

Hank could hear the siren in the background. "What is it, Willie?"

"Highway patrol called in a trash fire out at the north rest stop."

Willie had been sleeping at the fire station since he turned eighteen and his stepfather kicked him out. Brad Rister would be there tonight also. He slept there every time his wife kicked him out. Andy Daily, one of the night dispatchers across the street, would have caught a ride as well. Andy wasn't much of a fireman, but he was an adrenaline junkie and about to starve to death in a town the size of Harmony.

"I'll meet you there," Hank said, and closed up his phone.

Andy and Brad were levelheaded, and Willie could follow orders. They didn't need him to put out a trash fire. But Hank had been restless all night. He might as well go check everything out himself rather than lie in bed worrying about it. With a trash fire, there was always the chance it could spark a grass fire.

Glancing at his watch, he realized in an hour he would have been up anyway. He liked to get up and be at work before dawn when he was at the ranch. He'd work a few hours before coming in for breakfast with his mother and Saralynn. His sisters usually slept late, and his old aunts had their morning tea and bakery scones in their quarters.

As he took the side stairs outside his

room, he hoped he made it back for breakfast. Tuesdays, his mother left early to visit
the gallery in Wichita Falls that handled
her pots, but every other morning, the three
of them laughed and talked over pancakes
and eggs before they started their day.
Sometimes he thought his family circled
around him in endless rings, but at the
core were Saralynn and his mother.

When Hank pulled up to the north roadside park, he could see smoke rising gray
against the night sky. The huge Dumpster
was still popping with the heat, but the fire
inside had been put out.

His men had sprayed the dried grass
around the site to ensure that no spark
would start something far worse than a
Dumpster fire.

"What do you think happened?" Willie
asked.

"Some traveler tossing his trash along
with an ashtray, maybe," Hank guessed.
Dumpster fires weren't all that unusual. An
odd smell drifted with the smoke, making
Hank wonder if some animal had been
trapped in the Dumpster. Or maybe road-
kill had been tossed in.

He noticed one of the sheriff's cars pull

up beside the highway patrolman's vehicle, but Hank didn't move out of the dark. If Alex was here, she was on duty and probably didn't want to talk to him. For the second Saturday in a row he hadn't gotten a call from the bar. She'd stayed out of trouble. Part of him was proud of her, and part wondered if she was staying away from him.

Flashlight beams floated around an old station wagon parked near one of the picnic tables. The crack of a police radio crackled across the cold air.

Brad Rister approached Hank. "Should we try to determine the cause, or just wait and come back in a few hours when it's light? Both lids were down when we got here, so the fire had pretty much choked itself out. All we got was smoke; no flame when we popped the latch."

"Go on back and try to get a few more hours of sleep." Hank turned his collar up. "I'll stick around for a while."

Brad motioned for Willie and Andy to pack up.

Hank noticed the beam of a light moving toward him. He didn't move as Alex's tall, lean shadow materialized from behind the light.

"Fire out?" she asked.

"It's out."

"Mind if we have a look inside?"

"The Dumpster's probably still hot and smoking, but knock yourself out." He followed her and two highway patrolmen. "Any reason this can't wait until dawn?"

Alex didn't answer, but the patrolman said, "We found drugs in the station wagon. There is a possibility that the driver climbed out of his car for some reason and decided to light up in the Dumpster."

Hank frowned. "You think he caught himself on fire?"

"I've seen it before. In the car, out where we could see him if we passed by, wouldn't seem near as safe as inside the Dumpster. Only problem was he might have closed the lid."

Hank could fill in the blanks from there. A few years ago, the parks department had put on latches to keep animals out of the trash. A five-year-old could open the lid from the outside, but there was no way to open it from the inside. A few park workers had complained about almost having a heart attack when they opened the lid and an angry raccoon shot out.

Hank stood behind Alex as she leaned over and shone her flashlight in. One of the patrolmen did the same.

Hank didn't have to look. He had a feeling they'd find something dead inside.

Alex stepped back and, in the dark, no one else noticed Hank steady her.

"We'll need a crime unit," she said, fighting to keep her voice calm. "He's burned, but the cause of death may be asphyxiation."

"Or drugs," Hank added. "Does it really matter? He's dead."

No one heard him. They began talking about what had to be done. Hank walked back to his truck just as the sky started to lighten. With the door open, he sat in his Dodge and watched the show. Usually, he loved sunrise on the prairie, but the smoky haze in the air and the stench took the joy out of it.

He barely noticed most of the cars leaving. The sky was rose-colored when he heard someone come around the side to the open door of his truck.

"You can go," Alex said, then added, "Thank your team for coming out. Thank you for coming."

He didn't move or look at her. "I wasn't asleep." He almost added that he'd been thinking of her, or, more accurately, thinking of her in bed beside him.

She came closer. "I'm staying until the crime boys get here. There's no reason for you to have to stay."

He turned his head and found her only a foot away. The dawn reflected in her eyes. She stared; an ocean of words that needed to be said flowed between them, but neither had any idea how to begin. The memory of the way she'd felt in the restaurant with her leg pressed against his filled his tired mind, blocking out all else.

"You need something, Hank?" She raised one eyebrow slightly.

"Yeah, come closer." He was just tired enough not to be able to act like he didn't want her anymore.

She took a step closer, almost touching him, her eyes daring him.

Hank slowly lifted his hand and slid his finger around the back of her neck. He didn't tug her forward, but leaned out of the truck and kissed her lightly on the mouth.

When she stiffened, he moved away.

"You can shoot me out here if you want to, Alexandra, but I've been wanting to do that for a while." He had no idea what she'd do or say. He didn't care.

She braced her hands on either side of the open door frame and leaned in, kissing him full on the mouth hard.

His arm circled around her and tugged her in beside him as her mouth opened and the kiss deepened.

She broke the kiss, but she couldn't pull away. Her back was pressed against the steering wheel, and her front was pressed against him. "This doesn't mean anything," she whispered, as if to herself, not him. "Don't think we're even friends."

"Fine with me," he answered as his arm tightened, pulling her hard against him and covering her mouth once more.

He wanted to feel her heart pounding as she kissed him back, but all he felt was her bulletproof vest. The knowledge of where they were and who they were must have registered with her a second after it did with Hank.

He broke the kiss as she slid away. Neither of them looked at the other.

Hank started his pickup. She closed his

door with a slam. He didn't trust himself to look at her until he'd backed out and thrown the truck into gear.

He wasn't surprised to see her standing, legs wide apart, fists on her gun belt and glaring at him like she hated his guts. She deserved better than to be kissed in a roadside park crime scene. "Smooth," he mumbled, "really smooth." He could have at least said something. Women need words; men only need women.

After he'd used every swear word he could think of, it dawned on him that she'd kissed him with the same hunger he'd kissed her.

By the time he pulled up to the ranch house, Hank was smiling. Apparently neither one of them had a romantic bone in their bodies. A roadside park with a body forty feet away wasn't exactly a romantic spot. There had been no words of love, or even caring. They reminded him of wild mustangs mating. If they ever did make it to bed, their pillow talk would probably be cuss words whispered to each other.

He shook his head. He didn't care. She'd kissed him back; that was all that mattered. They might never sit down to a candlelight dinner, or go to a movie, or waltz in the moonlight, but the next time they touched, she wouldn't be wearing that damn vest and they wouldn't be in a public place.

When he walked in the kitchen, Saralynn and his mother were sitting down to breakfast in the kitchen.

"Everything all right, son?" his mother asked.

"Everything is fine," he answered as he crossed to the sink and washed his hands.

"Perfect," he grumbled beneath his breath, "but way too public." He could still taste Alexandra's lips on his mouth.

Chapter 17

THERE WAS A CHAIN OF COMMAND IN MATTERS of death, and Tyler Wright knew he was at the bottom. When people killed themselves or died under unusual circumstances, he was always the last one to get the body. Tyler had a staff of five. Two men who did the embalming and helped with funerals. One bookkeeper, one secretary, and one night host who worked after hours when needed. The Wright Funeral Home had a standing rule that whenever a body was resting in state, the night host, or Tyler himself, was there if the family wanted to come in, no matter the hour.

In all his years he'd never had to open the doors after ten P.M. more than a dozen times. Once a son drove in at two A.M. insisting on seeing his father before he was buried at dawn, and a few times widows wanted to sit up all night with their mate. But for the most part, the host worked a few days a week from five to nine P.M.

Since the beginning, the host had always been a man, usually a retired member of the staff. But for the past eight years the host had been Stella McNabb, a retired home economics teacher who knew everyone in town and, more important, remembered each of their names. Those she hadn't taught, she'd made home visits to when their children were in school. The U.S. census takers could have saved themselves days by just visiting Stella. She was sixty-three and pleasantly fluffy, and she cried with the mourners at every viewing. The perfect host for a funeral home.

Tyler liked Stella. He'd hired her on the spot when she'd answered his ad. The fact that she'd been the only one who answered might have been a factor, but Tyler liked to believe he'd hired her because she was the opposite of him. He'd start a

sentence with something like, "You know
that family that lives out by . . ." and Stella
would give him the names, ages, and sometimes ailments of everyone who lived under
the roof before he finished his sentence.

Tyler swiveled in his chair and looked
out his office window. He'd called Stella
an hour ago to come in and sit with a
family tonight. The old teacher was never
late.

Sure enough, Bob McNabb pulled up
as Tyler watched. The weekend farmer let
his wife out and drove away. He'd drive
over to the fire station and spend his time,
then be back for her at nine. Tyler often
wondered why he didn't just drive the five
miles home and come back, but then farm
folks thought of coming to town as an
event and made the most of every trip.

Stella was carrying a big plastic
container. Cookies, probably. The woman
could turn sugar, white flour, and shorten-
ing into heaven.

Tyler sucked in his stomach. He'd lost
ten pounds the past three weeks, but
avoiding Stella's cooking wouldn't be easy.

He stood and walked out to the lobby.

Stella had set the cookie tin down and

was working on the knot of her head scarf. "Evening, Tyler," she said in her sweet way.

"Evening, Mrs. McNabb." He might be more than twenty years out of high school, but he would never be comfortable calling her anything else. "Glad you could come in. The Trudeaus are having a family visitation at six. You think you can handle them all? There could be forty or fifty coming."

She smiled. "I can handle them. There's not a one of them I'd hesitate to thump on the ear if he got out of line."

Tyler grinned. He wouldn't have put it past her. "I've got work to do in the office tonight. I'll check in a few times." He'd already been out to the house to deliver a funeral wreath for the Trudeaus' door. The place looked like a bus terminal that had never been cleaned. Chairs and trash everywhere. It made sense to use the funeral parlor to welcome folks who wanted to pay their respects.

Stella finally got her scarf off, but her hair looked worse than if the wind had blown it. "I always felt so sorry for Mary Trudeau. By the time she stopped nursing kids, she was taking care of Martin. I'll say one thing for him, though. He fought that cancer." She patted her hair, trying to make it look like it did when she'd had it back-combed and sprayed several days ago.

She moved down the hall to where it widened into an area with coffee and bottled water. She set the cookies out on a plate and stored her container with a dozen others beneath the counter. "I'd better make the coffee early tonight. I may need some myself to stay awake. I've been having this dream over and over last night, and I swear I found no rest even if I was asleep. It's a vision, really, about a terrible storm coming. Last night, I saw a coffin coming out of the storm and we all know what that means."

"What?" Tyler asked as he finally broke down and picked up one cookie. Peanut butter, his least favorite. He'd eat only two.

Stella frowned. "When you see a coffin, it means someone's going to die."

He almost choked on the cookie fighting down a laugh. Finally he managed to say, "I've found that very true."

She didn't notice his distress. "My Bob don't believe in my visions, but I've traced my family tree and I've got Gypsy blood. It may not make sense even to me, but there's something to be said for dreams."

Tyler nodded without having any idea what she meant. He was always dreaming some version of a dream in which he woke up late and ran to the cemetery to do a graveside service and somehow he couldn't find the grave or, when he did, all the people were waiting and he noticed, too late, that he'd run into the crowd naked.

Wonder how Stella would interpret that dream? She'd probably think he was on drugs, or worse, that he was some kind of sleepwalking exhibitionist.

He said good-bye and rushed back to his office. He wanted to jot down notes and search the Internet before he e-mailed Kate tonight. They could talk about the meaning of dreams. That would be something new and fun.

Willamina, his housekeeper, had brought his supper on a tray and left it in the office. Pork chops with gravy, cheesy potatoes with gravy, and sweet corn with butter melting on top. He covered the meal and left it by the door while he ate two diet meal bars. He knew one was a meal, but he always had another for dessert.

It was seven thirty when Kate's first e-mail came through. *Evening, Ty, how was your day?*

He smiled. No one had ever called him Ty. *Evening, Katherine.* He was guessing Kate would be short for Katherine. If she could shorten his, he could lengthen hers. *My day's perfect now I can talk to you.* He'd been thinking about saying that for two weeks. *I had a dream last night that you were walking out of a storm toward me.*

Do you believe in dreams? she came back before he had time to pat himself on the back for being such an interesting person.

Do you? He didn't want to commit before she did.

As always, she didn't hesitate to tell him what she thought. *Sometimes I wonder if you're not more dream than real.*

I wonder the same thing. He thought for a moment and added, *Sometimes I wonder if you're not the only real thing in my life, my hazel-eyed dinner partner.*

She wrote that she was laughing, and he swore he could almost hear her.

They talked of crazy dreams they'd had over the years. Tyler hated to end the evening, but he had to check on the Trudeau family.

Until tomorrow night, he typed.

Dream of me tonight, she answered back.

I'll do that. He signed off, leaned back in his chair, and smiled. When he talked to Kate, he wasn't the overweight undertaker, he was someone special. He closed his eyes and tried to remember what she looked like, then realized it didn't matter. She was beautiful to him.

Chapter 18

SATURDAY AFTERNOON

SHERIFF ALEXANDRA MCALLEN WALKED through the old mission-style home on her family ranch. The place was covered in dust and smelled faintly of decay. Even though her brothers had fought leaving and her father had hated to move from the ranch, their mother had relocated the family to town years ago.

Both of the boys came back as soon as they could drive. First Warren, and now Noah. It was as if they belonged to the land, more than the land belonged to them. Their father helped Warren get started, but after his oldest son was shot, Adam

McAllen lost all interest in a ranch that had been in his family for generations.

Alex walked through the empty rooms, remembering how her mother had never liked living out here alone where she couldn't see a sign of civilization in any direction. Living on the ranch had been just one more thing her parents had argued about. Her mother had always claimed the land was worthless. Adam McAllen used this home only as his base camp between rodeos. He wasn't there enough to keep the place as a working ranch. Finally he'd given in, and the family moved to town. The fighting eased, but the scars were still there. They'd married young, then spent years having kids and fighting. Now, Alex thought, Dad lived in Amarillo and rarely returned and Mom lived bitter.

Alex looked at the blank wall that had once held a dozen family pictures. Almost all her memories of her father were the same. He'd come home after being gone on the rodeo circuit for months. There would be hugs and presents all around, and then that night she'd hear the arguments after her mother and father thought the kids were asleep.

Adam McAllen seemed to come home less and less. He must have lost at least one argument, though, because her mother never moved back to the ranch. At some point, Alex started calling her father Adam. When he did come back, he stayed on the ranch until the place got too dirty to use even for a night.

"Alex!" Noah yelled from the front entry. "You in here?"

Her kid brother's voice had changed, lowered, and for a second she thought it was her big brother yelling. Alex swallowed hard and answered, "I'm in the den, Noah."

He rushed in. "Thanks for coming. I want to show you the horses I'm getting today. The first of a future herd I'll have running over this ranch. Michael says, as long as he and Maria are still living on the place, he'll watch over them if something happens and I can't get out. He and Maria planted a garden out back of the foreman's house, so I guess that means they're planning on staying." Noah finally took a breath. "What you doing in the house?"

She ran her hand over the fireplace mantel. "I was just looking around."

"I know you remember this place a lot better than I do."

She smiled. "You were little when we left. Warren was fifteen. He threw a fit, cussing like I'd never seen, and I cried so hard I made myself sick. Mom said you joined in yelling with the pack. She claimed we all sounded like coyotes and she thought of just leaving us here."

"I wish she had," Noah said. "I love this place. I've already told Mom as soon as I turn eighteen, I'm moving out here."

Alex felt sorry for him. If ever a kid belonged on the open range, it was Noah. Growing up in town wasn't for boys like him. "What'd she say?"

"She said that it's probably in my blood, and the next time around she's going to marry a banker and raise kids who love the smell of vaults."

Alex put her hand on his shoulder. "She shouldn't be too worried. I'm only a half mile away at the cabin. If you get into trouble or start to starve, you can always make it to my place."

"You've got food?"

"Cheerios," she said with pride. "And, once in a while, milk."

They walked out of the house and down to the barn, laughing about how bad a cook their mother was and how it was no wonder they were both so thin. Last Christmas she'd made cookies out of artificial sweeteners and wheat germ. Even the birds wouldn't eat them.

The first thing Alex saw when they stepped into the barn was a beautiful Appaloosa mare and her colt. They were both chestnut brown with markings in white over their backs. The mare had a blaze of white down her face and the colt bore a star between his eyes.

"They're wonderful!" Alex bent down to touch the foal, who looked to be about five weeks old. He resembled a giant stuffed toy with his woolly coat called milk hair and big brown eyes. He stood upright, with his legs straight and far apart like a tripod.

Noah bushed his hand along the mare's neck. "It's time I started raising horses, Alex. Mom says I have to go to college, but by the time I get out, I could have a real herd of these beauties. Michael says we can run horses on this place as well as cattle, so the only upkeep will be vet bills and grain in the winter. He said he'd keep an eye on them if Mom makes me go away to school."

"And who will put in the hours of mucking out this barn?" she said, thinking they were lucky to have Michael and Maria on the place. Free housing in exchange for watching over the land seemed a fair exchange.

The mare nudged her shoulder, wanting attention. Alex laughed. "Where'd these beauties come from? They remind me of a horse Warren used to have."

"They came from my place," Hank Matheson said calmly as he stepped out of the tack room.

Alex did her best not to show how startled she was. It made sense that he was here. Someone had to have brought the animals in, and she hadn't seen a trailer parked out front. All Hank would have had to do was ride the fence line of his place, cross over Lone Oak Road, and bring them in using the back trail to the barn. All he'd need was a lead over the mare. The baby would follow.

Noah caught the brush Hank tossed him.

"The mare should look like Warren's

horse," Hank said without looking at Alex. "She's the granddaughter of his mare."

"Remember that filly Warren gave to Hank six years ago?" Noah brushed the horse. He patted her neck. "She sure did grow into a beauty, and this is her first foal."

"I sold Noah the mare," Hank said to Alex, "but I gave him the colt."

"That was nice of you," she managed.

"It's time," Hank answered. "He can handle them." Hank winked at Noah. "Can't you, Preacher?"

"You bet. This is the start I needed."

She smiled at her little brother. "I hope so. Mostly all he knows about horses is how to fall off."

After they played with the colt for a while, Alex decided it was time to head back to her cabin. She'd had a long day, a long week. Once home, she decided to take a quick shower and go into town for a meal and a drink. One drink, she told herself, maybe two and that was it. Her days of having Hank drag her out of the bar were over.

In the shower, she thought about Hank touching her leg in the restaurant. It hadn't been an accidental touch or a casual brush. He'd moved his hand under the table and slid his fingers down the side of her leg. She should have said something right then. Or maybe stormed out, embarrassing him, letting him explain to his niece why she had left.

If she'd taken action when he'd touched her, he wouldn't have kissed her at a crime scene and, more important, she wouldn't have kissed him back.

What did he think he was doing, flirting? Proving a point of some kind? Being funny?

She stepped out of the shower, dried off, tied on a wrap, and began drying her hair. If Hank Matheson was flirting, he was doing a terrible job. If he thought he was proving a point, he hadn't, and if he was being funny, near as she could tell neither of them were laughing.

Alex tried to keep the kiss they'd shared at dawn last Wednesday out of her mind. She couldn't blame that on him. Well maybe the first one, but not the second. She crossed to her bedroom and slipped into a pair of jeans and a shirt. There was no need to dress up; she wasn't planning to pick anyone up. She just wanted a meal and a few drinks tonight.

As she walked into the living room, the sun was low in the sky. The view out her huge windows was breathtaking, except for one thing: Hank sat on her front porch.

She stormed out. "What do you think you're doing here?"

He'd tied his horse to the railing. He looked different than he did in town. The Stetson was still there, but his long legs were strapped into chaps. The spurs buckled across his boots reminded her that he was a working rancher, not one who dressed for show. The dried bloodstains on his plain chaps left no doubt about that. The cuffs of his shirt were rolled to his elbow, revealing strong, tanned forearms.

"I haven't been in from work to clean up yet," he said, slow and low as if he thought he might frighten her. "But I wanted to stop by here first on my way home."

"You smell of sweat and horses." She leaned against the porch railing, waiting to hear what he had to say.

He stared out at the sunset. "You hate ranching like your mother did?"

Fighting to control her anger, she said,

"That's none of your business, but no, I don't hate ranching."

She wanted to add that what she hated was that everyone in town knew about her parents' troubles. It occurred to her that he might be worrying about her little brother. If the kid tried to work the ranch, he'd be stepping right in between her parents. "If Noah wants to make a go of the ranch, I'm all for it. I'll even help when I can."

She stood, arms folded, waiting for him to leave. He just stood there.

Finally, he turned and looked at her as if just noticing she was standing next to him. "You hungry, Alexandra?"

Alex hadn't expected the question. She didn't have time to lie. "I could eat."

He stepped off the porch and put on his hat as he tugged the reins free of the railing. "How about a steak over in Bailee?" He swung onto the saddle. "I'll clean up and be back in a half hour."

He kicked his horse and was gone before Alex thought to close her mouth. After all these years of knowing Hank Matheson to be one of the most predictable people in town, he'd surprised her. First touching her leg, then kissing her, and now . . . now what?

She was way out of practice, but she could swear the man had just asked her for a date.

Alex put on a little makeup and combed her hair as she tried to think of how to tell him they couldn't go out. He was over thirty. If he had decided it was high time he started dating, he'd have to look somewhere else. She knew she could never look at him without remembering he'd been her older brother's best friend.

Maybe she shouldn't have allowed him to kiss her. She must have sent the wrong signal. Of course, there was also the possibility he was just trying to be nice.

Thirty minutes came and went. Alex reached for her keys. He wasn't coming. Maybe this was all just a plan to keep her on the ranch. He probably thought she'd wait an hour or two, and then it would be too late to go into town.

Well, she'd fool him. Alex grabbed her coat and was out the door before she could change her mind.

Halfway down the steps, she saw his truck flying up the road. He cut the engine and was out of the cab before she could come up with a strategy.

"You were leaving?" he asked as he met her on the steps. Even in the shadows she could see the anger in his face. "You were walking out?"

"I thought you weren't coming." She took a step backward, ashamed of herself for not believing him. Hank might drive her crazy, but he wasn't a man who lied. They'd both be better off if she'd just tell him that she doubted they could talk to one another for five minutes without getting into a fight. They were fooling themselves if they thought they could have a conversation over dinner.

"Alexandra." He said her full name slowly. "I may be a lot of things in this life, but a liar isn't one of them."

She backed to her door and grabbed the handle, knowing she had to be honest. Whatever his reasons for asking her, this ploy wouldn't work. "Dinner was a bad idea, Hank. A real bad idea."

He was so close she could feel his breath on her cheek. "You're right," he said. "I'm not interested in food."

With only a slight movement, he leaned

down and kissed her. When she didn't protest, he closed the space between them, pressing her against the door.

He felt so right next to her that for a few minutes she just let feelings wash over her. It had been so long since she'd felt . . . a lifetime since she'd thought of anything but family and work. She couldn't count the Saturday nights in the bar when she'd gone in to drink and forget about all feelings.

Hank wasn't flirting with her; he was showing her exactly what he wanted.

His hands slid up the sides of her body, boldly feeling her. His mouth moved from her mouth to her neck, tasting her flesh. He was so close she felt his chest press against her each time he breathed.

This was Hank. She closed her eyes. She'd known him all her life. He'd spent years teasing her when she'd tried to tag along with him and Warren. He'd bossed her around when she was in her teens and he was in college, always accusing her of going wild. He'd held her brother's body in the middle of a road while she'd stood in the dark and stared. This was Hank.

If she kept her eyes closed, maybe she could forget everything but the feel of him molding her body, turning her on, warming her blood. God, it felt so good to just relax and let someone pull her to him. But this was Hank.

Slowly her body stiffened. "Stop," she whispered. "Stop."

He held her tighter for a moment as if fighting, and then he stepped away. "You want this, Alex. You want it as much as I do."

She held her head up. "I want it, but not with you. Never with you."

Bracing, she wouldn't have been surprised if he'd hit her. But he didn't. He simply swore under his breath and walked away. She stood, staring at the taillights until they vanished.

She'd hurt him worse than she'd ever hurt him in the hundred fights they'd had since Warren died. Alex knew it deep down, just as she knew him. He hadn't been offering a one-night stand. He'd been offering himself.

She had to stop this now, no matter how much it hurt them both. She couldn't let him make love to her and then find out

sometime later that she had been the reason Warren died. And she couldn't live
with herself if she slept with Hank without
being honest.

Alex crumbled on the porch and cried
like she hadn't cried in months. The kind
of sobbing that made her guts hurt. The
night three years ago came back to her as
if it were yesterday.

She'd just gotten her master's and come
home to celebrate. Everyone knew she'd
been waiting that night at Warren's office.
But no one knew that she'd talked Warren's partner into skipping the patrol he
should have been making with Warren so
he could entertain her.

She'd been having sex in her brother's
office when he was shot on a country road
without anyone to cover his back. The image of Hank fighting to save her brother as
Warren's blood ran across the road flooded
her thoughts.

Finally, as she knew they would, the
tears no longer came. Alex curled up in a
ball, feeling cold and drained but refusing
to go inside. If Warren's partner had been
with him, he might still be alive. She'd
wanted to celebrate that night, a walking

wild, half-drunk woman party looking for excitement. It had cost her brother's life, and she couldn't even remember the partner's name. He'd blamed himself and quit the force. But Alex knew who was at fault. She was. She'd come on to the guy. She'd begged Warren to let him stay at the office when the late call came in. She was the reason her big brother died on that back road three years ago.

Two months after the funeral, she'd run for sheriff and been elected. She'd turned her life completely around, but it took her a year before she could look at Hank and not see the tears she'd seen that night running down his face.

He'd fought to save her brother, even refusing to stop when the doctor said it was hopeless.

And she'd stayed in the darkness and watched. Frozen.

Chapter 19

REAGAN WAS CONCENTRATING ON HER MATH when Jeremiah passed through the kitchen. "It's almost sunset," he said and walked out the side door.

"He's worse than a freaking grandfather clock," she mumbled as she closed her book and followed him.

They had a routine. At sunset they always sat in the two west-facing chairs and watched. The only thing that had changed in the yard since she'd arrived six weeks ago was that now a pair of chairs faced all four directions. Jeremiah watched the sun rise and set every day. He watched the clouds. He watched the birds. He watched the dust blow. She had a feeling that if it ever rained, he'd sit outside and watch that, too.

Reagan decided nature was his TV.

She curled up in the blanket he'd left on what was now her chair and studied the sky. She'd never lived in a place where folks were so aware of the weather, but she liked this time of day. Watching the sunset was a routine, and she'd decided the third night she was in Harmony that she liked routine.

If Jeremiah had anything to say to her, he usually said it now. He wasn't one to waste time talking at the table when he could be eating.

"You passing in school?" he asked without looking at her.

"Yep," she answered. "Signed your name on my report card last week. I got all Bs."

"Good." He didn't sound like he cared one way or the other. "I was thinking maybe you should drive the truck in a few days a week and then you could get supplies on your way home, saving me a trip."

"I don't have a license." She tried not to let her excitement show. She'd been driving the truck around the farm and once to town to get a saw fixed, but she never thought she'd be able to drive it to school.

"You got a birth certificate?"

"Yep."

"That's all you need. Turn it in, take the test. If you have to do anything else, find out. If you're not smart enough to figure it out, you're too dumb to drive."

"You think I might be too dumb to drive?" She didn't want to tell him that her name wasn't Truman on the birth certificate.

"You're smart enough. I think you'll do just fine." He stood. "I'm going out to the shed. I'll be back in an hour or so for supper. Remember, you're cooking tonight."

"I remember."

She watched him fold himself into his little cart and head down the path to what he called the shed. In truth, it was a large metal storage building back behind a forest of aspen. It looked like it would easily hold a dozen cars.

She'd looked inside a few times for a glimpse of his collection. Of all the things she'd thought he would have collected, tractors weren't even on the list. These weren't the huge tractors she saw moving up and down the back roads; these were old tractors. The kind that looked like they should be in a museum. She had no idea why he had them—not a spot on the farm appeared to have ever seen a plow—but almost every night he spent an hour or so working on the engines and polishing. He'd never invited her in for a close look, but he didn't bother closing the door most nights, so she knew he wasn't keeping them a secret.

She'd found other collections in the house. One wall in what could have been called his office was covered with clippings of World War II. He'd framed each clipping and printed dates on the glass. None of them, as far as she'd read, mentioned Jeremiah, but she had a feeling they were battles he'd been in.

She also found a box of what had to be every card he'd ever been sent in his life. Old Beverly might have not wanted to live with him, but she'd sent her brother a birthday card and a Christmas card every year. He'd saved them all. Reagan guessed he'd never sent one in return.

There were probably other collections in the rooms she hadn't ventured into yet. She had her room, they always used the kitchen, and she'd made a place in the front room where he kept the rolltop desk with his money tucked away. She'd made up her mind the day he handed her his roll of bills that she'd never take a dime without leaving a receipt.

On Sundays, she liked to curl up on the couch in the front room and read. The light was good and she could almost feel the ghosts of all the dead Trumans around her. They weren't frightening, just sad, and the longer she lived in the house, the more she felt like they were her relatives. She'd learned the names of all the people in the old portraits. Jeremiah didn't seem to mind telling her about his ancestors. They'd talk about them after dinner sometimes as if they were still alive.

Jeremiah would say things like, "Wilbur wasn't worth a dime from the day he was born in 1890." Or "Agnes didn't know her directions. Half the school days, her pa would have to hitch up the wagon and go find her, knowing she'd taken the wrong way home. Worst wrong turn she ever made was marrying a railroad man. He'd leave every spring about plowing time and not come back until it was too cold to work outside."

Once, the old man made Reagan laugh
so hard she cried when he told her that his
father's brother, Mac, got kicked in the
head by a mule one summer and hopped
around like a rabbit for a month. "He was
just plain dumb," Jeremiah admitted. "Drow-
ned in water he could have stood up in
and walked out."

Reagan smiled at the story, feeling like
she knew all the people who'd lived in this
place. She made her way back inside as
the last sunlight faded. She wanted time to
try out another one of the recipes in Miss
Beverly's handwriting. She loved the
way Beverly added little hints at the bottom of each one, the little secrets that
turned a pie from ordinary to wonderful.
Reagan felt like the old woman was teaching her, one step at a time, to cook.

As she collected the ingredients, she noticed they were low on cocoa. The keys to
the old truck were on a nail by the door.
Reagan grabbed them, made sure she had
enough money, and decided to drive the
two miles to the gas station store. She could
be back in five minutes. Uncle Jeremiah
would never miss her.

The old truck started with a hum. She

circled the yard and bumped her way down the dirt road to the pavement. Night had moved in, and the big old trees lining the road hugged in around her.

Reagan kept her eyes fixed on the beams of light in front of her and told herself trees were not something she needed to be afraid of in this world. Not even huge old bushy ones whose tops pointed like aging fingers. On cold nights, when the wind whipped around, the tops seemed to shake their bony fingers at her.

She stepped on the gas and was going at least thirty when she swung onto the pavement and headed toward town.

Four minutes later she pulled into the tiny grocery store and ran in. It took another minute to find the cocoa and pay. Only one person was in the store besides the clerk, who had the bored expression of one who'd left mentally on break and forgot to take his body.

He gave Reagan the wrong change and turned to a woman of about twenty-five buying a crossword puzzle book.

Reagan smiled at the sad-looking woman and said, "Hi."

The woman's expression didn't change.

In fact, Reagan wasn't sure either of them even noticed her passing through the store. She probably could have shoplifted the cocoa and no one would have noticed.

Reagan climbed back in the pickup, deciding that if the invasion of the body snatchers passed by here, they'd skip the two at the gas station. Aliens would have better luck with mind control over geraniums.

Backing out of the drive, she noticed one car half a block away coming toward her, so she gunned the engine and headed home.

Halfway there, the car caught up to her and flashed red and blue lights.

For a second, Reagan thought of making a run for it, but in this old bucket she'd be lucky to make it to the spooky old trees.

She pulled over and waited as the lady sheriff walked to her window.

"You got some kind of trouble, Reagan?" Sheriff McAllen asked.

"No," Reagan answered. "I was just out of cocoa."

The sheriff laughed. "So you're cooking."

"Every other night." Reagan tried to sit up straight. The sheriff didn't have a ticket book in her hand, or handcuffs. That had to be a good sign. "I'm trying out some of my grandmother's old pie recipes. Uncle Jeremiah seems to think they're edible."

Alex McAllen put her elbow on the window rim. "Really. I remember her pies. If you can make them as good as she did, I bet Cass at the Blue Moon would buy them from you."

"Really?"

Alex backed away. "I don't want to keep you if you're baking, but you tell Jeremiah that he needs to get you signed up for driver's ed. Till then, stay off paved roads."

Reagan put the car in gear. "I'll do that." She couldn't believe she wasn't at least getting a ticket. "Tell your brother I finished the math homework."

Alex smiled. "You two competing?"

"Not much. I beat him almost every time."

"That's because he can only count to eight." The sheriff waved. "You keep making him work, Rea, will you?"

"I'll try." Reagan drove away smiling. In her whole life she never thought she'd have an officer of the law call her Rea like they were friends or something.

Chapter 20

TUESDAY

HANK DROPPED HIS NIECE OFF AT PRESCHOOL and headed straight for the sheriff's office. It had been a few weeks since he'd almost attacked Alexandra on her front porch. He'd seen her from a distance a few times and she hadn't shot at him, but he had no illusion she was over being mad at him.

He walked in past the dispatchers and clerks. "Morning," he said to Andy Daily.

Andy looked tired. Hank guessed he was just finishing his night shift as dispatch. Between manning the phones here four nights a week and staying at the fire station three, Hank wondered when the man slept. During the day he owned the town's two Laundromats, one in a run-down apartment building and the other a block from the mall. He didn't do much to keep the places up, but he kept enough machines running to make sure people came back.

Hank had noticed that Andy's pockets always jingled, and he wondered if the man dropped by one of his places every day and cleared a box of coins to use for coffee money.

Andy downed the last of his cup of coffee and hurried after Hank. "You here about what we were talking about last night?"

"I am," Hank, said trying to get his thoughts off Alex's porch and on to the problem at hand. "I'm filing a report with the sheriff this morning."

Andy nodded. "Like you say, it might be nothing, but better safe than sorry."

"I'll let you know what, if anything, we decide to do at this time. I like your suggestion that we go on full alert at least until it rains."

Andy smiled. He liked being included.

Hank reached Alex's door and turned. "There's coffee at the station if you want to

keep Willie company for a while. I'll be back
as soon as I'm finished here."

"I'll do that." Andy nodded one sharp
nod and turned on his heel.

Hank took a long breath and walked into
the sheriff's office.

Alex's secretary, Irene, was on the phone.
She waved him past her desk, leaving no
doubt that Alex was expecting him.

When he stepped into the sheriff's office, he was surprised to see the highway
patrolman from the night they'd found the
body in the Dumpster and one of Alex's
deputies.

The thought crossed his mind that she'd
planned it so they wouldn't be alone, even
though this was official business. He nodded at the two men and took his seat at
the round table Alex had in the corner of
her big office.

"Thank you for seeing me, Sheriff," he
said formally. "Trooper Davis. Deputy Gentry. Glad you could join us."

Alex stepped around her desk and took
the last chair at the table. "Let's get right to
business, Chief."

Hank fought down a smile. She'd never
called him Chief before.

"All right." He forced himself to look at her without emotion. He could play this game just as well as she could. "The boys at the fire station have been keeping a record of the fires we've had since the burn ban went into effect a few months ago. We've been lucky; none of the grass fires have happened around any homes, and most were small enough to be contained within a few hours.

"Leaving out cooking fires in town and a few boys playing with matches, I've marked all others." Hank spread a map out on the table, forcing Alex to lean closer. "All this is of little interest to law enforcement, unless you consider when and where the fires happened." He pointed at the first red X on his map. "This was the first one. Since then, the fires chart counterclockwise in a circle." He moved his finger. "Six fires in two months. All seemingly accidents. All sparking on relatively calm nights. All moving until they've completed three fourths of a circle with Harmony smack-dab in the center."

The highway patrolman stood and leaned over the map, and so did the deputy. Alex continued to make notes.

Hank moved his finger slowly. "This first one we thought might have been a cigarette tossed. The second one wasn't near a road, so we guessed dry lightning sparked it. We found no cause evident on the third and fourth. The fifth looked like it might have been a camper who didn't put out his campfire. The sixth was our Dumpster druggie."

Alex's deputy whistled. "Holy shit. If these are really being set, that means our druggie may have been murdered. Someone could have seen him crawl in the Dumpster to smoke and tossed something burning in before closing the lid."

Trooper Davis frowned. "We've no proof it happened that way. The crime report won't be in for another week or more."

"We've no proof it didn't," Gentry added.

"Six accidental fires in two months?" Alex raised an eyebrow at Hank.

"Not likely," he said. "But not impossible."

"And all forming a circle at what looks like about five miles from town."

"Impossible," Hank whispered knowing she was following his logic.

"And the next one?"

"If it follows the pattern, it's due to hit toward the end of the week, right about here." He touched a place on the map just southwest of town. "Only our luck may have run out. The weatherman tells me there's a strong chance of winds over thirty every night this week and no hope of rain. If someone sets a fire on a windy night, we don't have the manpower to contain it. Even calling in every county volunteer fire department, around thousands of acres could burn before we could stop it. With all the grass around here in the government's Conservation Reserve Program, a lot of the grass is long and thick. That kind of fire could jump a road."

"We have to keep this quiet," Alex reasoned. "And we have to prepare."

Hank smiled. Despite hating his guts, she believed him. The four of them began to work on what could be done. The highway patrols could concentrate southwest of town. They might not be able to stop everyone, but they could keep an eye out for trouble. The deputy said he'd station men at high points to watch for smoke, and Hank planned to have a full team sleeping at the fire station. Alex remained silent.

He had his doubts about the location. The circle wasn't exactly even. Some of the fires were closer to seven miles out, some only four. And if they were set, the guy wasn't always moving the same distance around his imaginary circle. Two of the fires were within sight of one another. Then there was the slim chance this was just coincidence, nothing more. Fighting grass fires was their most common problem. They were a curse to dry land. Between lightning and careless folks burning off trash, grass fires kept them busy. Spring was on the way and with the wind and storms, their busy season was about to begin.

But this time it didn't feel like coincidence. Someone was playing a game with them. Hank felt it.

If he was wrong, all he'd wasted was time. If he was right, he just might save lives. He didn't care whether he was a fool or a hero. He had to follow his gut.

When he stood, Alex finally spoke. "If you have no objection, I think I'll investigate each one of these fires."

"I've no objection." He looked at her, but she didn't meet his eyes. "My files are open, and I'll even go with you to talk to anyone."

"That won't be necessary," she said. "If I get lucky, I might find a small clue that your firemen overlooked."

Hank walked out with the other men, wishing he'd had a moment to talk to her alone. But . . . what would he say—that he was sorry about that Saturday night? Not likely.

He spent the day doing all he could to be ready if another grass fire sparked. When he left to pick up Saralynn, he had a headache bigger than Texas and he had to act like nothing was wrong.

Saralynn waited for him in her class-room as always. She could have used her crutches and made it to the front of the building, but he knew school always wore her out. Plus, she had to be very careful around other children and most animals. One bump, one fall could send her back to the hospital with another broken bone.

He always waited until the other chil-dren were gone before he picked her up. He knew she wouldn't have liked them to see her being carried in and out.

She was waiting for him with a pirate hat on and beads made of macaroni.

"You a pirate today?" he asked as he lifted her.

"No. I'm one of the lost boys and we're only pretending to be pirates."

Hank nodded at the teacher, who was busy gathering up all the scarves and cardboard swords that helped fuel Saralynn's imagination. "Mind if I take one of your pretend pirates home?"

"Go ahead and smooth sailing." The teacher winked.

Driving home, they stopped, as they always did on Tuesdays, at the Dairy Queen for a chocolate-dipped ice cream. His mind was full of worries, but he listened to every word his niece said, figuring that today his mother wouldn't be home to listen and his sister Claire would be too busy painting and his other sister, Liz, would just be too busy.

Sure enough, when they got home, Claire had locked herself in her studio to work on her new masterpiece called *Man on a Hook*. Hank didn't even want to think about the finished product. Last week she'd frightened him with a pencil sketch of a work in progress called *Mr. Dismemberment*.

He carried Saralynn all the way to the back of the house, where his two great-aunts lived. They had separate bedrooms and shared a bath and a sunny sitting room. They welcomed him but didn't stop their gin game. They played gin every afternoon, and at last count he noticed Aunt Pat owed Aunt Fat twenty-three hundred dollars.

He sat Saralynn in the sunny window seat and helped her pull out her coloring books. The aunts would take care of her, spoil her with sweets, and keep her occupied until Claire finished her latest mutilation of man on canvas or his mother got home.

Hank stood. "I got to go back to town," he said. "I will not be back for supper tonight."

They both nodded absently.

Saralynn said reassuringly, "I'll remember to tell Grandma."

He looked at her framed in the afternoon sun. Her blond hair almost looked like it was on fire, and the thought that someone was out there setting fires made him sick to his stomach.

Hank was at a full run by the time he left the house to get back to the fire station.

Chapter 21

REAGAN CUDDLED INTO NOAH MCALLEN'S jacket and shivered as she watched one bull rider after another fall off. This Friday night was nothing like the last few rodeos. No families, no snack truck parked nearby with hot chocolate and hard, barely edible burritos. No friendly atmosphere.

Tonight, the wind howled out of the north and the air seemed thick with dust. She fought to keep her curly hair out of her face and stuffed it back into the hood of the wind jacket she had on underneath his coat. She should have brought something to tie her wild mop back because she'd never get a comb through it when she got home.

She'd taken to thinking of her hair as tumbleweed styled. The new hair products made it shine with health, but nothing seemed to tame it. In foster care, she'd always kept it short, like a fuzzy red football helmet on her head, but she hadn't cut it since she'd been in Harmony. It almost touched her shoulders now.

Reagan swung her legs, trying to keep warm on the hard, splintery wooden bleachers. She couldn't even remember the name of the town they'd passed through before they reached the rodeo grounds. A few of the same kids she'd seen last week, at the Guyman rodeo, were in the stands. She'd noticed Brandon Biggs smoking at the end of the rickety bleachers. He didn't look in her direction, but she was sure he'd seen her. The crowd was so small it would be hard to miss anyone.

Most of the kids from Harmony hadn't made the three-hour drive tonight. Noah said several of the guys thought the prize wasn't worth the gas to come so far, but he took every chance to ride he could get.

He had tried to talk her out of coming, warning her that it was the worst school district in the state, and that half the time a fight broke out at the end.

Reagan had set her books on the hood of his pickup and faced him, or rather his chest. "Then you'll need someone to cover your back, Preacher," she said, her hands on her hips as if she'd fight him if he didn't stop arguing.

Noah had laughed, bending down until they were eye-to-eye. "You're right, Rea, I can think of no one else I'd rather have on my side in a fight than little old you. Come on along if you're brave enough."

That had settled it. They'd climbed into his truck and hit the road. She'd already told Uncle Jeremiah she would be late because it was Friday night, so he wouldn't be expecting her.

Now, as she watched the sun set against a brown sky, she wished she were home. Noah was busy at rodeoing and spent little time sitting beside her. When he wasn't riding, he was helping out in the chutes or talking to the other riders.

The announcer yelled that Preacher McAllen was up next, riding a bronc named

Blue Thunder. Reagan turned to watch just as the gate swung wide.

Noah's long body jerked and popped as the horse whirled. With one hand in the air and his hat crammed down, his body bowed as if boneless in the saddle. Reagan felt the pain with him as she clicked off the seconds in her mind. Five. Six. Seven. Another hard buck. His hat flew, but he held on.

She was on her feet when she yelled, "Eight," just as the buzzer sounded and Noah dropped his arm and leaned forward on the powerful animal.

Pickup men moved in on either side of the still-bucking bronc. Their horses were big, well-trained animals, and despite the condition of the arena, the two seemed skilled at their jobs tonight.

Noah grabbed one man's waist and hung on long enough to be out of stomping distance before he slid to the ground, stumbled backward, but stayed on his feet. The riders shooed the horse toward the open corral gate.

Reagan ran toward him as he picked up his hat and moved to the fence. "You made it!" she yelled. "You made the full time."

He grinned down at her through the fence. "I do now and then, you know, Rea. Don't look so surprised." He stepped on the bottom board of the arena fence and swung himself over to stand next to her. "If I'm going to go pro someday, I got to start staying on. That's my plan. Besides, I didn't want to hit that ground. I've seen blacktop softer."

Reagan laughed. "It was worth coming and waiting out in the cold to see that ride. You looked great. I was so worried I swear I could feel my heart pounding in my throat."

Noah looked at the almost-empty stands. "I'm glad you were here. Nobody else was. Now I've got someone to back me up when I brag and tell what happened." He messed up her unruly curls with his big hand. "I'm glad I let you talk me into you coming along."

The rodeo came to an end and Noah collected the buckle, and then they piled into the truck and headed home.

As they passed back through the little no-name town, Noah asked, "Want to stop for an ice cream? I feel like celebrating."

"Sounds good," she said, still shivering.

"As long as we can run the heater on the way home."

They pulled into a hamburger place, and he was still explaining how he'd planned his ride tonight as they took the back booth.

"What are you going to do when school's out?" Reagan asked after the waitress took their order.

"I got it all planned out. Hank said I would work part time at his place. With the money I make, I'm going to start buying stock for the ranch. When my brother was alive, he ran a hundred head on our land and had dreams of twice that. Mom says the ranch isn't worth the taxes on the place, but I think if I had a stake I could make it work. We have a couple, Michael and Maria, living next to the main house in a place that used to be the foreman's quarters. They stay rent free for watching over the ranch. Michael said he'd keep an eye on any stock I had grazing."

"Why does your mother hate it so much?" Reagan didn't care about the cattle; people interested her more.

"Dad told me once she hated the land more than she loved him. Whatever that means." He shrugged. "Sometimes I think they just got married to fight. Everything about them is polar opposite. She's from Dallas, never rode a horse till she met Dad. He said she thought the only cowboys left played football. I asked my brother once a few years before he died why he thought a rodeo cowboy and a Dallas cheerleader would marry, and his said he'd explain it to me when I was older." Noah frowned. "I'm older now, but he's gone."

"Are your folks divorced?"

Noah laughed. "Hell, no. I guess they figure if they divorced and married someone else, they'd just make two more people miserable. Alex says Dad pays the bills on Mom's house in town, and he sent checks regularly for her schooling. Mom works at the Lady Bug in busy seasons to make a little extra money, but she's got a small trust fund that's enough to keep her in new cars every few years."

"Why didn't your dad move back to the ranch after she left?"

"He's got his life in Amarillo, I guess. He was from ranching folks, but I think the only part of it he really loved was the competition. Now, folks say he's a workaholic.

To tell you the truth, I don't know him very well. I know he loved the rodeo, but he didn't really teach me. I think it was just in my blood. I don't remember him being around much."

Reagan smiled. "He must have come home at least three times."

It took Noah a second to figure out what she was implying. He looked down. "Yeah. I guess he thought he wasn't needed after Mom had us kids. You should meet her; she turned into a supermom when it came to raising kids. Dad probably thought with all the relatives in town, he wasn't much needed. I think of him as kind of a jack-in-the-box father. He pops up now and then."

"You like him?"

Noah smiled. "I respect him. Since he's never been around, I can't say as I miss him." He leaned back. "What about your dad?"

Reagan was saved from lying by the arrival of banana splits in tiny red boats.

As they ate, the place filled with high school kids, loud and traveling in small packs. While Reagan watched them, Noah stole every other bite of her ice cream.

"We'd better get out of here," he said in

a whisper. "Too many people around bothers me. I see a few of the guys I rode against tonight, and they weren't happy about me winning the buckle."

"I'm still hungry," she whispered back.

"I'll buy you a malt on the way out."

She grabbed his jacket and folded it over her arm, holding it tightly as they moved through the crowd. Noah looked back and offered his hand.

Reagan didn't take it. She wasn't into holding hands. He didn't seem to mind. He just ordered the malt, and by the time he'd dug the money out, it was ready.

They made it almost to his truck before a shout stopped them.

"Preacher!"

"Get in the truck," Noah ordered her as he turned to face trouble.

Three shadows moved toward them, kicking up the white dust of the parking lot as they rushed.

Reagan, making no move toward the cab of the truck, tried to see around Noah as he widened his stance.

The local boys had been at the rodeo, but all three wore leather football letter jackets, not denim. They weren't part of the rodeo, they were just locals. Boys a few years past high school but still refusing to grow up, she guessed.

All three were older than Noah.

She couldn't make out their faces, but the way they spread out told her this probably wasn't the no-name town's welcoming committee.

"You came a long way to take our prize," one said. "My little brother was riding tonight, and he was hands-down the pick to win until you showed up."

"Look." Noah stood his ground. "Your brother is more than welcome to come down to Harmony's rodeo and compete for our buckles."

They'd spread out enough so that Reagan could see one of the guys clearly. He wasn't tall, but had a hard kind of beefiness about him.

Noah could no longer keep an eye on all three, so he spoke to the one in the center, who seemed to be the leader. His voice was low and calm, but not friendly.

It crossed her mind that these three were the most incompetent thugs she'd ever seen. They were trying to frighten Noah and her, but they didn't look like they knew what to say. These boys should have stopped by some of the foster homes she'd been in for a course in bullying.

Finally, the one nearest her laughed. "Is this your girl, Preacher, or your little sister?"

Reagan glared at him. She hated not looking her age, and she despised it when others mentioned it.

"She don't look old enough to be out this late, Preacher. Maybe we should turn you in for pestering a kid?"

"Yeah, maybe you're some kind of child molester," another one shouted.

Reagan sensed it now. Noah might not have been angry when they tried to bully him, but he didn't like them picking on her.

"Lay off," he said. "She's a friend."

"Cute." The guy moved closer, puffed up like a horned toad. "Reminds me of those Ewoks in *Star Wars*. She's got the wildest hair. What color is it, anyway?"

As his big hand reached out toward her, Reagan decided she'd had enough. She threw her malt directly at his chest.

The paper cup exploded, sending the cold cream from his face to his boots.

Out of the corner of her eye, she saw

the other two moving on Noah. All Reagan could do was think about keeping the one before her from joining his friends. She began kicking the beefy guy as he swore and screamed and backed away, trying to wipe malt out of his eyes.

She doubled her kicks, landing several against the back of his knees, making him almost fall as he twisted and turned to avoid her assault.

He finally stormed away, calling her every name he could come up with.

When Reagan turned, she was expecting to see the other two beating Noah, but they were just standing five feet in front of him, frozen.

It took her a moment to realize what had stopped them.

Standing on the bed of Noah's truck was Brandon Biggs with a pipe in his fists long enough to do some serious brain damage.

Noah slowly turned until he also saw what had stopped them. "I don't need your help, Brandon," he said. "Get out of my truck."

Brandon smiled. "I ain't here to help you, Preacher. I'm here to save these fools before they get too close to that girl of yours. I'm still doctoring the scabs on my leg from the last time I talked to her."

Brandon swung out of the truck bed without turning loose his pipe. "Why don't you take her home while I finish talking to the Fraser boys? We've been waiting for weeks to discuss a problem we had the last time they visited Bailee. I figure to-night is as good a time as any to settle things, and I'd appreciate you butting out of my business."

The Fraser boys were already backing away when Noah pulled Reagan toward the truck. He opened the driver's-side door, pushed her inside, then climbed in behind her.

"Should we leave Brandon? Those guys are older and there are three of them." Reagan couldn't believe she was worried about the troublemaker.

"Brandon can take care of himself. Trust me, he lives for this kind of stuff."

"Are you two friends?"

"No." Noah backed the truck into the road. "But I don't hate the guy like a lot of kids do, so I guess that makes me as close to a friend as Brandon's ever had."

"I'm sorry I hurt him now."

Noah laughed. "You got his attention. Sounds to me like he respects you, Rea. It appears my girl is tough."

"I'm not your girl," she snapped. The last thing she wanted in the world was to be someone's girl. She knew what that meant, and little of it was good, from what she'd seen. "And stop acting like that creep has a crush on me."

He looked at her as if trying to read her in the low glow of the dash lights. "What's bothering you, Rea?"

She waited a minute, then decided to be honest. If it ended the friendship, so be it. She'd been fine before she met Noah McAllen, and she'd be fine if he walked away and never spoke to her again. "I think we need to get a few things straight."

"About me turning into a werewolf?" he asked. "I've been trying to figure out what you meant."

"No, not that. Well, partly, but not all." She wasn't making any sense. "Rule one," she started over. "I don't like people touching me. Not you. Not anyone."

"I kind of noticed that," he answered.

"And I don't want to be called some

guy's girlfriend like I belong to him or something."

"All right. We stay just friends. Fine with me."

She thought for a moment, then added, "And you be straight with me. Don't ever try to play me."

"Agreed," he answered. "I try to be straight with everyone. I don't have the brains to remember lies."

"Okay, tell me. Why do you want to be my friend?"

Noah shoved his hat back. "I don't know, really. I just saw you out on that bench one day eating lunch all by yourself, and I wanted to get to know you."

"Because you felt sorry for me?"

"Because I already know everybody else in the school, but I didn't know you. Because you didn't look busy." He laughed. "And you didn't look like you'd make it easy."

She smiled. "And you don't like doing things easy."

"You guessed it."

They spent the rest of the way home reliving the almost-fight, making it longer and more exciting with each telling. They talked.

She waved good-bye from the porch as he pulled away, even though she knew he couldn't see her in the dark. Uncle Jeremiah would never waste electricity by leaving on a light.

After the pickup had disappeared, she stood looking at the moon and thinking that for the first time she could remember, she felt peaceful.

It couldn't last, she reminded herself. Nothing ever lasted. The only thing she knew for sure about people was that eventually, they'd let you down.

Chapter 22

TYLER WRIGHT WENT INTO THE POST OFFICE TO make his weekly complaint that someone was working all the crossword puzzles in his magazines before they reached his mailbox. But in truth, his heart wasn't into complaining today. For weeks he hadn't had time to do more than flip through the magazines, and then it was for discussion topics, not the puzzles. He had other things on his mind.

Correction, he had one thing on his mind . . . talking to Katherine. He'd decided his mystery lady was more a Katherine than a Kate, though if he ever did meet her again, he thought he'd call her both. Katherine when they discussed interests they had in common, Kate when he teased her.

As he waited his turn, then stepped up to the counter, Johnny Donavan, the postmaster of Harmony, was ready for him. "I know. I know, Mr. Wright. Someone is reading your mail."

"Not reading it. Writing in it," Tyler answered. "I buy those magazines for the foyer of the funeral home, and they look used the day I get them."

Johnny pressed his lips together and smiled, making wrinkles wave across his cheeks all the way to his ever-growing ears. "Well, Mr. Wright. It's not as though your customers are going to read the magazines. Or, for that matter, complain."

Tyler hated funeral home humor. He hated it when people introduced him as "the last to let them down" or "apt to give you grief."

He tried another tactic. "Who sorts the mail, Johnny?"

"You know as well as I do that Ronelle Logan does the downtown mail. She has since her daddy got her the job four years ago."

"Could I talk to her?"

"No." Johnny shook his head. Not all of his chins kept up with his face. "Last time you tried that, she was sick for two days and her mother came in to give me a piece of her mind. And believe me, Mr. Wright, you don't want a piece of that woman's mind."

"I don't want to upset Ronelle." Tyler smiled. "I just want to give her this. I picked it up in Lubbock the last time I was there."

Johnny frowned. People were always bringing in little gifts for him at Christmas. Cookies, cards, even gloves now and then. But no one had ever given Ronelle anything. It looked downright suspicious even if he didn't know why.

"Just tell her it's from a friend," Tyler said. "I don't even want her to know it's from me."

"Well, I guess it would be all right." He took the envelope, moving it slightly as if guessing the weight. "I'll have to look at it first."

"I didn't seal the envelope," Tyler answered, wondering if he'd have to put postage on the package before Johnny would deliver it to the back room.

The postmaster opened the flap and tugged out a large crossword puzzle book. "*The Best Crossword Puzzles of 2005 from the Country's Top Newspapers*," he read.

"I'll look for 2006 when it comes out."

Johnny nodded and shoved the book back inside the envelope. "I've never seen one so big. She usually brings in those little ones she gets at the gas stations."

"Neither had I. They sell them at the big truck stops." Tyler smiled. "I'm hoping it'll last her a while."

"It might, but she considers crosswords a timed event. If it ever makes it into the Olympics, we'll lose her to the glory, I'm afraid."

"It'd be Harmony's loss." Tyler tried to look like he meant the lie.

Back in his car, he picked up the copy of a hand-drawn map of an old cattle trail. A librarian at the state capital had sent it to him, guessing he'd love to study the details marked down more than a hundred years ago.

Friday afternoon, the sun was shining, and he had no funerals pending. Life didn't get much better, he thought. He'd decided over breakfast to take the afternoon off and wander the back roads. If he got lucky, very lucky, he'd see an indentation in the earth where thousands, maybe hundreds of thousands of cattle crossed this land before fences barred their way to the rail-heads in Kansas.

Just thinking about walking on the exact spot where early settlers had walked always made Tyler smile. His father had loved his-tory and made bedtime stories out of the legends of this part of the country. After his father died, Tyler spent months writing down all the stories he remembered, but in the end they only made him sad when he real-ized he'd never have children to pass them on to.

Tyler checked his watch. If he planned it right, he'd miss dinner but still get back in time to e-mail Katherine. As he drove out of town he thought of how much he knew about his Kate, and how little at the same time.

He knew she was allergic to shellfish and liked to eat barbecue with her fingers even though it was messy. She'd said she loved rainy days when the earth was sleepy. She thought she was fat. She'd read *Gone*

With the Wind every summer since she was fifteen and had never seen any of the Harry Potter movies. She collected crystal snowflakes for a Christmas tree she said she never had time to put up.

Tyler waved to a farmer mending fence as he turned off one farm-to-market road and onto another.

There were so many important things he didn't know about Kate. He didn't know how old she was. He knew she rented a two-bedroom apartment and she could hear planes flying over, but he didn't know the town. He knew her favorite movies and TV shows, but he had no idea what she did for a living.

Something important, he bet. She was a worker, he sensed that. And, as much as she dreaded work, sometimes she was dedicated to it. The few times she'd had to leave, or been late e-mailing, she'd said that it couldn't be avoided. Once she'd said she was in D.C., but she hadn't told him why. They'd talked of the capital but never of her career.

He knew if he asked, he'd open the door for her to do the same, and he didn't want to tell her he owned a funeral home in a small town she'd probably never heard of.

Tyler passed a highway patrolman parked near the crossroads and decided he'd better pay more attention to how fast he was going and stop thinking about Katherine. But he knew that was impossible. She was in the back of his mind all the time.

She was like honeysuckle in a garden. Most of the time you didn't even notice it among all the flowers, but the smell was always there, welcoming. Katherine was like that in his head. Tyler laughed and hit the steering wheel with the palm of his hand. He couldn't believe his thoughts. If he wasn't careful, he'd be writing poetry.

As he passed the McNabb place, he thought about Stella and Bob, who'd been married for forty years. Some folks thought it strange that Stella, an educated woman, being the high school home economics teacher, had married Bob, who had barely made it out of high school. But they fit together. More important, they seemed to really like each other. Bob waited outside in the car for her every time she kept the funeral home open at night. Tyler had never heard either one of them say a cross word to the other. Stella knew and talked to everyone in town. Bob waved, and that seemed enough.

Tyler wished not for what they had, but that he and Katherine could continue to have what little they had for a few years.

If he could just have that much, it would be enough.

Chapter 23

HANK MATHESON WALKED INTO THE BLUE Moon Diner with no illusions that Alexandra had called him to have breakfast. She'd been all business when she'd said, "Seven, tomorrow morning at the diner." The only question in his mind was why not one of their offices?

The place was deserted. The usual old guys who had breakfast every morning during the week weren't here because on Saturdays the senior citizens served a free pancake breakfast and Sunday they'd all have coffee and doughnuts at the church before Sunday school. The two days away from the diner gave the old men new stories to tell Monday.

With the regulars gone and no one in the downtown offices grabbing a meal before the start of a workday, the place looked closed. If Ronelle hadn't been at her usual tiny table at the door, Hank would have thought Cass, the owner of the place, had simply left without turning off the lights or locking the door.

"Morning, Ronelle," he said as he passed by.

She didn't look up from her crossword puzzle book.

When Hank took a seat in the back booth by the windows, Cass yelled to him through the pass-through window, "What'll you have? Ain't got no waitress this morning, so you'll have to fend for yourself."

"Just coffee for now," Hank yelled back. "I'll get it."

He stepped behind the counter and poured himself a cup. He could see through the window that Alex was pulling up her Jeep beside his truck, so he poured her a cup as well.

She hit the door moving fast. Ever since he could remember, Alex was like a storm.

Warren used to complain about his kid sister, but Hank had always been fascinated by her. She was a woman who took life at full speed. Warren and he used to laugh that boyfriends had the half-life of Kleenex around her. She changed majors twice a year until Warren talked her into settling on criminal justice, and then she'd gone all-out straight through to the terminal degree, a master's. Just like her big brother. Only for Warren, the career path had proven terminal.

Hank shoved the memories aside as Alex slid into the seat across from him and unzipped her jacket.

"The boys from the crime lab found a few things that point to the possibility that you're right about the fires being set. They also said whoever did it had some knowledge of fires and a good sense of place. The guy's exact words were, 'Our arsonist knows the lay of the land.'" She met Hank's stare. "There's a good chance he's either in law enforcement or one of your volunteers at the station."

"Shit," Hank said under his breath.

Alex took a sip of the coffee, then added sugar, giving him time to think. "I'm starving," she murmured, more to herself than him.

Hank stood and walked to the pass-through. "Two specials, Cass."

"Ain't got no specials on Saturday," he yelled back. "I can make you up two breakfasts, but you'll have to take what you get."

"Two surprises," Hank agreed, knowing that he'd eaten everything on the menu in this place, so nothing would be too shocking. "With whole wheat, scrambled, well done, and dry," in case any of those words applied.

"You got it," Cass answered. "I'll ding the bell when your order's ready. Pick it up fast if you want it hot."

Back at the table, Alex smiled up at him, but the smile didn't reach her eyes. He wanted to pull her close and tell her everything was going to be all right. They'd make it through this trouble. But he knew she wouldn't welcome sympathy. She needed someone she trusted to talk things out with, and he guessed he should be thankful that she considered him that. They might fight about pretty near everything, but they'd never lied to one another.

"There's more, isn't there?" Hank asked.

She nodded and waited until he sat down before she said softly, "The highway patrol has one suspect who isn't either one of my men or one of yours. Right now they're calling him a person of interest."

Hank relaxed. "That's good news, I guess." He didn't want to think that one of his men could be setting fires, even though he'd heard about it happening a few times over the years.

"No," she answered. "Not good news. Their person of interest is Tyler Wright."

Hank shook his head. "That's not possible."

"I feel the same way, but they've got records of people seeing him driving by at least three of the fire sites just before the fires."

Hank leaned forward, staring right at her. "I'm not buying any of this."

"You'd rather believe it's one of your men, or mine?"

Hank downed the bitter news along with his coffee and stared at the scarred wooden table between them. "Maybe my theory is just that, a theory. Maybe all these fires aren't related. We've had six grass fires before in two months. Even the results on the Dumpster fire couldn't prove that it had been set by someone other than the druggie. Maybe . . ."

She leaned closer. "I know Tyler is your friend, Hank, and you stand with your friends to the end."

His head shot up, and he knew she was thinking the same thing he was at that moment. He'd been the first to the scene that night Warren was shot, and the EMTs had had to pry his friend's body away from him. Hank had been a full-grown man, educated and trained to deal with anything, but he couldn't, wouldn't let his best friend go. In those moments, he'd believed with everything he had that if he could just hold on tight enough, fight hard enough, he could keep Warren from dying.

Hank saw the sadness in her eyes. The heartache he'd seen since that night. It had been three years, but now and then the pain twisted like an embedded spur.

Cass broke their silent standoff by clanking two plates on the table. "I got tired of ringing the bell. Eat up, folks," he said, then walked away.

Alex looked down at the mound of food. "I'm not hungry anymore," she said.

"Me, either."

"I'll want a list of all your volunteers dating back ten years."

Hank nodded. "You'll have it in an hour."

"You staying at the station today?" She zipped her jacket. "You still got that feeling another fire's coming?"

"Yes to both."

She slid to the edge of the booth. "I'm staying close today, too. I'll be working in my office if a call comes in."

"Dinner tonight, here," Hank said in a flat voice. "We'll go over any detail we find in a file. With our phones transferred to our cells, we'll get any calls."

"Fine." She looked at her plate of food. "With our luck, Cass will warm all this over and make us eat it for dinner."

Hank stood, dropping a twenty on the table. "Call me when you're ready."

She climbed out of the booth, and for a moment they were standing so close they would have touched if one had shifted. Neither moved.

A river of unsaid words flowed between them, and neither knew how to cross. Hank had sworn after last week that he wouldn't be the one to try again. He stepped back, reaching for his hat.

"It's not Tyler," he said. "I'd stake my life on it."

"I'll still check him out."

"You do that, Sheriff." Hank tried to keep the anger from his voice. It wasn't fair to be mad at her for doing her job. But he knew it would be a waste of time. A man who kept a quarter in his vest pocket just in case he ran into a four-year-old princess wasn't the kind of man who set fires.

They walked past Ronelle, bidding her good day. She ignored them both.

Chapter 24

BOB MCNABB HAD NEVER CONSIDERED HIM-self much of a farmer, but he leased ten acres five miles outside Harmony because Stella wanted to live in the country. He drove back and forth to wherever the Texas Department of Highways and Public Transportation sent him every day for thirty years to do highway maintenance, and then he retired and drove Stella around. When he was alone in the car, he liked listening to western novels on tape. He'd probably checked out every one the library stocked at least twice.

When Stella retired from teaching, she

began practicing what she'd preached all those years. She canned and made jams in the fall, quilted all winter, and gardened in the spring. She belonged to every ladies' club in town and served as queen of the biggest Red Hat Society in the panhandle. She taught the youth classes at the Baptist church on Sunday nights, worked part-time at the funeral home when Tyler Wright needed her, and volunteered at the Pioneer Museum on the Square.

Bob took on only one hobby: raising long-eared rabbits for the tristate fair every year. Stella, having been a professional, wasn't allowed to enter her quilts or canned goods or even vegetables, but Bob could enter his rabbits. He had ribbons all over one wall of his small barn. Stella's favorite joke was to introduce him as a rabbit wrangler.

Tonight, he could hear Stella singing with the radio as he walked outside to smoke his one cigarette of the day. They made a pact years ago. He'd cut his smoking down to once a day, except after making love, and she'd stop bothering him about the habit. He'd thought it was a good rule, but to be honest there were a few times he'd

have sex just to get to the cigarette afterward. Stella must have figured it out, though;
about two years ago she stopped being in
the mood. Bob didn't know if she was no
longer attracted to him in that way, or if she
thought she was improving his health.

He lit up and walked out by the barn.
The land next to their few acres was leased
for grazing, but it had been so dry lately
he hadn't seen cattle on it.

Bob strolled all the way to the fence post
watching the evening sky, wishing he'd see
a cloud. Without rain, the warmer days
coming would be even hotter. Even with the
sides of the barn open, the rabbits would
suffer, and Bob couldn't afford to buy air
conditioning for pets. A few days last year
when it had been well over a hundred, he
and Stella had brought in the rabbit cages.
They'd stacked them in the kitchen and
bathroom tub, but it had been a mess.

He looked up, smelling something in the
wind.

Someone burning trash, he thought, then
remembered the burn ban. Anyone would
be a fool to burn, knowing the fine.

Then he saw something black moving
across the short grassland a few hundred

yards beyond his fence. It moved like the shadow of a black cloud, shifting unevenly as it crawled toward him.

"Fire," he whispered with an intake of breath.

He stared hard. The dry stubby grass burned so quickly, he could barely make out the flame between the smoke and the earth.

Fire!

Bob crushed his cigarette with his foot as he turned and ran back toward the house. "Stella!" he yelled. "Call the fire department."

She came to the door and stared at him. Then, behind him, she must have noticed the smoke. Her face seemed to go pale as the moon in the evening light. She put one hand over her heart, then took a quick breath and disappeared.

Bob ran to the barn and began loading up the cages as fast as he could. He had his van full by the time she came around the house with the garden hose. A gray fog of smoke drifted between them. The black ground cloud had moved twenty yards closer.

He took the hose from her hand, wishing

it would stretch past the fence. "Get in the van and drive across the road with the rabbits. I'll wet the fence line down."

Stella had never taken orders well, but for once she didn't discuss his plan. She climbed in and gunned the engine. For a woman who never liked to drive, she looked like a racer flying down the road.

Before she was out of sight, a pickup turned down his drive. The McAllen kid, Bob thought. He'd seen the boy pass by on his way to the old worthless McAllen ranch ever since the kid could see over the steering wheel. Everyone said he was a good boy despite being as crazy as his old man about the rodeo.

Noah McAllen jumped from the truck before it stopped moving. "How can I help?"

Bob motioned to the old washtub he used to clean up the rabbits for show. "Grab that and bring it to me, then get all the feed sacks you can find in the barn."

By the time Noah found a half dozen sacks, the tub was full of water and two more neighbors had arrived. They knew what to do. Noah might be only a kid, but he learned fast and did twice the work of the others.

One man cut the fence with pliers he kept on his belt, and they all stepped into the field beyond Bob's property. Barbed wire wouldn't stop the fire; only a road would, and Bob and Stella's home lay between the fire and the road.

The four men took wet sacks and formed a line about twenty feet apart. Each man had to hold the fire line so that it didn't reach the thick grass of the yards and flower beds or beyond to the house and barn.

Bob worked as fast as he could, knowing that even if they held the fire, it would eventually bend and come up the sides. There wouldn't be enough men to stop it then. Four men could hold one side of his property line, but it'd take a dozen or more to save the place.

The black smoke burned into his lungs and his face, and Bob's hands felt sunburned in the heat.

He was aware of Stella even in the smoke. He'd hoped she would stay with the van, but he knew it was in her nature to come back and join the fight. She was passing out soaked sacks and tossing burned ones into the tub. She moved with the hose, spraying the men down as well as the ground when they came near enough for her to reach them. The fire constantly pushed them backward. Before long they'd be at the fence line. Bob tried not to breathe deeply as he fought harder.

The sound of sirens filled the air moments later. Bob felt like it had been an hour since he'd first seen the fire, but it couldn't have been more than ten minutes. The sheriff's car pulled in first, and then the fire truck crossed the grass and headed toward the open spot in the fence.

Another pickup, loaded down with men with shovels, pulled up near the house. The men jumped out and ran toward the fire line, holding their shovels high like ancient Scots going to battle.

Bob stepped back as the fire hose came to life, spraying water over the grass in a twenty-foot sweep.

Men with shovels dug a ditch in the ground between the barn and the grass. If fire came again, it would have to jump the line to reach the barn.

He stared and watched, knowing how close he'd come to losing his home, Stella's quilts, the rabbits. If he hadn't seen it coming when he did . . . he couldn't think about what would have happened.

"You all right?" someone whispered as Bob felt a hand rest on his shoulder.

He turned and smiled at the sheriff. He had no words. *Thank you* seemed an empty bucket, considering what they'd all done.

She seemed to understand. "Your wife went in the house to wash up. The boys will take care of making sure it's out. You look a sight."

When he didn't move, she added, "It's over, Mr. McNabb. You can rest now. It's over." She put her arm around him and tugged him toward the porch.

"Your little brother was here when I needed him," Bob managed. "Without him . . ."

Alexandra smiled. "I know. I'm proud of him. He's a good kid."

Bob nodded. "The best, if you ask me. Tell him I said so."

"I sent him inside to wash. You can tell him yourself."

Bob took a few steps toward the house and stopped. He stared at the open door, with Stella moving around the kitchen.

They didn't have much. Didn't even own the house they'd lived in for half their marriage. But when he thought about losing everything, he realized just how rich he was.

He walked in, his face and clothes black with smoke. Walked right up to Stella and kissed her on the mouth like he hadn't done in years.

As always, she understood him and moved into his arms. They were alive.

When she tugged away, he asked, "How are the rabbits?"

"They're fine."

"I meant for you to park the van across the road and stay there."

She shrugged. "I know, but I couldn't see sitting with the rabbits while you were just down the road fighting to save the house. If those rabbits had died, we'd have dinner, but if you'd . . ." She couldn't finish for crying.

He held her tightly and smiled. He felt the same.

People were moving all around now, washing up, doctoring burns on their hands and faces, rolling up the fire hose, but he didn't care. Bob leaned close against her ear and whispered, "I think tonight, when we're alone, I'd like to make love to my wife."

She giggled just as she had when he'd first mentioned the idea forty years ago.

"And," he added, "I don't think I'll smoke a cigarette afterward, if you've no objection."

Chapter 25

ALEX CHECKED THE SECOND-DEGREE BURNS ON her little brother's hands and face. "You got too close without gear."

Several of the firefighters in the country kitchen agreed with her.

Noah tried to pull away. "I didn't exactly have time to go shopping for the crisis." Immediately he looked like he regretted snapping back. Unlike her, Noah was usually even-tempered. "When I drove up and saw the smoke coming toward the McNabb house, I only thought about helping."

"Next time," said Hank, who had joined them, "wet a bandanna and tie it around

your face. Dunk your hat, too, if you get a
chance."

"And wear gloves," Alex ordered. "Mom's
going to have a fit about you getting
singed."

"I'm not hurt," Noah insisted, glaring at
his bossy sister. "I've had sunburns worse
than this."

Alex chose not to argue with him in front
of everyone. They could both see the blis-
ters rising on the backs of his hands.

She nodded a thank-you as Stella
passed, offering everyone iced tea in
mason jars. When Noah joined the other
men, Alex walked out into the night, where
the smell of smoke was still thick in the air.
Usually, this time of night was her favorite
part of the day, but now danger drifted in
the wind as if whispering of more trouble
to come.

When she reached the fence, she heard
Noah's truck and knew he must be leaving. The fire truck started backing through
the mud toward the house. It was over. In
a few minutes the night would be still and
quiet again. And, thanks to the breeze,
free of fire.

Alex knew it was Hank who walked up

behind her. She didn't turn but whispered into the smoky stillness, "You were right. You warned of a fire tonight."

"Yeah, and I hate that I was," he answered, resting his arm on the fence post. "If we'd been five minutes later, the McNabbs would have lost their home."

"McNabb told me he knew you'd come." She smiled. "He thinks you hung the moon, Hank. Told me you were like a son to him."

Hank shifted. "He never told me that. I think a lot of him and Stella, too, good people. If he were twenty years younger, I'd give him this job and stay on my ranch long enough to make some money."

Alex shook her head. "No, you wouldn't. You'd find something else to keep you busy. You're nothing but a Boy Scout, Matheson. Always trying to help people."

He didn't deny it. "You're nothing but a wild child, McAllen. If you hadn't been sheriff, you'd probably been an outlaw."

She didn't argue. She'd made her share of dumb choices.

They were both silent for a while, and then he added, "I hate the thought that someone is out there starting these fires.

We have all we can handle with the accidental ones started by lightning or backfiring cars, or downed transformers. We don't need a nut running around setting them on purpose."

"If the wind had been stronger tonight . . ." she began.

"We'd be standing beside ashes," he finished.

On impulse, she gripped his forearm and closed her fingers around the solid muscles a few inches above his wrist. "You're not in this alone, you know; we'll fight this, Hank. We'll fight it together." All the problems they had between them— all the past that haunted them—didn't matter. All that mattered was stopping whoever was setting the fires before someone was killed.

His hand closed around hers. "There's nothing else we can do here tonight. I'll call in help first thing tomorrow morning and we'll find the point of origin. Maybe our firebug got careless and left a clue."

"Until then," she said, wishing she could see his face in the darkness, "I'll have a patrol out here making sure no one sets foot on the land. As far as I'm concerned, this entire burn is a crime scene and I'm treating it like one."

Someone yelled, "Chief!"

Hank turned, pulling away from her touch. "Tomorrow," he whispered, as if someone might be close enough to hear.

She nodded, then realized he couldn't see her any better than she could see him. "Name the time?"

"Seven, your office for coffee. The team should be here by eight and we'll find out where this fire started."

He walked toward the house, but she stayed in the shadows. She wanted to stand there and listen to the wind, feel the heat still in the earth, smell the smoke. Somewhere near was a criminal who was trying to destroy her town, and she planned to get to him first.

Chapter 26

REAGAN SAT DOWN BESIDE JEREMIAH IN WHAT she thought of as her chair. The darkening sky seemed muddy tonight, but the air was far too dry for it to be fog. She swore this part of Texas sometimes had negative humidity. The air just sucked what little moisture there was out and turned it into dust mites.

"There's a fire northwest of here," Jeremiah said to himself. "I can smell it."

"Any idea what's burning?" She'd learned he could read the atmosphere better than a crossbreed of a weatherman and mystic.

"Grass, I think, just grass. When trees burn, they leave the smell of heartbreak in the air."

"Oh." She tugged her blanket around her, thinking she'd always wondered what heartbreak smelled like. "How far away do you think the fire is?"

"It's out by now. All we're getting is a drift of the smoke in the wind."

She looked at the silhouette of him a few feet away. Even in the night she could see his bent, crippled-up frame. Like an old tree root, he seemed to draw life from the earth. There was not one ounce of doubt in her mind that he loved his apple trees more than he'd ever love any human.

"You ever have your heart broke?" she asked, just for something to say.

He was so quiet, she wasn't sure he planned to answer, and then he surprised her and said, "Once."

Reagan waited. For Jeremiah, the flow of conversation was more like a drip.

"I was engaged to a Matheson girl before I left for the war. I thought she was about the prettiest gal in the state. She called me Dimples and giggled every time she said the word. I suspect that would have gotten irritating in time, but when I was eighteen I remember thinking it was cute."

"Really." Reagan leaned over the arm of her chair and looked at him upside down. "Was this girl any kin to the Mathesons in town?"

He didn't answer, but she could feel the look he was giving her even in the dark. It was the one that silently said she was dumber than a chipped rock.

"Oh, of course. You grew up around Mathesons with their ranch bordering us near the apple trees." It occurred to her that if he'd married the girl, the Truman name wouldn't be down to two. Now, when he died and the town figured out she wasn't a Truman, one of the founding families would be gone. Completely gone. The thought hurt Reagan's heart. How would she tell people that her family was extinct?

"So, what happened to the giggling Matheson girl?" she asked him as she shoved aside her thoughts of being alone again.

"When I got back from the war, she said she was more interested in a career than me. Became a grade-school teacher and lived with her sister in town until they both retired and moved out to Hank's ranch where they grew up."

Reagan had heard Noah say once that Hank lived with a houseful of women, but she never thought one of them might be Jeremiah's old flame. "Did you ever go over and say hi?" Hank's ranch was within walking distance.

Jeremiah didn't answer, but she thought she saw him shake his head.

Finally, he said, "I didn't have nothing to offer her. My land ain't hardly fit for farming, and I never wanted to nurse a bunch of cattle. If it weren't for those apple trees my father planted a hundred years ago, I would have starved by now. The government pays me to let all my grass go back to nature. Even sent me seeds years ago." He looked out in the darkness as if he could see his land. "I like the idea that the native grasses are growing up, making my place look like no one ever settled here."

"If you like the natural land so much, why have all those tractors?"

He laughed. "Do you wake up ever' morning with a certain number of questions you have to ask?"

"No. What about the tractors?"

"I fixed trucks in the army; never carried a rifle all my time in the war. I got so good at it I could tell what was wrong with a motor when they pulled a truck into the garage. When I got home, old tractors were about the only thing around to work on. Working on them was easy, and it passed the time. I used to do work for everyone around, even bought all kinds of old farm equipment and fixed them up to sell, but when newer models came along, they weren't so much fun, so I quit and just kept the old ones I liked."

Reagan almost giggled. Jeremiah had just said more words than she'd heard him utter in weeks. "Would you show me them?"

"Sure." He patted the dog's head and the dog stood. "Maybe tomorrow before supper. I think we'll turn in now."

The old dog and the elderly man moved silently toward the house. The dog that had no name but Dog was never far from Jeremiah's side. The few times she'd gotten up earlier than Jeremiah, she'd seen the dog on a rug just outside the old man's door.

Reagan curled into her blanket. She

loved it here. Each day a piece of her soul dug deeper into the soil of this land along Lone Oak Road. She wasn't sure if it became more of her, or she was slowly becoming a part of it, but she knew she'd never leave this place completely no matter what happened. A part of her would always be here.

She watched a pickup turn off the main road and recognized the sound of Noah's truck.

Jeremiah moved up the steps. "Tell that boy to change his spark plugs. Engine's missing."

"I will."

"And tell him he's welcome to a slice of leftover pie. He gets any thinner I'll mistake him for a sapling."

"I will." Reagan smiled as she stood. Jeremiah liked Noah McAllen even if he did complain.

"Don't let him talk your ear off, girl. We've got work in the orchard tomorrow."

"I won't."

Noah's pickup pulled to a stop just as she heard the kitchen door close. Jeremiah might like Noah, but that didn't mean he planned to be sociable.

She saw the white of the bandage on his left hand as he walked toward her.

"Are you hurt?" As he approached, she tried to see his face beneath the shadows of his battered cowboy hat. "Did something happen?"

He stopped several feet away. "Now don't start babying me, Rea, or I swear I'll leave. I just got a little burn. It's not even blistered in but a few spots. Between my sister and my mother I've had all I can take of being pampered. I came over to tell you about the fire at the McNabbs' place tonight."

"I know about it."

"You know?"

"Sure, Uncle Jeremiah said he smelled smoke. Grass fire, right?"

"Right. What else did the old man say?"

Reagan smiled. "He said you could have some pie if you wanted."

They moved toward the kitchen door. "You know something," he said as he held the door with his good hand and let her pass under his arm. "Food seems to come with being hurt. I never noticed it before."

She slid the pie tin toward him, sat down on the seat next to him, and handed him one of the forks.

The kitchen was still and silent, like the night. With no TV and a radio that got only three stations, she was glad for the company.

He told her all about the fire while they finished off half a chocolate pie.

He moved his bandaged hand to rest on the back of her chair, just above her shoulder, and she didn't mind. Maybe she was getting used to his nearness. Maybe she knew he meant nothing when he drew closer.

"I did something good tonight, Rea, and it felt really great."

"I wish I could have been there."

"Me, too." He stared at her for a few seconds and added, "Want to go with me to Dallas next week? There's a PRCA rodeo and for once, I'd be going just to watch. Several of us are skipping school after lunch and heading down, but it'll run too late to drive back on Friday. There's a church that opens their doors and lets us sleep on bedrolls in their fellowship hall. Last year there were kids from all over the state sacked out on bedrolls. The rules are strict, but you'll—"

"No," Reagan said without hesitation.

"But—"

She didn't give him time to try to talk her into anything. "Uncle Jeremiah is feeling bad. He's got a cough. I'd better stay close."

Noah nodded, but the look in his eyes was skeptical. "You're still afraid I'm going to turn into a werewolf or some other kind of monster, aren't you?"

"No." The word came too fast to be complete truth. "I just don't want to be that far away from home."

She hated it when he got that kind of smile that said he'd read her mind. He couldn't read her thoughts. He couldn't know . . . he didn't know anything about her. Yet he understood.

"All right, stay home, but you're missing a good time."

She'd heard those words before in another place, another time . . . and they'd been wrong.

"Well"—he tapped her shoulder—"how about watching me ride in two weeks? The rodeo is right here in Harmony, close enough for you to walk home."

"I'll be there."

When she stood to wash the pie pan,

she noticed him looking at a calendar on the wall by the door. "You marking off the days to something?"

"Not me, Uncle Jeremiah. Every morning he crosses one more day off."

"It's a long time before Christmas. What do you think he's marking?"

"I have no idea. He hates talking at breakfast and by evening I've forgotten about it." She frowned. "If I were guessing, I'd say he's marking off the days until I leave. I don't think he's really gotten used to the fact that I might stay."

She tugged Noah out of the chair by his unbandaged hand and walked him to the porch.

Just before he headed down the steps, he turned, shoved his hat back, and leaned close as if to kiss her on the cheek.

She moved away, looking down, not wanting to see his face.

Neither of them said good night. He just walked to his truck and drove away while she watched.

"Don't get close," she whispered to the night. "Never let anyone close." She watched at the taillights faded. "Not even Noah."

Chapter 27

HANK WENT BY THE FIRE STATION WHEN HE CAME back from the McNabb place. He showered, then made sure all was in order.

Willie Davis was so pumped Hank almost had to peel the kid off the ceiling. He'd been around a year, but this was the first real firefight he'd been in. Luckily, Andy Daily was still at the station running off copies of pictures he'd taken when they were fighting the fire. He seemed to enjoy rehashing the details as much as Willie did. He finally had to leave to walk across the street to the city dispatcher's desk. Hank had a feeling Andy would have no problem staying awake tonight.

Adrenaline still pounded in Hank's blood, too, so instead of going home, he headed down North Street for no reason. The fires, or rather the fact that someone was setting them on purpose, ate away at his gut. He took the crimes personally, as though each were committed against him.

Since his father died when he was a kid, Hank had always thought he had to take care of things. His branch of the Matheson family didn't have much money, but Hank had the original land old Harmon Ely had given his great-granddad. Somewhere a few generations back, his ancestor had managed to buy out the others. Every other relative moved to town or away except his branch of the family tree.

He had cousins who worked in the bank and one who owned the Ford dealership. Cousins taught school at every level. One second cousin was a lawyer, one the youth minister at the Hilltop Baptist Church. Almost everywhere he looked in town, he had a relative who worked there, but none wanted to ranch, except him. Hank's father must have handed over the last gene for ranching before he died. Maybe that's why Hank understood Alex's brother Noah so well; he knew how the kid felt about the land.

The day Hank graduated from college, his mother signed the ranch over to him with the understanding that the big rambling house would always be home to family. His two sisters would always have a place to come home to, but Hank held the title to the land. Which, as it turned out, was very smart, otherwise some ex-brother-in-law would now own a slice of the Matheson ranch.

His mother had been selling her pottery for as long as he could remember, but she never mixed that money with ranch funds, except once to build on to the house. Which, considering his two great-aunts and two sisters who all came home to roost, hadn't been a bad idea. She had her studio, a low adobe-style building off the garden, and Hank had his barn out back, far enough away that the ladies didn't smell his horses.

He'd also closed off one upstairs wing for his bedroom and study. All the women said they understood, but Hank had the feeling

that if he ever left the door to his wing unlocked they'd have his socks matched and
underwear folded before he was out of sight
of the house.

Some years the money from the ranch
barely kept the taxes and utilities paid, but
Hank knew he'd never sell. In good years
he'd buy a new truck, repaint the barn, and
improve the stock. In bad years, he'd hang
on and hope.

His mother had her business but when
Hank got home from college, the ranch was
all his. She took care of the house. The
aunts managed the flower beds, which grew
larger every year. Claire, Saralynn's mother,
painted in the attic, and no one was quite
sure what Liz, his younger sister, did. She
had two college degrees and had been telling people she was studying to take the bar
exam, though Hank had yet to see a law
book around the place.

As Hank turned around at the end of
town, his thoughts turned dark. Hank liked
order. He liked everything to make sense
in his life. He liked reason, but this time
reason told him that if the arson followed
around, closing the circle, his ranch or one
close might be the next target.

He laughed without humor. Right now nothing made sense; why should the arson? Hank was crazy about a woman who hated him. His two divorced sisters were settling in, planning to never leave. His niece grew weaker every day. The police thought his good friend was a person of interest.

For a man who liked order, Hank was batting zero.

When he passed the Blue Moon Diner, he noticed Alex's Jeep parked across the street on the back row of the Buffalo Bar and Grill parking lot. She'd almost hidden it in the trees that lined the alley, but he knew it was hers.

Hank swore and pulled in beside the Jeep. Alex seemed to be determined to make his long day endless. He thought that a minute ago everything that could go wrong already had, but he'd forgotten it was Saturday night.

He walked in the smoky bar and looked around. He was hoping she'd ended her habit of coming here on Saturday nights, but that would be too much to ask. If she was drunk, she'd be wild and hard to handle, but he'd do it. He'd get her home safe, sober enough that he could leave her, and then walk away, cussing himself for caring one way or the other what happened to her.

Saturday night Buffalo's always had a band playing, and the place was usually packed. Tonight was no exception. The bar smelled of sawdust, sweat, and beer. Lights blinked along the dance floor, offering only flashes of light. The low rattle of conversations blended amid laughter and the sound of bottles clanking.

Alexandra wasn't at her usual place at the far corner of the bar. In fact, she wasn't anywhere. When he finished his second lap around the place, Hank wondered if he'd been wrong about the Jeep being hers. A tall blonde wearing a sheriff's badge wasn't an easy person to miss.

The thought crossed his mind that she might already have left with someone. He checked his watch. Even if she'd come straight from the McNabb place, he didn't think she'd had time to get drunk enough to go home with someone yet. Besides, one of the bartenders would have called him if she was acting out, not because they owed him any favors, but because they all respected Alex and didn't want to see her make a fool of herself.

He spotted her walking out of the ladies' room. She hadn't noticed him yet. She walked toward the dance floor, stopping only long enough to gulp down the last half of a beer, and then she stepped into some cowboy's arms. They began to two-step across the floor. He was dressed western, but not with clothes that had ever seen a day's work on a ranch. He also seemed far more interested in showing off his dancing moves than in his partner.

Hank watched her for a while. She seemed to be enjoying the dancing, but she wasn't talking to the guy whirling her around. She wasn't even looking at him. Her eyes were closed as she moved to the music.

When the song ended and the cowboy stepped away, pointing toward the bar, she shook her head and turned her back to her partner.

Hank's boot hit the dance floor wood hard as he moved forward.

He saw the anger in her eyes the second she spotted him, but he kept walking straight to her.

"Are you checking up on me again?" she snapped when he was close enough for her words to be private.

"No." He tried to smile, but couldn't pull off casual when she was glaring at him. "I came to dance."

Without giving her time to comment, he circled her waist as the music started.

She didn't move. "I don't want to dance with you."

He tugged her against him and moved her as if she were a mannequin. "Just close your eyes again, Alexandra, and pretend I'm the nobody you've been dancing with all night."

To his surprise she took his suggestion. Her body began to move with his, her hands rested on his shoulders, and they danced.

First one, then another, then another. Hank hadn't danced except at a few weddings since college, but the good thing about country music was that the dances he'd learned in bars near campus seemed to still fit. As with all bands toward the end of the night, the music got slower.

Alex slid her hands down his back and hooked her thumbs into the waist of his jeans.

When she rested her head on his shoulder and breathed against his throat, Hank drew her closer and she melted into him like warm butter.

He pushed her hair away from her face with his chin. "How about we take a night off from hating each other and just relax? I'm too tired to fight. Why don't we just pretend we're strangers?"

"I don't want to fight anymore," she whispered. "And I don't hate you, Hank, I just don't . . ."

"I know, baby, I've heard it all before. All I want to do tonight is dance with you."

He felt her nod of agreement and moved his hand slowly down her back. He didn't want to dance at all, but if she'd stay in his arms, he'd give it his best shot.

She felt so good against him. Without the vest he could feel her chest rising and falling against his. She fit perfectly in his arms, just as he knew she would. He rested his hands at her waist and moved his thumbs over her last few ribs. He thought of teasing her about being too thin as he'd done a hundred times when they were growing up, but he didn't want to tease her tonight. He just wanted to hold her against him.

She was tall and lean and stronger than most men he knew, but right now, in his arms, she was all woman. No gun. No badge. No smart mouth. Just pure woman, leaning into a man.

What he wanted to do with her would probably shock even wild Alexandra. When she'd been sixteen, he'd reminded himself he was four years older and she'd think he was a pervert if he flirted with her. When she'd been twenty and having her fun with every man she liked, he'd reminded himself he was her brother's best friend. Hank felt like he'd been watching over her and wanting her all his life.

When the band took a break, he closed his hand over hers. "How about I buy you a beer and we split some wings?"

She shook her head. "I want my own basket of wings."

He smiled, tugging her off the dance floor. "You got it. Find us a table and I'll order the wings at the bar."

She looked up at him, her grip tight on his hand. "Before I forget or reality comes crashing in, thanks for the dance. It was nice."

Before he could react, he tasted the

touch of her lips on his mouth, and then she was gone, vanishing into the crowd.

It took all his self-control to head toward the bar. He ordered the wings, grabbed two beers, and went to find her.

The third time he circled the bar, he accepted the fact the she'd ditched him.

Frustrated, he walked outside to clear his head. He expected to see the empty spot next to his Dodge where her Jeep had been parked. But the Jeep was there.

Letting his eyes adjust to the night, he looked around. The noise of the band tuning up for another set drifted from behind him. It crossed his mind that Alex might be playing a trick, or worse, teasing him, but that wasn't like her. She hadn't been drunk enough to pass out in the restroom or think she could walk home, so she had to be somewhere near.

He set the beers on the railing and walked toward her Jeep.

He'd guessed right. She was sitting in the front seat with the door open.

Hank thought he knew women, but Alex was from a planet all of her own. She didn't get her hair done or her nails painted. Half the time he couldn't tell whether she wore makeup, but to him she was sexy as hell.

"You trying to run out on your wing order?" he asked as he rested an elbow on her Jeep's door. "Or maybe me?"

"Neither," she answered. "I couldn't find a table so I thought I'd come out here to think."

"About what?"

She looked up at him with those less-than-innocent blue eyes. "About how we might as well do it and get it over with."

"What?"

"You know what, Hank. The tension between us is so strong I swear I can see it in the air sometimes." She stood and tugged her T-shirt free from her pants. "Right here, right now. You've got more room in your Dodge than I do in the Jeep, so let's go there."

When he didn't speak or move, she added, "Or we can do it standing. It's dark enough between the cars."

She was so close when he inhaled, he breathed her in. He felt her hands brush his middle and move to his belt. She began tugging the buckle loose.

He leaned to kiss her, but she turned

away. "Don't waste time. Let's get this over with."

Hank had wanted her so long his brain couldn't function. After all this time, suddenly, she wanted him, right here, right now.

He dug his fingers into her hair and twisted his hand into a fist, then tugged hard until her face lifted and she met his stare. "Stop it, Alexandra. Stop it right now."

She raised an eyebrow. "You don't want me, Matheson?"

"You know I do, but not like this." He realized that *like this* might have been the only way she'd ever had it.

She pushed away. "Well, if you're waiting for me to wear a strapless dress and a pushup bra and bat my eyes all evening before I finally surrender, you're out of luck. I'm not that kind of woman."

Hank remembered once Warren had slugged a guy in a bar for commenting about Alex. The drunk had said he could tell she was from rodeo people. She wouldn't let a man stay on her longer than eight seconds.

Hank pulled her head toward him, ignoring her protests, and kissed her hard, then

whispered against her lips, "You're not any
kind of woman, Alex; you're an original,
and I wouldn't want you to be any other
way than just how you are." He kissed her
softer, then moved to her ear and added,
"We're not making love for the first time in
my truck."

She pushed on his chest, and he let her
go. "What makes you think there will ever
be a second time, or a second offer?"

"I'm betting on it." He buckled his belt,
wondering if he wasn't a fool for turning
her down. Half the men he knew had an
any-woman-any-time-offered rule they followed, but Hank knew he wanted far more
from Alexandra. "Tuck that shirt in and let's
go eat our hot wings and warm beer."

"You're not my big brother," she snapped.

"Damn right about that." He grabbed her
shoulders and pushed her against the Jeep.
While she protested, he kissed her again.
He tasted when passion sparked once more
in her and felt her move against him, trying
to be even closer than they had been on the
dance floor.

He slid his hand inside her T-shirt and
cupped her breast, then broke the kiss
and listened to her rapid breathing as he

pressed his palm against her soft flesh. He liked the little sounds of pleasure she made as he molded her in his grip.

With his last ounce of control, he pulled away and said in a voice that came out more harsh than tender, "I'm not your brother, Alexandra, and there *is* going to be a second time, but not here."

He stepped back from her. "We're going inside and having a drink like old friends, or half the town will be talking about us tomorrow."

Alex straightened and said in a low voice, "Have I mentioned lately that I hate you?"

"No, but it's about time. I thought for tonight we were calling off the war."

She looked like she might argue, then turned and followed him into the bar. He had no idea if it was the food or the drink that made her return, but he had a strong feeling it wasn't him.

Just before they reached the door, Hank realized he'd been talking to Alex all her life, but he'd never talked to her like a lover. He risked looping his arm around her neck. "One more thing, Alexandra, I think you're about the sexiest woman alive just the way

you are. If you ever did consider that strapless dress and pushup bra, my heart probably won't be able to take it."

She jabbed him in the ribs. "You missed
your chance. Now all I want is a meal. And
you'd better not drink too much, Chief; you're
due in my office at seven."

She was letting him know everything
was back to normal.

He followed her inside, letting her set the
ground rules. They talked about the fire as
they ate, and then she walked to her Jeep
with her cell phone to her ear. He had no
idea who she was talking to, probably dispatch. She climbed in her Jeep, closed the
door, and waved as she drove away.

Chapter 28

TYLER WRIGHT PACED THE HALLWAYS OF THE funeral home. He had to try and find a reason that he could accept for his Katherine not answering any of his e-mails in three days.

He could think of none. Depression followed him like a shadow.

He turned the corner and passed down the hall with empty viewing rooms on either side. If he didn't come up with an answer he could live with, he'd wear out the carpet.

Turning right again, he walked past the offices and copy room, thankful that his

grandfather had built Wright Funeral Home
in a square. At least he didn't have to decide which way to go. The brothers who'd
built the place had actually been wise: By
making the hallways run along the outside
frame, they could easily put in private sliding pocket doors between the rooms, allow-
ing them to move anywhere in the building
without being noticed. The last thing a griev-
ing family wanted was to have a casket
pass by.

On each corner, the hallway widened
into a seating area large enough to hold
twenty visitors waiting to pay their respects.
Tyler now stopped at each corner to catch
his breath before storming off down the
next hallway.

After he'd passed his office the third time,
he gave in and decided to check his e-mail
once more. It was almost midnight. He had
little hope she'd answer this late, but tomorrow seemed a lifetime away.

He stared as the latest e-mail came up.
The subject line read, *Sorry*.

He hesitated, then clicked.

**Sorry, Ty, things are crazy here at
work.**

He wrote back, *I've missed you.*

272 Jodi Thomas

I've missed you, too. More than you know.

He read the words several times before answering, *These last few days have made me realize how thin the thread is between us. If for some reason you didn't write, I'd have no other way of reaching you. I could lose you forever.*

He waited, staring at the screen, wondering if he'd already said too much, been too bold. Lost her. All she'd have to do was click Erase a few times and everything they had would be gone.

I understand, she wrote. Nothing moved for a minute, and then she sent, *I suggest a plan. If for any reason one of us disappears and doesn't answer back, the other agrees to go to Quartz Mountain on the first Monday of the month for three months and have dinner. If the other never e-mails or shows up to dinner, the one at the dinner table will order a drink and toast what we had with a smile and promise never to try and find the other.*

Tyler wanted her to tell him who she was, where she was, any other way to contact her, but he knew if he did, somehow what they had would change, and he couldn't risk losing her.

You have my word. If you disappear, I'll go for three first Mondays and have dinner on the mountain. I'll toast our friendship.

What if it's you who breaks this off, Ty?

It won't be.

She didn't respond. After a minute, he added, *Hope all at work is better.*

It's a mess, she answered. *Sometimes I wish I could just dig a hole and bury my job.*

I know how you feel. He laughed so loud in his study he was glad no one, not even the dead, could hear him.

He then settled back in his chair and told her of a woman he'd met who had a collection of a hundred clothespin dolls with faces all painted and dresses made to fit the wooden clothespin.

She laughed.

He didn't tell Katherine that the lady's family decided her collection should be buried with her. Tyler strongly suspected not one relative wanted to continue the hobby.

Katherine told him about having car trouble and having to deal with a mechanic who suggested changes she knew she didn't need. She described growing up with a father who made her change her own oil and rotate her tires. He ran their house like it was a boot camp. She told of being able to make a bed a quarter would bounce on by the time she started school.

Tyler was impressed. He'd always considered himself being very mechanical when he refilled the wiper fluid, and he'd never made a bed in his life.

They talked for an hour before she wrote, *After midnight, have to get some sleep.*

Me, too, he answered.

Tomorrow. Good night, dear one. If I ever disappear for a few days, trust that it will not be by choice on my part.

I feel the same. Good night, my Kate.

He stared at the screen for a while. He was someone's dear one.

Chapter 29

ALEX REFILLED HER COFFEE CUP AND SAT BACK down at the table across from her deputy, Phil Gentry, and Trooper Davis from the highway patrol. They were both men with experience, trusted men. Davis followed his gut feelings and now and then stepped on a few toes, but he'd asked for this assignment, so she knew it mattered to him. Phil Gentry had been with the department in Harmony for more than twenty years and always thought out every possibility.

Trying to concentrate, Alex figured she was the weak link in the team. She couldn't remember what they'd been talking about before she went for coffee. Translation, the only man she truly saw in the room this morning was Hank Matheson. He seemed all professional and distant, as if nothing had happened between them in the parking lot of a bar last night.

For once she wished she'd had enough to drink the night before to have trouble remembering what she'd done. Unfortunately, she remembered every word, and worse, she remembered every touch. It had all started with the way Hank gently handled her on the dance floor. No one had ever driven her so crazy with such an easy touch. He'd brushed her, pressed against her, moved with her through song after song, but he'd never taken it beyond the limit. If he had, she could have stepped away. She might even have slapped him and stormed off the dance floor. As it was, she'd been the one making a fool of herself.

"If our arsonist follows the pattern," Hank said, tapping the map on the table without looking at her. In fact, he hadn't really looked at her since he'd arrived exactly at seven. "I figure he'll strike in about ten days, maybe two weeks."

The others agreed with his assessment. Alex downed a big gulp of hot coffee, knowing her concentration was off. Hank had been ready to work this morning and so had she—in theory. She couldn't help wondering if last night lingered in his thoughts the way it did in hers. She remembered the way he'd touched her breast, not like a man exploring, but more like a man who knew exactly what he wanted. The man before her now was nothing like the man who'd kissed her last night.

Hank circled a spot on the map with a highlighter as he said, "I'm guessing right about here. I could be a mile or two off in any direction, but this guy is playing some kind of game, and it looks like Harmony is in the center of his target. When he finishes roping us in, he'll head for town."

Alex leaned forward. The area he thought would be hit next took in one corner of the McAllen ranch, half of Hank's land, and part of the old Truman place on Lone Oak Road, along with four other small places scattered in between.

"What do we do that we're not already doing?" Trooper Davis asked.

"We could ask the farmers to plow a fire

break between the farms. That, and the roads will keep most fires from spreading." Hank frowned. "If flames reach the CRP grass here, and here, it's tall and thick. That kind of fire might jump, even a road or a plowed line."

"I could get county crews to mow anything along the roads," Alex suggested.

"That'll help, but we don't want to cause our arsonist to get suspicious. He might move somewhere else, and we can't watch every mile of road. I'm thinking right now he has no idea we're on to him."

"We don't know much," Alex admitted. "We don't know what he'll do once he's made his circle."

"And," Hank added, "if he panics, he could set more than one fire at a time."

"We need rain," the deputy said.

Hank straightened. "We can pray for rain, but we plan for fire."

They all agreed.

"One last thing." Hank finally glanced at her, but she saw no emotion in his stare. "On the outside of this circle, a mile or so farther out from Harmony than he's ever set a fire, there's a small branch of the Palo Duro." Hank hesitated, pointing to what looked like a root running across the map. The Palo Duro Canyon ran for hundreds of miles across the flat land of upper Texas. The canyons grew shallow and small, branching out in thin veins cutting into flat land. There were long stretches of miles where no roads had ever been cut.

"If our firebug sets a fire at this rim of the canyon, there are no farms close and no roads to get the trucks into the area fast. A grass fire could burn wide before we could get to it. I've got two trucks at the station, but we can't battle a fire line miles long and have any chance of putting it out before it reaches a fence, much less a road."

Deputy Gentry leaned forward. "What if we had Wild Derwood fly over those sections a few times a day?"

Hank shrugged. "Who'd pay for it? The fire department runs on volunteers, and last I checked the city and county budgets had no extra funds."

"If we requisition money, everyone in town would know about it," Alex added. "Whoever is setting these fires would love all the talk. This kind of guy lives off the excitement. He could be right in the middle of us and we'd never know."

"Right," Hank agreed.

Phil Gentry smiled that fake smile he always used in poker games. "Wild Derwood would love to be on the volunteer fire department, Chief."

Hank frowned. "Derwood's crazy. Everyone knows that. He stole his dad's Cessna and went joy riding when he was twelve. He flies over the cemetery every Sunday to wave at his mom, and his favorite topic of conversation is clouds. A few years back he told me he was born with cloudaphobia and had to fight like hell to overcome it. I think he may have gone too far in the other direction."

"He brought the plane back safe that day he was twelve, so we know he's a good pilot. And good pilots always watch clouds," Gentry said, "and you can't fault a man for loving his mother."

"That doesn't make him sane." Hank folded his arms. Everyone at the table knew Derwood also occasionally smoked the weeds he grew in his backyard, but no one mentioned it or they'd have to deal with the problem and in so doing lose the town's only good pilot.

"So, if his only flaw is insanity"—Alex

looked from Phil Gentry to Hank—"what does that make him?"

Hank frowned.

Phil smiled. "A firefighting volunteer."

Alex choked down a laugh. Hank looked like he'd swallowed a horned toad. She knew he didn't want Derwood around the fire station, but he also saw Phil's point. One plane could do more good at spotting a fire than twenty men.

She watched Hank fold up the map and shake hands with the other men as they moved to the door. He didn't say a word to her. She told herself everything was back to normal. Last night had been a lapse into a place neither of them planned to go.

If and when she was ready to get involved with a man, it wouldn't be Hank Matheson. He'd always seemed so much older than she was. When she was sixteen, going to her first dress-up dance, he and Warren had been like two fathers, questioning the boy, taking pictures on the porch. Half the conversations she'd had with Hank in her life had been when he was telling her what she should do or ordering her to listen to her brother or telling her to grow up and act like a lady.

Alex frowned as she took a seat behind her desk. She hadn't acted like much of a lady last night. But then, he wasn't exactly acting like a big brother.

She knew they should put this attraction for each other aside, but when this was over she had a feeling a different kind of sparks were going to fly.

"Alex." Hank's voice snapped her back from her thoughts.

"Yes." She grabbed a pen and spent a few seconds looking busy before she glanced at the door. She couldn't help but notice he looked a little hesitant. "What is it?"

He took one step into her office and stopped. "I told Noah he could come over to the station this afternoon and I'd start his training. I want him more aware of safety before he stops to help out at another site, if that's all right with you?"

"It's a good idea." She knew no one in her family could stop Noah. She'd been a wild child, but her little brother was both wild and brave, a far more dangerous combination. "Thank you, Hank."

"No problem." He leaned against the wall. "You know, when he learns enough to go on a call, I'll do my best to keep him out of harm's way."

"I know." She smiled. "He's stubborn."

Hank gave her a pointed look. "It must run in the family."

He was five feet away and she swore she could feel his hand on her breast. This man drove her mad. He wasn't her type. He knew every fault she had, every wild thing she'd ever done. She wasn't looking for a man, and if she were, it wouldn't be him.

She liked her men reckless and out of control with the taste of danger on their lips. Hank was steady and solid. How reckless can a man be who lives with his mother, two sisters, two great-aunts, and a four-year-old? The man had so much baggage he needed his own U-Haul.

Last night in the parking lot was probably as close as he'd ever come to being out of control. And even then, he'd been the one to stop, to think of what a scene they'd make, to think of her.

The memory of how he'd handled her in the dark flooded back, and she felt fire in her cheeks.

She looked up and saw that he was still

standing by the door staring at her. "What are you looking at?" she snapped.

"You," he said, and his slow smile told her he had guessed what she was thinking.

He turned and walked out of the office.

Alex put her elbows on her desk and held her forehead in her palms. "That's it," she whispered. "When this is all over I'm going to check myself in for observation. I'm losing my mind." She slapped her forehead. "Or, maybe I'll go flying with Wild Derwood and let him tell me about clouds while we fly over the cemetery and wave at his mom."

Chapter 30

REAGAN SAT IN THE PACKED STANDS OF THE Harmony rodeo waiting for the bull riding to begin. Everyone in town was at the rodeo grounds tonight, and most had come to see Noah "Preacher" McAllen ride. She'd heard talk that many thought he might just be a better rider than his father, Adam, had been. Adam McAllen had put Harmony on the map in his youth. When he'd ridden in the national finals, it was said that more than a hundred folks went to Las Vegas to see him win.

Adam McAllen was a legend. Even when he moved to Amarillo three years ago and

separated from his wife, he still told reporters in interviews that he was from Harmony.

Reagan didn't care about Adam
McAllen. All she cared about was his son.
She hadn't seen Noah except at school
for almost two weeks. Since the night of
the fire at the McNabb place, Noah had
been hanging out at the fire station when
he wasn't training for this one eight-second
ride tonight.

At lunch, he'd told her all about it, until
she felt she knew as much as he did about
how to fight fires. She also learned that
both his sister, Alex, and Hank Matheson
were worried that there would be more
fires. Hot, dry weather warned of it, and
spring seemed to have nothing but hot,
dry days coming one after the other.

She and Noah had sat on the tailgate of
his pickup one afternoon and planned
what would have to be done on Jeremiah's
place if fire came. Reagan hated the thought
of it. She didn't mind that the spooky old
trees to the main road might have to be
cut down, but she didn't like the idea of
scarring the earth with a plow. Jeremiah

loved looking out over his land and it wouldn't be the same if they plowed a fire line.

She pulled her thoughts away from the threat of trouble and watched people wandering around the grounds. Some of the middle school kids in front of her hadn't seen any of the rodeo. They were too busy walking from one end of the stands to the other, or talking, or hopping from bench to bench. Three blond girls about fourteen were dressed like they thought they were going to a beach party and had gotten off at the wrong stop. Even though it was after dark, they still wore their sunglasses.

Little kids played under the bleachers, and a group of men were taking a smoke break over by the parked cars. Reagan almost preferred the "no name" rodeo to this one. Too many people. She recognized most of their faces, and most smiled or waved at her, but she really didn't know them.

Speaking of too many people, Brandon Biggs stepped on the empty seat next to her with a hard pound that wiggled the entire bleacher. He had on army-style boots and a jacket the local giant must have lent him. Brandon could have wrapped it twice around his stocky frame.

"Mind if I sit down?" he asked.

"If you'll behave yourself," she answered.

"If I accidentally forgot, the scar on my leg from the heel of your shoe would remind me."

"How did things go the other night after we left?"

"Me and the Fraser boys had a real nice visit." He leaned over. "They're nothing but trash, you know."

She snorted. Whatever.

As the announcer introduced the next rider, two of the three middle school blondes stood up. Brandon yelled for them to sit down or they'd be needing the dark glasses to hide a black eye.

The girls squealed indignantly, but sat down.

The first bull rider managed to hang on to the count of seven.

When the cowboy hit the dirt, Brandon stood.

"I better move on. Everyone knows you're Noah's girl."

She thought better of correcting him.

"Brandon," she smiled, "before I get mad at you and forget it, thanks for what you did the other night."

He stood just a bit straighter. "You're welcome."

She watched him push his way down, pestering a few of the middle school kids just for the hell of it.

The announcer yelled that Preacher McAllen was the next rider. Reagan stood up.

Noah came out of the chute spinning on a bull that looked like he'd breathed in smoke and couldn't wait to blow it out. She'd never seen one buck so high. Noah's free hand reached for the sky as he gripped tight, and the battle between man and bull went full force.

With snot flying, the bull turned left toward the gates, snorting and heaving, and then suddenly twisted right.

Noah tumbled as if snapped off as quick as an icicle breaks.

He rolled, but the bull was still kicking in a tight circle.

Reagan screamed as Noah's body curled and twisted beneath the animal.

Noah was on the ground, fighting to

crawl free, but the bull kept turning like a mixer, catching him with every turn. The clowns she'd watched and laughed at took on their real job, bullfighters. They moved in, trying to get the bull's attention. The first caught a horn in his side and slammed into the chute gate; the second tumbled backward on the uneven ground.

For one heartbeat there was no one near to help Noah.

The pickup men couldn't get close and the bull paid no attention to the last rodeo clown, a kid in training, as he waved and danced like a medicine man around a fire.

Reagan couldn't breathe. She counted seconds in her head as if at some point there would be a bell and the round would be over.

"Don't let him die," she whispered.

As if in answer, a tall man jumped down from the back fence and swung his hat at the bull. When that didn't work, the man spread his arms wide and rushed forward with his chest.

The animal charged the stranger, his horns pointed straight at the red shirt beneath the man's western suit.

Like a matador in the movies, the

stranger jumped out of the way a second before the bull reached him. A heartbeat later, the riders had their ropes, swinging them like whips as they turned the bull toward the corral.

It had all happened so fast, yet the seconds had seemed endless. Reagan began to shake as the bull charged into the corral. Nothing had prepared her for such panic, such violence, such fear. For those few seconds with Noah under the bull, the entire world seemed to be holding its breath.

She watched Noah, expecting him to stand and wave that he was all right, as all the others had done.

But Noah lay curled in the dirt like a broken toy cowboy. His hat was gone. Dark hair mixed with shiny red blood covered part of his face.

The stranger who'd saved him knelt at Noah's side. The crowd fell silent. Everyone watched as the doctor ran out with his bag. A circle of men all knelt around Noah, blocking any view from spectators. Behind the chutes, emergency lights flashed through silent air and an EMT van pulled to the edge of the arena. The announcer's voice seem to whisper in the air, "Preacher may need your prayers tonight, folks."

Reagan pushed her way from the stands and headed toward him. By the time the stretcher was brought onto the grounds, she'd crawled through the fence and was almost to Noah.

She saw his face, gray-white as they lifted him carefully and began to carry him out. She tried to see him as they put him in the ambulance, but there were too many men, all taller than she was.

The sirens sounded as she screamed his name, but Noah couldn't hear her. For a moment in the chaos, she couldn't hear herself.

The door closed and red lights flashed. She heard someone yell to call the sheriff and let her know her brother was heading to the hospital.

Reagan backed away to the shadows of the bleachers. She shoved hot tears off her cheek. Noah was all right, she thought. He had to be.

The rodeo went on, but people had lost interest. She waited in the darkness, not wanting to talk to anyone or see anyone.

She wanted to be with Noah. She wanted to know what was going on. She crossed her arms around her and wished she could hug away the pain she felt inside. If this was what it felt like to care about someone, it hurt too much.

"You all right?" A voice came out of nowhere.

She turned and saw Brandon. "No," she said. "Where's the hospital?"

"It's all the way north on North. I pass it every time I come in from Bailee. You sure you're all right?"

Reagan shoved her fingers into the pocket of Noah's jacket. She felt his truck keys, as she knew she would. "I'm fine. I'm going to check on him."

Brandon opened his mouth to say something, then changed his mind.

She circled beneath the bleachers and crossed the darkness to where Noah had parked his pickup.

"Eight," she whispered to herself. "He was only on the ground eight seconds."

Chapter 31

ALEX WISHED SHE WERE AT THE RODEO INSTEAD of driving the back roads looking for any sign of a spark. It had been two weeks since the last fire. If trouble was going to flame, it would be soon. The guy they were looking for had set maybe as many as seven fires in the past three months. Either he was hooked on the adrenaline of what damage each new one might cause, or he loved to watch the flames build and grow. She could almost see him in her mind, planning, waiting maybe for more wind or a time when he thought no one was watching.

Waiting for her to blink.

She had no intention of blinking. This was her town, by blood and by occupation. She wouldn't let someone destroy it. She glanced at the man beside her and knew Hank felt the same.

In the past dozen days, she'd seen Matheson about ten times and talked to him on the phone at least twice a day. Neither had mentioned the parking lot episode. She had no idea if he thought about it as much as she did. Hell, it had become her favorite bedtime story on those nights she didn't fall asleep before her head hit the pillow.

Alex stopped her cruiser at the crossroads of Lone Oak Road and the county highway. Hank got out with his binoculars while she stepped to the front of the car and searched the horizon. They'd been riding together for two hours, both constantly checking in with all other spotters. They'd had a feeling it would be tonight, but now she had her doubts.

Hank wanted them to go together over what he called the eye of the circle. He was guessing they'd be able to spot something first, and if they did, both could be in contact with their people at once. With luck, if a fire started, the police could cut off all exits out of the area and the fire department could move in fast. Putting out the fire would be first priority, but catching the criminal would run a close second.

"Nothing," Alex said for the tenth time in an hour.

"Nothing," Hank echoed.

They both knew that all the other fires had been set before nightfall. It was almost an hour after dark. If someone had set a fire, it would be burning bright enough to be seen for miles on a clear night like tonight.

"I'll check and see if Derwood's called in yet." He lifted his cell and nodded toward her radio.

She understood. She picked up the receiver to call dispatch.

She could hear Hank talking as she waited for dispatch to answer. One ring. Two. Three.

"Derwood called in ten minutes ago," Hank reported as he snapped his phone closed and circled to her side of the car. "Nothing. He's making another flyover, then I told him to call it a night." Hank sounded tired. They'd been chasing a ghost every night since the last fire. Both were exhausted.

She'd thought tonight would be the night, almost wished for it, so they could catch the criminal and this all would be over. Even going back to changing the lightbulb outside Dallas Logan's house looked good compared to what she had been doing.

Fourth ring, then just as the fifth one dinged, someone picked up at dispatch.

"Alex," Andy's voice scratched across the radio. "Sheriff McAllen!"

"Here," she answered as she reached into the car to turn up the speaker so Hank could also hear. "What's the problem? Any fire?"

"No fire," Andy was almost screaming at her. "All quiet in that area, but, Sheriff, your brother, Noah, is on his way to the hospital. He was hurt at the rodeo."

Alex dropped the radio and grabbed her binoculars resting on the hood.

When she turned back to her door, Hank was already there, shoving her aside. "I'll drive. You call in and see if you can find out anything."

She ran to the passenger side. Andy

had patched her through to the ambulance by the time Hank hit eighty miles per hour.

"He's breathing," she echoed what the EMT said. "Looks like a blow to the head and multiple wounds on his arms and legs." Alex paused, then added, "I heard."

"What?" Hank glanced over at her. "Alex, what else?"

She looked at him, but didn't really see him as she repeated the driver's words. "My dad's riding in the ambulance with Noah. Adam was at the rodeo."

Five minutes later, they were pulling up to the county hospital. They jumped out and headed inside at a full run. The ambulance had emptied its load, and everyone had disappeared behind the emergency room doors.

The waiting room and desk were deserted. The place looked old and tired. Alex felt she was walking through death's parlor; she kept moving.

They ignored the sign that read AUTHORIZED PERSONNEL ONLY at the next set of swinging doors.

Adam McAllen, tall, thin, and gray-haired, stood alone at the end of the hallway that was marked NO ENTRY. He looked strong as a statue, but she didn't miss the worry in his deep blue eyes. He was dressed like the successful businessman he was, except for the blood that was spattered across his jacket and the dirt-stained knees of his trousers.

Alex didn't move into her father's arms. There had been too many times he hadn't been there for her. Her brothers might have come to terms with their father leaving their mother, but Alex never had.

Adam held his daughter in his stare but made no move to touch her. "They took him straight to the operating room to do the examination. Both doctors on duty are with him."

"What . . ." Alex wasn't even sure which questions to ask.

"I don't know anything," he admitted. "But I think it would be wise to call your mother."

Alex wanted to scream that he should call his own wife. After all, they were still married even though he never called her anything but *your mother*, and they hadn't seen each other more than a dozen times since Warren's funeral three years ago.

But there was no time for that. Noah was all that mattered right now.

Alex walked to the windows and dialed her mother.

IN A MATTER OF MINUTES, THE LITTLE WAITING area was filled with friends, family and high school kids. If anyone in town had need of the emergency room tonight, they'd have to fight their way in.

The crowd parted as Frances McAllen rushed in. She was wearing a peach jogging suit and looked fit enough to step out on the fifty-yard line and cheer at the Dallas Cowboys football games. Thirty years of being a mother might have turned her hair silver-blond and carved tiny wrinkles around her eyes and mouth, but she was still a beauty.

Frances went straight to her husband.

To Alex's surprise, her father put his hand on her mother's shoulder and talked to her softly.

The room went silent and Adam's words drifted like smoke through the air. "He took a blow to the head, Fran; I think that's what concerned the doc most. The other injuries look like they'll heal."

Fran leaned against Adam's shoulder and began to cry. A river of ice set Alex's spine. It was a scene she'd seen once before three years ago. Warren had been dead when they lifted him from the road, but they'd still loaded him into the ambulance and brought him here. Her parents had stood just as they were now, her father talking softly, her mother crying. Two people who never got along in the calm of life clung to one another in crisis.

Alex pushed her way through the crowd. There wasn't enough air in the world for her to breathe. She made it outside and away from all the bright lights. She couldn't watch her parents. Not again. She couldn't look for Hank, either. If she saw Hank now, all the memories of Warren's death would flood back and she couldn't deal with it, not with Noah hurt.

Once she passed the doors, the only dark place she spotted was a shadowy drive leading to a back parking lot behind the hospital. Alex almost ran to it.

One person stood in the center of the drive. She saw him too late to choose another direction. Hank. He'd found the darkness before her.

Part of her wanted to turn and run. Part of her knew this one man would be the only one to understand. He'd walked the nightmare once before. He'd hear the echoes of it again.

He turned to her and opened his arms. She stepped into his embrace, needing the strong hug her father had never given her.

He pulled her close. Holding her to earth as he always had.

They stood for a while. When she felt the silent tears running unchecked down her face, she pulled back. "It's too much like . . ."

"I know," he answered.

He pushed her hair out of her face. "Noah isn't Warren. We don't know much, but we know one thing: Noah's alive."

She nodded. "Promise you'll stay until we know more?"

He smiled. "Of course."

They moved apart and walked back into the waiting room, where she joined her parents. Everyone else in the room was talking, but she felt she was floating in a silent bubble with her parents. The only thing keeping her sane was Hank ten feet away, keeping an eye on her. She had a feeling if she bolted again, he'd be right there to meet her in the shadows.

Finally, the doctor emerged with a status report. Noah seemed to be out of danger. He had two cracked ribs, multiple bruising, and a concussion. They were keeping him for a few days to run more tests.

Alex closed her eyes and breathed.

Her parents went in to see Noah, and Alex encouraged the friends and relatives to go home. The doctor had insisted on no visitors.

When the last one left, she turned to Hank. "Thank you. For being here."

"You're welcome," he responded, his hands in his pockets. After a moment, he added, "I called in ten minutes ago. Still no sign of fire."

She'd forgotten about the fire. "Good," she managed. "I think I'll ask if I can go in and say good night to Noah."

Hank moved toward the parking lot. "I'll be here when you get finished. Take your time."

"You don't have to wait." She frowned. She'd appreciated his presence tonight, but that didn't make them a couple.

He smiled. "Yes, I do. You're my ride back to my truck."

"Oh." She felt stupid. "Of course. I'll be out in a few minutes."

In Noah's room, her parents were on either side of the bed. Her mother clutched Noah's hand in both of hers. Her father stared at his sleeping son with tubes taped to his arm.

"I can't stand seeing him like this," Frances whispered. "His riding days are ended."

"We'll talk," Adam also whispered in his gruff tone. "He'll wear a helmet and a vest from now on. He should have had one on tonight."

Alex let them leave without her, knowing they'd be arguing as soon as they stepped outside the door.

"Hold on, little brother," she whispered to Noah, as she must have a thousand times when they were growing up. She threaded her fingers through his. "Hold on tight."

Chapter 32

"I KNOW YOU'RE THERE." NOAH SOUNDED LIKE he had a sore throat. "You might as well come on out."

Reagan thought of staying in the corner between the blinds and the shelving filled with supplies. Maybe he'd go back to sleep and when he woke again he'd think he'd dreamed he had seen her hiding.

"Rea, come on out."

She looked at the door. A nurse wandered in now and then, but she'd heard a racket in the hallway and knew that another round of customers had arrived at the emergency room. Slowly, Reagan slipped from concealment and approached Noah's hospital bed.

"You look terrible," she whispered.

He raised his left hand. The back was blue from where it had been stomped on, and the fingers were swollen double in size. Three or four stitches laced across a cut at his wrist.

"I probably look better than I feel," he said. "My side is killing me and I feel like one of the doctors, the fat one, is sitting on top of my head."

Reagan smiled. "He is. You want me to tell him to get off?"

The corner of Noah's mouth twitched. "Any chance you want to hug me, Rea?"

"No, and even if I did, I'd have trouble finding a place on you that's not bruised, bleeding, or bandaged. They could use your body for the model in a new Operation game."

Noah lifted his right arm. There was a bandage from his elbow to his shoulder, and his hand had tubes taped to it. "I don't like this."

"Me, either." She scrubbed at her cheek. In fact, she hated seeing him like this, all broken and pale.

"Have you been crying?"

"No," she lied. She'd waited until every-one left, not knowing what else to do. When a dozen people from a bar fight stormed in, all the hospital staff had their hands full. It hadn't been that hard to slip between the doors and find Noah. She'd planned to just talk to him a minute, but she'd waited an hour for him to open his eyes.

His cracked lip twitched again. "You were worried about me."

"No, I wasn't." Reagan ducked into the shadows as the door opened.

Noah closed his eyes.

A nurse whose name tag identified her as Georgia Veasey looked at the moni-tors, adjusted a few bags, and left. Before the door closed, they heard someone down the hall yell that someone had thrown up in room three.

Reagan reappeared and finished her sentence. "I wasn't worried about you, I was just worried I wouldn't have anyone to eat lunch with. I've kind of gotten used to you bothering me."

"You should go on home. I'll be all right." His words came slow, like someone who hadn't slept in days.

"No," she said simply.

"You think I'm lying? I'm just waiting until you're gone so I can die."

She bit her lip. "I wouldn't put it past you."

He smiled weakly. "You're staying then? No matter what I say?"

"Until they kick me out. You're not much in the way of a friend, but you're all I got."

He moved his left hand away from his body, making room on the bed. "You may not like any touching, Rea, but I could sure use someone next to me about now. You look tired enough to drop, plus you're the only one left around."

She hesitated, glancing at the door.

"What are they going to do," he asked, "kick you out five minutes earlier? They'll do it anyway; you might as well rest until she comes back."

She crawled carefully up beside him and stretched out next to him, her hand gently crossing below the bandages on his ribs.

He sighed and kissed the top of her head. "It's over, Rea. You don't have to cry. I'll be around to bug you tomorrow."

She closed her eyes, and they both fell asleep to the rhythm of the machines.

Fifteen minutes later, Nurse Veasey opened the door to check Noah's bags. She froze at the sight before her. A Truman was curled up against a McAllen.

Everyone born in Harmony knew that the youngest, and soon to be the last, Truman had come to live with her great-uncle out on Lone Oak Road. Georgia hadn't seen the girl up close, but there was no mistaking that wild red hair.

Georgia smiled. The kids were close in age, about sixteen or seventeen, but he looked double her size. The girl was curled close, barely touching him with her hand resting on one of the few spots on his chest not bandaged. They were both sound asleep.

As a nurse, she should wake the girl and tell her to get out, but Georgia couldn't. Everyone knew Trumans and McAllens never spoke, not for years and years. Yet here they were, curled up together like a lion and a lamb. Only from what she'd heard from her husband, who taught English at Harmony High, the girl was the lion.

Georgia slowly closed the door, knowing it would be an hour or more before she got all the drunks now piling into emergency sorted out, doctored, and sent home to sober up. Let the kids sleep until then. She'd see they weren't disturbed.

The feud, if there still was one, could wait for another day.

Chapter 33

Uncle Jeremiah walked through the back door and into the kitchen. He crossed to the sink and washed his hands, then sat down to breakfast.

Reagan had made French toast, which he ate without comment.

"Where's the McAllen kid?" he asked between bites with the same disinterest with which he asked everything.

"Maybe he spent the night here," she answered, just to see if Jeremiah would bother to look up from his food.

"He didn't." The old man kept eating. "If he had, you'd have set another place."

Reagan smiled, guessing that if Noah walked into the room in his underwear, Jeremiah would simply tell him to pour himself a coffee and keep eating.

"Noah was hurt last night at the rodeo." She whispered the words, hoping that would make them sound not so frightening.

Now Jeremiah looked up. "He all right?"

"He will be. I stayed with him until midnight just to make sure he didn't die, then I drove his pickup home."

"I thought you two might be planning to leave for parts unknown in that old junker of his."

"Nope." She passed him the syrup. "I think I'll just go to see him as soon as the dishes are done. I won't be long and I'll work extra fast to make up the time I'm missing in the orchard."

Jeremiah nodded as he refilled his cup. "The sheriff told you not to drive until you passed your driving test."

"I know, and since Noah's her brother, she's bound to notice when I drive his truck back into town to check on him this morning." She stopped and waited.

Like a slow cooker, he stewed on what

she'd said a while before he asked, "You
want me to drive you in?"

"Would you?"

He nodded. "But I'm not going in. I don't
like hospitals. I went in one back in eighty-
seven with one problem and came out with
two." He reached for the calendar on the
wall behind the door and marked off the
date. "Month is sure going by," he mumbled,
and put the calendar back on its nail.

Reagan hurried to finish as she added
between bites, "If you drive me, we can
stop at the bookstore and I'll go in and get
you a new copy of the Dallas paper. That
one you got in the front room is two months
old."

"Fair enough," he echoed. "I can start
reading it while you visit."

A half hour later she walked into Noah's
room.

He was sitting up in bed talking to several girls from the cheerleading squad.
They all had their uniforms on and giggled
at everything he said.

Reagan made no attempt to announce
her presence; she just stood at the door
and watched.

"That last hug made me feel a lot better,

Arlee." Noah smiled at the girl in a goofy way she'd never seen him smile.

"You want another one?" She laughed. "We're all happy to do whatever we can to help out the sick."

"And brave," one of the other girls said. "That was so brave."

"No." A blonde beside Arlee pushed closer to the bed. "It's my turn to give him a hug."

Reagan wanted to throw up. They giggled and talked on for five minutes. Most hadn't been at the rodeo last night, but apparently visiting someone in the hospital was a free pass out of church, so they'd all decided to put on their uniforms and cheer him up.

Reagan knew there was no substance to the group. Not a redhead among them. But Noah didn't seem to notice. She slipped down the hall to the restroom, not wanting to see or hear Harmony's boob trust in action.

She stepped into a stall and leaned against the wall, wishing she'd taken up smoking once when she'd been offered a cigarette. If she had, she'd have something to do right now besides wait.

The restroom door popped open, and giggling came from just beyond the stall door. Reagan had no trouble guessing who had come in. From the voices, three cheerleaders were now far too close to her.

She didn't have anything against cheerleaders. The last two schools she'd been in, none of them had bothered her. In fact, Reagan—and girls like her, she guessed— were invisible to the popular girls. They weren't boys to flirt with or cheer on. They were no competition. Reagan and her kind didn't matter.

Reagan closed her eyes and wished she could close her ears. The girls were talking about Noah. One said he had bedroom brown eyes. Another said he was too thin. Two out of the three claimed he'd be worth having a few nights' fun with, and then they giggled. The third said not to bother; she wouldn't be caught dead in his old truck, plus he had no butt.

After they left, Reagan stood in the stall for a long time. She hated that they talked about him like he was some kind of toy they'd just noticed. She hated what they said, and she hated even more that she cared.

When she stepped back into Noah's doorway, he was alone. For a moment, he didn't notice her, and she saw how tired his eyes looked and the pain in his face as he tried to shift in the bed.

Then he looked up. A smile came just a bit slower than usual to his lips.

"Morning, Rea," he said. The bruising on him looked even darker than it had last night, but his color was better.

"How are you?" she asked, feeling angry for no reason.

"Better. The doc came in and said I can go home in a few hours, but he wants me to take it easy for a week or so."

"You were lucky." She crossed her arms and didn't move closer.

"I know, but it feels like maybe I'd have been luckier if I'd drawn another bull. One of the guys who dropped by told me this morning that it was my dad who jumped in to get the bull to quit dancing on me. He said it was a sight; everyone was screaming and yelling. They all thought I was dead for sure."

"What else did he say?" That every girl in town seemed to have noticed him? That they all thought he was a hero? That two-thirds thought it would be fun to go out with him?

Noah raised an eyebrow. "What's wrong with you, Rea?"

It had taken him a while, but it finally seemed to dawn on the brain-dead cowboy that she wasn't happy.

"Nothing," she lied.

"Why are you standing at the door? What's happened? Did they tell you something about me that they didn't tell *me*?" He looked worried. "Hell, I'm probably dying and the doc's not telling me 'cause I'm not eighteen yet. Or maybe they just found out I'm contagious and that's as close as you're allowed to come?"

Rea resisted smiling. "You're not dying, at least not that I know of, and I don't think being dumb enough to climb on sixteen hundred pounds of fury is contagious."

He relaxed back on his pillow. "Thank God. I'd hate to die and not know it."

She laughed now and moved to his bedside. "Shouldn't joke about it."

"S'pose not," he said, turning his hand palm up to her.

She didn't take his hand.

Without taking offense, he lowered his

offer. "So, how about telling me what's got you so upset this morning, other than seeing that I'm better?"

"I heard them talking about you in the restroom."

"The nurses?"

"No." She laughed. "Worse. The cheerleaders. One said you had bedroom eyes, whatever that means."

"Which one?"

She glared at him. "I don't know; they all sound alike to me. They all *are* alike. I swear there's probably a factory in China that turns them out by the thousands every year and ships them all over, pompoms in hand."

He didn't seem to be listening. "Did they say anything else?"

"One said you didn't have a butt."

He frowned, and she almost felt sorry for him. Then he said he'd noticed none of them had that problem, and she wanted to hit him on one of the few spots available to her.

"You're mad because they came up," Noah said. She could almost see his brain working it out. "You're jealous."

"I am not. I couldn't care less if they hug

you and make a fuss over you and talk about how they wouldn't mind . . . oh, never mind."

"Wouldn't mind what?"

"I'm not telling, so don't bother to ask and I'm not jealous. I've told you before I don't want to be your girlfriend, just friends, so what do I care? Go ahead and date them. Date all of them at once if you like."

"For just friends, you don't look or sound very happy." He stared at her as if he'd just discovered a lizard person living under her skin. "Let me get this straight—you don't want anyone thinking you're my girlfriend. You don't want me touching you, even holding hands, because you figure I'll turn into some kind of werewolf if I do, but you don't like any one else touching me, either. I'm sort of off-limits to the world, like some kind of global quarantine."

She'd had enough. If he thought he was confused, he should try looking at the world through her eyes. Without warning, she stormed out of the room.

She heard him call her name, but she didn't stop until she was outside. There, she breathed out hard like a deer trying to clear human scent from her lungs.

Uncle Jeremiah was sitting on the bench ten feet from the exit. "How's the—"

Raising her hand, she shouted, "I don't want to talk about him."

Jeremiah stood slowly and nodded. "Fine."

He drove Noah's truck back to the ranch and passed the house as he pulled the old piece of junk straight into his museum of a barn.

"What are you doing?" she asked.

"I'm going to clean up this engine before it sputters so hard the damn thing falls out in protest."

"Why? It's not your problem."

Jeremiah stepped out of the cab. "I know. When he's driving, I don't much care, but I don't want him having any trouble when you're riding with him."

"Why?" She decided she had no knowledge of men from sixteen to eighty-six.

"Because," he said without looking at her, "you're the only niece I got, and I don't want to lose you in a wreck."

Reagan's heart took his words like the kick of a bull. For a few seconds she couldn't breathe. He'd claimed her. Uncle Jeremiah had claimed her as his kin with no one else around, and she hadn't even asked or begged.

She climbed out of the cab and walked around to where he'd lifted the hood. "I'm staying," she said. "I just want you to know, I'm staying here forever, so stop waking up every morning thinking I'm leaving."

"Good," he said in his usual bland tone. "Hand me that wrench."

Chapter 34

HANK LIFTED SARALYNN ONTO HIS SHOULDER and moved through the Tuesday morning crowd at the Blue Moon. His tiny niece waved at everyone as if she were riding on a float, then giggled when they waved back. Most, from the three-piece suits to the overalled farmers, smiled at her. The few who didn't, Hank mentally marked down on his waste-of-flesh list.

"What are we today?" Edith asked as she wiggled past them with four plates of food.

"She can't talk, Edith," Hank whispered. "She's a mermaid, and everyone knows they can't talk around humans. All she can do is wave and look beautiful."

The waitress nodded, as if he made perfect sense. "I'm guessing she'll want the usual with a little seaweed on the side."

He winked and moved on. As he watched the people, mostly men this early in the morning, he couldn't help but wonder if the arsonist was among them. Could a man who looked so much like every one of them be thinking of destroying not just their land, but their way of life? Hank had heard of small communities in the Texas panhandle that faced a disaster and never recovered. The buildings left standing simply marked the boundaries of ghost towns.

Hank pushed the dark thoughts aside and headed toward the only empty booth. He noticed Willie and Trooper Davis at one table, but even if they'd invited him to sit down, he didn't want to talk about fires in front of Saralynn. The young man and the old trooper made a strange pair, but because they were both named Davis, Hank guessed they were somehow related. In this town, it would be hard to find a jury made up of people who didn't know or weren't related to just about anyone who committed a crime.

Last year he'd had to take Aunt Pat in for double parking in two handicap spots and she'd known every person in court, even served as a character witness of one and paid another kid's fine because she swore he came from good people and should know better than to run a red light.

Hank looked around and thought what he always thought. His town. His people.

He lowered Saralynn slowly, as always taking care not to bump her leg braces on anything, then sat beside her. "How about I order for you today?"

She nodded and folded her hands, fingers outstretched, over her chest.

"Morning," Tyler Wright said as he slid into the other side of the booth. "Mind if I join you?"

Hank had to admire the man; he always asked, even though they'd been eating meals across from one another once a week for probably ten years. "Morning, Tyler. How's business?"

"If it gets any slower, I may take the day off and go for a drive. Nobody wants to die in good weather, but wait for the first cold

spell with snow flurries and we'll have the
hearse heated up and running all day." He
grinned as if the lack of work didn't bother
him in the least. Hank had to admit the
chubby little undertaker seemed happier
lately than he'd ever seen him.

Hank thought of asking Tyler to watch
for fires, but he held back. Trooper Davis
had planted a seed of doubt about the funeral director. Hank told himself he didn't
believe a word of it, but he still hesitated
inviting Wright into the inner circle.

"What do you do on these drives?" He
tried to make the question casual.

"Mostly I just like to get out in the fresh air
and think. Sometimes I look for signs of the
past. Every man or animal who ever crossed
this land, and believe me most just crossed
without thinking of staying, left a footprint
somewhere, and I like thinking once in a
while I'll find a sign of that passing."

Hank told himself there was nothing odd
about that. "Tyler, do you know of anyone
who might want to harm our town?"

"Sure, every tourist who eats at the truck
stop just south of the hospital."

Hank smiled. No locals had eaten at the
gas station/curio shop/restaurant since a

month after it opened, when the meat-loaf sent a dozen people to the hospital. After that, everyone thought it lucky the two buildings were so close together.

After Edith brought their coffee and juice, Tyler fished in his vest pocket and found a quarter. "It's not a new one, darling," he said to the mermaid next to Hank, "but I've heard it's waterproof and that's very important to you these days."

Saralynn laughed.

Tyler tugged a tiny felt bag from his pocket and passed it over. "I found this. You might want to keep it safe in here."

When Saralynn opened the bag a tiny glass bead, like the ones Hank had seen in fake flower arrangements at the funeral home, fell out.

Tyler's eyebrows shot up as if he were surprised. "Oh no, I must have left a dragon's tear in that bag so long it turned to clear stone."

Saralynn beamed. "A dragon's tear. May I have it?"

Tyler nodded. "It's magic, you see. If a mermaid holds it, she can talk."

Hank fought down a groan. He played along with Saralynn's fantasies, but Tyler was adding to them. Pretty soon Hank would be having breakfast with a wood nymph and a troll.

Tyler chuckled at Hank's frown as if he'd read his mind.

Hank knew beyond all doubt that he wasn't looking at an arsonist.

When Edith plopped down the plates, the mermaid's pancakes were circled in seaweed that looked a lot like parsley.

His niece began planting each tiny branch on top of her pancakes and watering her garden with syrup.

Knowing Saralynn had lost interest in the conversation, Tyler asked Hank, "How's the painter in your family doing? I hear she'll have a show soon."

Hank spread jelly on his dry toast. "She's very creative, I'll give her that. Her latest is called *More Coffee, Dear.* It's a man floating in a huge coffee cup, facedown."

Tyler had his cup halfway to his lips. He reconsidered and sat the coffee down.

Hank smiled. "Hey, it beats the one she did of a guy impaled on a wall by a remote control. It was called *Last Change.*"

"Sorry I asked," Tyler said as he concentrated on his oatmeal.

After breakfast, Hank took his mermaid to school, then dropped by the station. He had tons of work to do at the ranch, but he still couldn't believe the firebug hadn't started another grass fire. It didn't make sense. Why would he go three-fourths of the way around Harmony and stop?

When Hank pulled up, Alex was getting out of her car across the street.

"Mind if we talk a minute?" he called to her.

She shrugged with a frown.

Just once Hank wished that she'd look glad to see him, but he guessed it would be too much to ask in this lifetime.

He knew that Alexandra wasn't a morning person, but where he was concerned, she wasn't Miss Sunshine in the afternoon or evening, either. Hank held out little hope for the night.

They walked to the handicap ramp beside the entrance to the city offices, seeking the shade of the old oak. Legend was that the oak had been brought to West Texas by Harmon Ely himself when he hoped to settle here and then send for his family. But his family had all been killed in a raid near the border, leaving Harmon alone and bitter. The three men who worked for him—Truman, Matheson, and McAllen—all sent for their wives, and as the years passed, Harmon watched their children grow and play beneath the tree he'd brought for his children. Some in town thought that was why he willed all he had to the men who worked for him.

"Something's bothering me," Hank began. "I've been reading up on arsonists, and they don't just stop. Maybe they're frightened off, or maybe something makes them stop, like a car wreck or something else happening that's more exciting and draws them to the action. But we've had no one to close in on and make nervous enough he might stop, and nothing's happening of any interest around here."

Alex crossed her arms as she leaned against the railing. "So now you're upset because our little terrorist hasn't come out to play?"

"Something like that." He realized how odd he must sound. "Maybe he's just laying low. Hell, maybe he just ran out of matches and has to wait until payday."

"You'll drive yourself crazy guessing," she offered. "The only thing exciting that happened in the past few days was my little brother almost dying at the rodeo. I swear everyone in town has been by to see him. Half of them bring cookies. Add to that, my dad's still here fretting over Noah worse than Mother does."

Hank didn't want to talk about the three-ring circus that was usually going on at the McAllen house when Adam came back. He'd heard about Adam and Fran enough from Warren when they were younger. "The rodeo and the fires couldn't be connected."

She met his eyes. "Or could they? Half the town was at the rodeo. Maybe our arsonist was there, or was working one of the booths. Maybe he watched the whole thing."

"Or maybe he was pulled in to handle the crowd, or drive the ambulance, or take a shift at the hospital?" Hank tried to think like an arsonist. "If the guy sets fires for the excitement, he just might have found his fix that night at the rodeo, or afterward at the hospital."

An hour later they were sitting in Alex's office making a list of everyone they'd noticed in the waiting room at the hospital. Most were relatives and friends, but Hank remembered seeing a few he didn't know, and when he described them, Alex couldn't think of anyone she knew fitting the description.

Alex stood and grabbed two juices from the tiny refrigerator under her desk. She handed Hank one and sat back down across from him. "Now, we list everyone we know who's been around for the fires. If one person keeps popping up, maybe we've got our man."

"Someone besides me and you and Kenny from the paper?" Hank grinned.

"No. We list everyone *including* me, you, and Kenny." She picked up her pen and pointed it at him. "And for now, we keep this between the two of us. No one else. If we're wrong and this list gets out, it would hurt someone innocent. If we're right, we can keep an eye on any suspects without them being aware of it."

It was almost noon by the time they'd made lists of everyone involved in every fire. Alex had run checks of arson arrests over the past twenty years, and Hank had gone over his notes of every fire that had happened near Harmony in a year. Two firemen, besides himself, had responded to all the fires. Willie Davis, who never missed anything that happened at the fire station, and Andy Daily, who was sleeping at the station every night he wasn't working dispatch for the sheriff's office. Kenny, the newspaper's only reporter not using a walker, came to take pictures of the fires, but the flames were usually out by the time he made it to the scene.

Neither Alex nor he realized how long they'd worked until Alex's secretary poked her head in asking if the sheriff wanted lunch.

Alex hesitated, while Hank answered, "No, we're heading out to one of the burn sites. We'll pick something up on our way."

When the secretary backed away, Hank lowered his voice. "If I'm reading Willie's notes right, three of the early fires were called in by the same person. His name is Zackery Hunter and he owns a gas station out where two county roads cross. This was early, before we thought the fires were connected, so we didn't ask as many questions as we should have."

Alex smiled. "So now we should go out there and talk to him. Did he see the fires, hear about them and call in, or set them?"

"Exactly."

By the time they'd made it to Alex's cruiser, Trooper Davis pulled up beside them and decided to tag along. Hank had been around the man a few times. He seemed like a by-the-book officer, but there was something about him Hank didn't care much for. He jumped too fast. Rushed in when he should hesitate. Hank also had the feeling that Davis considered himself an expert on just about any subject. If this had been a hundred years earlier, Davis would have been a bounty hunter, Hank figured.

He felt, more than knew, that Alex didn't care for the man, either. Maybe it had something to do with Warren three years ago. Hank couldn't be sure, but he thought he remembered seeing Davis the night Alex's brother died, but there were so many highway patrolmen around that night, he couldn't be sure.

From the way Davis said the word *Sheriff* every time he addressed Alex, Hank sensed the trooper felt the same way about her as she did about him.

On the way over, with Alex driving, Hank found himself staring at the place just below her ear. If he leaned over and put his mouth exactly there, he might feel her pulse pounding in her throat and smell her hair at the same time.

And that time would be one second before she slammed his head into the windshield. He groaned. He was just guessing here, but he doubted she wanted him nibbling on her neck while she drove out to question a witness.

"What are you thinking?" she asked as she made the last turn and headed for the country store at the crossroads.

What he was thinking was, how do women know just the right time to ask that question? Can they sense when a man's thoughts step over the line, or are they just guessing that something is up because he gets some kind of strange glaze over his eyes? Or maybe men are so often thinking about things they won't talk about that it's a good question to ask anytime.

He answered with the first plausible response that came to mind. "I was thinking it's not going to be this easy."

They pulled into the crumbling parking lot of the little store. Country Corner had been there for fifty or more years and didn't look like it had been upgraded since the grand opening. It sold gas and snacks mostly, along with beer. The only thing that kept it going was the fact that it was halfway to anywhere from this point. For those who wanted to travel the back roads, it was the only restroom stop, ice cream break, or pay telephone around.

"I can't believe he has that old thing." Hank looked at the phone booth. "Who doesn't have a cell these days?"

"Cell service is iffy out here."

Hank checked his phone just to make sure he could be reached if needed. Between the fires and Saralynn's medical problems, he was never without the phone on his belt.

Trooper Davis joined them as they went into the store. Hank didn't miss the fact that Davis checked his gun as if expecting Bonnie and Clyde to be waiting just beyond the door.

The place was empty except for the owner.

Zackery Hunter sat on a stool behind the counter reading a magazine he quickly shoved out of sight. "Hi, folks. Just taking a drive, are you?" When he smiled, his teeth were so yellow Hank swore he must color them.

Alex, as always, was all business. She flipped open her notepad and began asking questions. Davis tossed in a few, but Hank just watched. Zackery was a talker and stretched out every answer as much as he could. He hadn't seen the fires; they'd only been reported by folks coming by. He was left of one, right of the other. The third, he heard about from a farmer who saw the smoke from his place, but Zackery called it in anyway.

Alex made a list of each of the people who'd stopped by to even talk about the fires.

Zackery scratched his stubble. "The funeral director from Harmony stopped by for an ice cream, but he always takes the back roads and I seem to be his ice cream stop. Sometimes I see him twice, three times a week. I remember on the third fire, he was so interested in where it was he forgot to eat the Nutty Buddy and it started dripping on my floor."

Hank looked down, thinking that from the looks of the floor, the remains of the ice cream were still there.

"You think Tyler Wright might have expressed an unnatural interest?" Davis asked.

"I don't know," Zachery said. "I guess so, or maybe he was just making conversation. He's a nice guy, and last I heard loving ice cream ain't no crime."

Hank didn't miss the look Davis gave Alex. Davis hung back and motioned for Alex to do the same as they left a few minutes later. Hank walked on toward the car. He couldn't hear, but he sensed they were arguing.

A moment later Alex stormed past him. She'd climbed in and slammed her door even before he reached the passenger side.

When Hank climbed into her cruiser, Alex was gripping the stirring wheel so hard her knuckles were white. "He wants to bring Tyler in for questioning." There was no need for her to explain more.

"Tyler is not our man," Hank said.

"I don't think so, either, but I've got to go along with Davis. It's a lousy lead, but it's the only thread we have."

Hank pulled a Nutty Buddy ice cream out of the bag. "Lunch?" he asked.

Alex's smile didn't make it up to her eyes. "Thanks."

Chapter 35

TYLER WRIGHT TALKED WITH A COUPLE WHO wanted to do pre-need arrangements. He was a retired professor from over at Clifton College, and she'd been an accountant for a small oil-drilling company. They'd bought a place out on Twisted Creek years ago and were finally settling down to becoming one of the nesters who stayed at the creek year-round. Neither fished. He was a bird watcher and she quilted, but they both loved sitting out in the evening and watching the water.

Since they were about an equal distance from Bailee, Texas, and Harmony,

they picked Harmony to be their last resting place. Tyler often expressed pride in
the town's cemetery. Early on, his grandfather had suggested that everyone who
wanted to could plant a tree in memory of
their loved one who had died. Wright Funeral Home would even order the tree and
see to its planting—which not only brought
in extra profit, it also made Harmony's Cemetery stand out as a place of beauty
among so many of the dried-up, tumbleweed-
collecting cemeteries in the area. There
were a few cemeteries on the plains where
the ground was so dry and hard it was impossible to dig a six-foot hole.

Tyler smiled at the old couple as he tried
to remember what they'd said their names
were a half hour ago. He had it written in
the pages of notes somewhere. He really
had to make an effort to remember details.

As they looked at caskets, he fought
down a laugh as he thought of something
funny that Kate had said last night. He
wished he could hear her words and not
just read them. She'd had a nice voice the
one time they'd met. A solid voice, not whiny
or too high. The kind of voice a man doesn't
mind listening to.

Tyler remembered every detail about what she'd told him in her e-mails. Last night she'd said that sometimes she was so tired she'd just toss off her clothes and crawl into bed without even thinking about her pajamas.

After they'd said good night, he'd tried it—though he couldn't toss off his clothes, he had to hang them up, and he did leave his underwear and socks on when he went to bed. He had a wonderful night feeling free and thinking of Katherine.

The professor picked a wooden casket, his wife a metal one that sealed. Tyler did all he was supposed to do. He said all the right things, but he also counted the minutes until they left.

He wanted to go back and read through the e-mails from last night. Tonight was Tuesday, and for some reason they always talked about food on Tuesday. She said she loved to cook but never had enough time. He said he was learning, though unless sandwiches and cereal counted he'd never cooked anything.

The old couple left. Tyler stood on the steps smiling and waving as he thought that he might tell Katherine he collected coins.

He might even tell her about his little friend, Saralynn. Thanks to Hank's bringing her to breakfast, Tyler felt like he'd watched her grow up. Sometimes, he thought he saw death's shadow standing just behind her, but she always made him smile, so it was easy to forget about the shadow.

Tyler had signed up to have each new quarter issued sent to him so he could give it to her. Last Christmas he'd given Saralynn a map of the United States with a spot for each quarter. She'd been delighted. She was a smart little four-year-old, and he wanted to tell Katherine all about her.

The sheriff's car pulled into the first slot in the funeral home parking lot. Alex McAllen and a highway patrolman got out. Tyler waited in the wind as they neared.

"Afternoon, Sheriff," Tyler smiled. "Trooper." Tyler thought his name was Davis. They'd talked a dozen times over the years. Or tried to, Tyler remembered with a frown. Davis wasn't a man who seemed to like small talk, unless it was about himself. There were very few people Tyler met that he didn't like, and this man was one. Strange, how he'd remember that name and not the names of hundreds of nice people he came across.

Alex didn't smile like she usually did as she climbed the steps to him. "We were wondering, Mr. Wright, if you might come down to the station and answer a few questions."

Tyler smiled. "I'd be happy to, Sheriff, just let me tell—"

Davis stepped forward and tugged his handcuffs off his belt. "You're going with us right now, Wright."

"That won't be necessary," Alex snapped.

Davis looked like he might argue, then stepped back.

Tyler's first thought was that this trooper didn't like Alex. Maybe because she was a woman, maybe because she outranked him. Tyler had no idea how it worked, but the man obviously wasn't a gentleman if Alex felt she had to order him around.

The next thought slammed like a shovel between his eyes. Davis was arresting him. Handcuffs! He'd never had handcuffs on in his life. His parents would not only roll over, but climb out of their graves in anger at the disgrace of their only child being handcuffed and dragged off the steps of Wright Funeral Home.

"I don't understand." Tyler focused on Alex, wishing he could see her eyes through the dark glasses she wore.

"We just need you to answer a few questions, Tyler. It's nothing, really." She touched her hand inside his elbow. "Please come with us."

He'd seen enough cop shows to know it was *not* nothing. "Do I need an attorney?"

"I don't think so," she said, "but I'll call one if you'd be more comfortable. There is nothing wrong or unusual about having an attorney with you."

"What is this all about?" Tyler's only crime for his entire life had been speeding. For a second it crossed his mind that maybe talking about sleeping with nothing on might be some kind of Internet crime. If he were arrested for that, it would be even more embarrassing then speeding down the back roads.

He looked back at the house, then toward his car, not knowing what to do. Hide. Run. Go with them. The sheriff tugged off her glasses as if she understood.

344 JODI THOMAS

Alex's eyes softened as if she saw his fear and didn't want to shame an innocent man. He felt overwhelmingly grateful to her for that.

She tugged his arm gently with her hand. "We just want to see what you know about the fires, Tyler. We need your help. Please, come with us."

"Oh." He calmed. He could handle help. He was good at helping. "Then I'll do all I can, Sheriff." He took a breath, wondering: If he'd almost panicked as an innocent man, what would he do if he were ever charged with a crime he'd actually committed? He'd die of a heart attack on the steps. His only chance of living a long life was to follow every law. That did it, he reasoned. His speeding days were over.

Davis frowned when Alex opened the front door of her cruiser and waved Tyler in.

Tyler had sat in police cars many times. Once in a while families took a long time between the funeral and the procession to the cemetery. When he'd been a boy he'd often gone with his dad and loved asking all kind of questions about what everything did in the car. But today, he just sat next to Alex for the two-block drive to the station and wondered why Trooper Davis was so upset.

This would definitely *not* be on his list of subjects to talk about with Katherine tonight.

Chapter 36

REAGAN AND UNCLE JEREMIAH TOOK NOAH'S pickup back after school Tuesday. The old guy had it running like new. Jeremiah might move slowly, but he knew his way around an engine. He'd also let her help, explaining every step even if she didn't understand most of what he'd said.

She wanted just to park the pickup in front of the McAllen house and leave, but Jeremiah told her to go in and hand over the keys while he drove to the parts store for oil.

Walking up to the door, she tried to remember exactly why she was mad at Noah.

Not because he got hurt. Not because he'd asked her to give him a hug. He probably didn't even remember the night of the accident and how she'd curled up next to him and slept until the nurse had tugged her away about midnight and told her to go home.

Reagan really couldn't be mad at him for hugging the cheerleaders; after all, he was hurt and tied to a bed. If anything, they took advantage of him. However, he could have protested a little harder.

It was the sheriff who answered the door, and for a moment Reagan tensed. Then she remembered that Alex McAllen was Noah's big sister and had already been nice to her several times.

Alex invited her in. Reagan had sat in the truck a few times when Noah had driven by his house to pick things up, but she'd never gone inside. The first thing that surprised her was that everything had an order about it. The house was one of the smaller old homes in what she was sure had once been the nicest part of town. Noah said that his mother bought it with a small inheritance from her grandmother, and his dad paid the bills.

Reagan couldn't help but think he'd done a fine job of keeping his family in style even if he didn't live with them. The place had that maid-twice-a-week look she'd seen a few times. Only problem was she was the maid when she'd seen houses like this, or rather one of her foster mothers had been. Her mom-of-the-month would bring a few of her foster kids along to help out. Reagan had never minded the work. It was easy and she could pretend that she lived in a house where the plants were all real and nothing was broken.

"Noah's in his room," Alex said. "First door on the right up the stairs. I'll bring you two some root beers before I leave. Try to cheer him up, Rea. He's been down for two days."

"Is he hurt bad?" Maybe she'd missed something at the hospital.

"No, just his ribs, and they'll heal. He was lucky."

Reagan climbed the stairs. The first door was open, a big airy room with floor-to-ceiling windows along one wall. Noah sat on the side of his bed picking at a scab across his elbow. He wore a pair of cutoffs that showed off hairy legs. A bandage circled his chest and another covered the top half of one arm, but the rest of him looked lean and tanned, but not as thin as she thought he might have been.

"Don't do that," she scolded. "It'll leave a scar."

"What'd you care? In rodeo no one minds a few scars." He glared at her. "I haven't seen you in days."

"Two days," she corrected as she dropped her backpack. "And I brought you something."

"What?" Curiosity overtook anger.

"Homework," she said, and he groaned.

Laughing, she moved to his side. She couldn't resist patting his unruly hair, which looked like it hadn't been combed or washed since he danced with the bull.

"I'm sorry," she whispered. It was the first time she'd ever said those two words and meant them.

He didn't pretend they were talking about the homework. "So am I, even though I still don't know what I did to make you so mad. Probably nothing," he reasoned. "I've always heard redheads are like that, firing up for no reason. It's probably something I'll have to get used to if you decide to hang around."

"It had nothing to do with my red hair, you idiot."

He frowned and shook his head slowly. "See what I mean?"

"It wasn't my hair. It was something you did, I just can't think of what it was exactly."

"Well, when you think of it and get all mad again, warn me that temper of yours is coming, would you, Rea? I'm injured, you know; I might need a little more time than usual to get out of range."

She giggled and fought the urge to hit him.

The sheriff came into the room and handed Reagan two drinks and then ordered Noah back into his bed. "Mom says you're to stay in bed until tomorrow morning."

"I'm all right, Alex. I swear. I can't stand all this resting. It's driving me nuts."

Reagan saw the pain in his movements as he followed his sister's orders even as he protested.

"Now stay there." The sheriff pointed her finger at him. "I have to get back to my office and talk to someone. I don't have time to nurse you and referee for Mom and Dad, so don't call me like it's some kind of great emergency again." She pulled a chair from the desk and put it beside the bed. "Your friend can stay ten minutes, no more." Alex looked at Reagan. "He needs rest."

Reagan nodded. "Ten minutes."

Alex left, and they listened to her bounding down the stairs and out the door. Whatever or whoever was in her office, she couldn't wait to get back to it.

"Where does it hurt?" Reagan asked.

"Everywhere," he admitted. "And if that's not bad enough, my mom and dad have been taking turns yelling at me. My mom tells me what I'm not going to do, and my dad tells me how I'm going to do it next time. They're downstairs in the kitchen now having coffee and talking about me. If you hear yelling, run. I called Alex and begged her to drop by just to check on them. Once in a while when it gets quiet like this, I worry that one of them has finally choked the other into silence."

Reagan laughed. "It couldn't be that bad."

"You don't know. They're both hard-headed and stubborn. Mom thinks she knows all about raising kids and takes every injury we get personally. Dad just thinks he knows everything, period."

"But they both love you."

Noah shrugged. "I guess, but lying around the house is more of a pain than being bruised." He settled his arm over a pillow and studied her. "We friends again, Rea?"

"Yes." She smiled. "But I'm not here to listen to you complain. If you climb on those bulls, you got to figure sometime one of them is going to stomp on you. I've calculated that with no more brains than you have, you won't suffer much damage to the head, and the rest will probably heal. But if you're going to complain, stop riding bulls."

"Thanks for coming just to cheer me up." Noah rubbed the spot between his eyebrows. "You're not thinking of going into nursing, are you? A fellow could die real easy with your bedside manner."

She giggled. "Anytime, and no, I'm not thinking of going that direction, but with you for a friend I'd probably get lots of practice in. Want to hear what's happening at school?"

"Sure." He leaned back and closed his eyes. "And don't leave out any conversations you heard about me."

She told him everything she could think of that had happened in the two days of school he'd missed. When she got to what the cafeteria was serving, she noticed his long slow breaths and knew he was asleep.

She glanced at the door and saw the tall, thin man who'd saved Noah from the bull standing in the doorway. Part of her felt like she was looking at Noah thirty years from now. Same blue eyes, same unruly hair, same long frame.

"You're my son's friend," the stranger said in a low voice that rumbled like faraway thunder. "The one he calls Rea."

Reagan nodded.

"You want me to try to talk him out of riding?" he asked.

It was a strange but honest question, and she answered directly. "No."

"Why not?" He leaned against the frame of the door as if he had all the time in the world to talk to her.

"He loves it. It's in his blood. It's all he thinks about. Maybe it's not fair to shatter a dream, even one that knocks him around now and then."

"So, Rea." He said her name slowly like Noah did when he was talking and thinking at the same time. "What should I do? His mother wants me to tell him rodeoing is finished."

Reagan stood. "Teach him to ride. All he's ever had was a weeklong camp last summer in San Angelo. You could teach him more. I know you probably think he'll stop if you don't show much interest, but he'll never stop. He wants to go all the way to the top."

Adam McAllen looked at her a moment, then nodded. "I'll give it a try, kid, but you got to promise me you'll be there for him when he falls. No matter what I teach him, if he rides, he'll tumble."

She had the feeling they were making a pact. "I'll try."

He straightened. "That's all any of us can do. Try. Sometimes I think it's not the winning or the losing, or even the right and wrong of things, it's the trying that makes us keep on living and hoping."

She heard the toot of Uncle Jeremiah's horn. "I have to go; my uncle is back."

"Tell Truman that Adam McAllen said thanks. He'll know what I mean."

"All right." She ran down the stairs. "I'll come back tomorrow."

"You do that," he said from the landing.

When she climbed in beside Jeremiah, she told him what Adam McAllen had said.

"What'd you do that he thanked you for?"

"Don't remember," Jeremiah answered, and Reagan knew he was lying.

That meant she'd probably never know. Not that it mattered. She was glad to know that sometime, somehow, Jeremiah had helped Adam out and that Adam was grateful. In a strange way, she admired both men for keeping it to themselves.

Someday, she decided, she'd do a kindness for someone like that and never tell anyone about it. Never even expect a thank-you.

Chapter 37

HANK STOOD ACROSS THE STREET AND WATCHED
Tyler being led into the sheriff's office. The
funeral director's shoulders were rounded,
his head down. He was so nervous, he
stumbled over one of the steps.

Thank God Alex hadn't handcuffed him.
Hank had tried to talk her out of letting
Davis bring Tyler in, but at least she hadn't
embarrassed the man in front of the entire
town.

Trooper Davis was grasping at straws.
He claimed Tyler fit the profile. No close
family around. No solid relationships. If anyone stood to benefit from a fire, he might.

Hank didn't buy any of it. Tyler once had family here. His roots ran deep in this town. He did have solid relationships. True, he wasn't married or dating anyone, but then neither was Hank, and no one was arresting him. And last, after Hank had seen the careful way Tyler closed the body bags of burn victims over the years, he found it impossible to believe the man would start a fire just in the hopes of getting a few more bodies for funerals.

Hank was halfway across the street when Alex shot out of the building, heading toward her car.

"What's up?" he asked, as if he had a right to know.

"I put Tyler in my office. Davis is checking in with his supervisor. He thinks the Texas Rangers need to be called in to talk to Tyler because the fires cover more than one county. He's working his way through proper command now. I have to run home and check on Noah, then I'll be right back."

"What can I do?"

She hesitated. "Off the record, you can go sit in my office and make sure Davis doesn't question or harass Tyler while I'm gone. Irene will stand her ground, but Davis

might try to pull rank and bully her. I don't
want him talking to Tyler about anything
before I get back."

She was gone before he could ask how
he could stop Davis. Tying up an officer of
the law wouldn't work. Slugging had some
appeal, but it would only bring more trouble.
Davis was the kind of man who wore on
people. If he decided to deck the guy, he'd
probably have to get in line.

Hank ran up the steps, deciding he'd
stop Davis even if he had to start shouting
that there was a green alien in Harmon
Ely's old tree out front. If Davis had to lock
him up for being nuts, it would give Alex
time to get back.

When he walked into the secretary's office, Irene surprised Hank by handing him
a tray. "Would you take this in to Mr. Wright?
I'm on guard, but I thought he might enjoy
a cup of coffee and some of my banana
bread. The poor dear looks upset about
something."

Hank had been in this office every day
for more than a week, and Irene had never
offered him banana bread. "Any way I might
have a cup of coffee, too?" He smiled but
knew it was wasted. Irene Lewis wasn't a

woman easily charmed out of her banana bread.

"I'll bring you one when I have time." She pointed him toward Alex's office.

Hank found Tyler sitting at the round table by the window, looking like a man waiting for his last meal.

He frowned when he saw Hank. "They brought you in, too?"

Hank shrugged, playing along with Tyler's assumption. "I was told to wait in here until the sheriff got back." He hated seeing his friend so upset and tried to cheer him up. "Should we start planning our escape? I'm not sure what we did, but I hear the Rangers are riding in after us."

Tyler smiled and let his hands uncoil from the arms of his chair. "I'm sure they just want to ask us questions." He seemed to be talking more to himself than Hank. "Everything will be settled in no time and we'll be home for dinner."

Hank played along as he passed Tyler the cup. "I am worried. Trooper Davis isn't friendly on a good day, and today must be one of his worst."

"I know what you mean." Tyler took a piece of Irene's bread from the little plate.

"I swear I thought he was going to hand-cuff me. Imagine that." He took a bite and seemed to breathe in the bread. "I always love Irene's banana bread."

Hank grabbed a slice and downed it whole before he added, "Me, too."

Irene hurried in with a cup of coffee for him, then hurried out, closing the door behind her. Hank thought he heard Davis's voice just as the door closed.

"What do you think they got the couple of us for?" Hank asked.

Tyler was back to his pleasant self. "I have little idea. Sometimes on the back roads I drive seventy-five."

"Most of the time I go about eighty. When I get a ticket, I always consider it supporting the highway system."

Tyler relaxed in his chair. "Alex said something about asking me questions, though I can't see how I could help her with anything she's working on."

Hank's mind finally put the pieces together. "You know the back roads, Tyler. You study maps. Maybe she needs your expert skill." As he said the words, something else became perfectly clear: Tyler drove the back roads following maps, not setting fires. If he crisscrossed this part of the country, it was only logical he'd be seen near the fires.

"I'm not an expert. Half the time I get lost and spend an hour trying to find my way back to a road sign." He took another slice of bread and leaned back. "I do find some interesting trails, though. For example, the other day I found the markings of an old wagon road across the back of your place. It might have been used to haul off all the buffalo bones left lying around after the buffalo hunters came through. Back behind your house is a ravine that could have trapped hundreds of buffalo. Hunters could have shot them, stripped their hides, and left their carcasses rotting. By the time this land was settled, there would have been nothing but bleached bones left."

Hank also took another piece of bread. "I think I remember my grandfather telling me about when he was a boy, how his father had hauled away bones to buy supplies the first winter after he inherited the land from old Ely. I'll never look at my back door again and just see the sunset."

Tyler laughed. "I heard Ely left the three families land, but no money. Some say he

gambled the last of his cash away the
week before he died, and the gambler who
won it left town the morning of Ely's funeral."

"That's probably right. They say the Trumans came from Virginia and brought some
valuables with them, but the Mathesons
and the McAllens were dirt poor, working for
what the old man paid them. Ely had land,
but they say he spent most of what he had
had trying to build a town around his trading
business." Hank knew they were talking
about something they both had heard every
detail of, but sometimes it's calming just to
talk.

Tyler seemed to feel the same way.

Hank was relieved to hear Alex in the
outer office yelling at Davis. She was back,
and she'd straighten out this mess.

Tyler was telling Hank about trails he'd
found where old Model Ts had hauled dy-
namite out of a few sites where men had
drilled for oil in the thirties when Hank felt
his cell phone vibrate. He flipped open the
cover and put it to his ear.

"Chief!" There was no mistaking Willie's
excited voice. "Derwood spotted smoke in
the canyon."

"How long ago?" Hank stood, shouting so loud Willie could probably hear him from across the street. He wouldn't need the phone.

The kid rattled on about how fire would climb the walls of the canyon. It could come out anywhere. They were fighting a monster now.

"Breathe, damn it, Willie," Hank shouted. "Get your gear on and make sure the call goes out to every volunteer. We'll need every man. Do you understand, every man!" For this fire, they'd need the dozen who always showed up and the thirty who never managed to make it.

He realized he was firing orders far too fast for Willie.

"I'll be right there." Hank closed the phone, tossed it on a pile of maps and papers, and stared out at the cloudless sky. Hank couldn't see a hint of smoke, but he could feel trouble moving in fast.

Tyler joined him at the window. "Fire?"

Hank nodded. "I've got to go." He hated the thought of leaving Tyler. On impulse, he turned and grabbed his friend's arm. "I'll be back. This will all get straightened out."

Tyler nodded. "Don't worry about me. You be safe."

When Hank exited through the outer office, everyone already knew there was fire in the canyon, and they were darting around and yelling. Andy was on dispatch, but he tossed a radio at Hank as he passed.

"I'll be there as soon as I can, Chief," Andy shouted. "I've got to help clear the calls first."

Hank nodded. Andy was always at fires; he'd be there as soon as he could pass the dispatcher duties along.

Hank brushed Alex's side with his hand, and she turned into him close. One look told him he didn't need to tell her how serious this might be.

"Let Tyler go," Hank whispered.

She shook her head. "Davis wants him locked up immediately. The best I can do is insist he stay in my office."

"Why? He couldn't have set this fire." Without turning loose of her, he began moving toward the door.

"Maybe not this one, but the others." Alex's voice was tight, as if she hated saying the words. "The state crime team found a quarter at three of the sites, and we both know he always carries quarters in his pockets."

"Pretty flimsy evidence." They were at the windy front door. Hank filled his lungs, swearing he could now smell trouble rolling in over the dry air. "Every man has change in his pockets."

"Not change. Only quarters."

"It's not enough to hold a man for arson."

"I know, but Davis thinks it's enough for a long talk."

"Then lock him up in your office." He tugged her closer for a fraction of a second before he let go and stepped out into the sun.

"I'll meet you at the canyon," she said.

He ran across the street, through the dry heat and dirt-filled wind whirling around him.

Chapter 38

REAGAN TURNED HER CHAIR TOWARD Jeremiah's and handed the old man one of the ice creams she'd bought when she'd done the shopping.

"What's this?" he grumbled.

"Ice cream on a stick," she answered. "Don't tell me you've never had it."

"Never thought to ask for it." He stared at the treat as if he were about to accuse her of poisoning him. "Why'd you buy it?" He took a bite.

Reagan thought for a moment, then said, "Where I've lived before, there were never enough of these to go around. There would always be a few of these good kind and lots of flavored frozen water. By the time the box got passed to me, all that was ever left was frozen water."

"Do you like frozen water?"

"No."

"What did you hate most about those places you lived?" He looked at her as if truly listening for once.

"I hated having to say thank you for everything given me. New clothes, used clothes, even the food on my plate. I was supposed to be grateful. And I was," she rushed on, "but sometimes they weren't giving it to me, they were just giving stuff away and I was handy."

He was silent for so long, she wondered if he'd dozed off, and then he said, "Buy more of these ice creams when you go to the store. In fact, keep the freezer stocked with them until you get good and tired of them."

"All right." She giggled.

"And get some of that frozen pizza I've seen. We need to keep it on stock for that boy who keeps coming around. I've heard it's fattening, and he could use some meat on his bones."

"All right." In all the weeks he'd never told her what to buy. He'd always said to buy the supplies she thought they needed. Now he was turning in an order for junk food.

Noah's pickup rattled down the lane at about half the speed he normally drove.

Reagan stood in alarm.

She watched as Noah pulled up close to their chairs and slowly climbed out of the truck. He didn't look any better than he had when she'd seen him after school.

"What are you doing here?" Reagan ran and pulled the old green wicker rocker off the porch. It was all they had with pillows in it.

He slowly folded into the chair. "I needed to talk to you, and you two don't have a phone between you."

Jeremiah looked up at her as if he hadn't noticed the bandaged, bruised boy sitting next to him. "Add that to the list. Order a phone. I have no idea how to do it, so figure it out. But I don't want any calls unless it's an emergency, so you might want to get one of those cell phones I see stuck to half the drivers' ears nowadays. You can use it and not give the home number to anyone, and I mean anyone." He pointed with his head toward the green rocker.

"It *is* an emergency," Noah said, "or it might be soon. There's fire down in the canyon on the other side of the Matheson place. If it reaches the grass, we could have trouble moving fast across dry land. Since I've been helping out at the fire station, they put me on the list to call, even knowing that I probably wouldn't be able to suit up and fight."

"You're hurt," Jeremiah said. "Only reason I can think of they'd put you near a fire is for kindling."

Noah shook his head. "It's mostly just a few bruises. Nothing really. We've got the fire to deal with now."

Jeremiah stood. "I'm not worrying about any fire till I know it's coming. My momma always said never waste worry, you never know when you'll need a bucket load of it and only have a thimbleful left." He headed toward the house, then turned and yelled as if Noah's injuries might have left him deaf. "You take care of yourself, boy."

"I'll try, sir," Noah yelled back. "You and Rea might think about moving out for a few days until this is over."

"I'm not leaving." The old man shifted to Reagan,. "You might want to give him a couple of those ice-creams-on-astick of yours."

"Please, don't feed me," Noah protested.

Jeremiah glared at the boy as if Noah had just proven he was some kind of rodent and they might want to put out traps, then headed on toward the house.

Noah leaned over and said quietly, "Does he ever say anything nice like hello or good-bye?"

"Nope," she answered honestly, "but now and then if you listen real close, he does say something nice."

Noah leaned back and closed his eyes.

"You shouldn't have come," she whispered. "You're supposed to be in bed. The doctor told you to rest for a week."

"I had to get out of the house. I've got to clear my head." He scrubbed his scalp, sending hair flopping across his forehead. "I don't care what the doctor said or how it hurts. I couldn't stay there, and this was the only peaceful place I could think of to come."

"I'm glad you did," she said, "but your house is great."

Noah leaned forward. "It's not the house. It's what I just saw there. Rea, it was horrible."

She couldn't imagine what could be so bad that he'd leave. Violence, murder, and a few hundred other terrible sights came to mind. "Tell me," she said, wishing she didn't have to hear what he saw. She had enough of her own nightmares haunting her dreams.

Noah put his head in his hands and began, "I thought I'd go down the back stairs and sneak into the den without anyone noticing. I thought I'd play a few video games before Mom found me and sent me back to bed."

He pressed his palms against his eyes, as if trying to push out an image. "The sun was streaming in the kitchen windows. The hallway was in shadows, but I could see to move past my mom's bedroom to the den. When I heard little noises."

"What kind of noises?"

"Strange kinds of noises. Kind of like someone is hurting and laughing at the same time. Like they were being tickled to death, or something."

Reagan waited.

"Then I took a step and saw in my mom's room . . ."

"And," Reagan whispered, afraid of what he would say.

He looked up at her, horror in his eyes. "I saw my parents having sex. I'm scarred for life."

Reagan laughed. "Did they see you?"

He shook his head. "They were too busy at the time. All I can figure out is when the doc said for me to go home and go to bed, my parents must have been listening. It wasn't even dark, Rea, and they were rolling in the sheets."

Reagan giggled. "Preacher, sometimes you're downright adorable."

Chapter 39

As the fire engines pulled out of the station, Hank climbed into his Dodge and followed. If the fire was running the canyon's length, he'd need to put the trucks at the two ends, and then he'd need his pickup, loaded down with supplies and equipment, to get from one end to the other. No proper roads ran to where a canyon dropped down like a giant crack in the flat earth, but with the prairie so dry the Dodge would be in no danger of getting stuck.

While he drove, dispatch patched him through to Wild Derwood, still in the air.

"Right now all I see is smoke, low in the

canyon." Derwood's words bounced through the phone. "Left wall. Little movement."

Hank swore he heard the man giggle before he asked, "Does this make me a full-fledged firefighter?"

"Yes, but we're not finished." Hank wouldn't have been surprised if Derwood took off to tell his mother. The guy had been crazy so long no one even talked about it anymore. In Texas, being nuts was a more dominant character trait than any illness and Derwood was a prime example.

"Give me the orders, Chief," Derwood shouted through the radio. "I'm ready to do my duty."

"You've got an hour before dark!" Hank shouted. "Keep watching until you get low on fuel. There's a chance the rock along the wall will stop the burn. We'll be up top if it climbs. What I need you to tell me is which way it moves."

North, it could break out near McAllen land. South, it would hit his spread and then Jeremiah Truman's place. East or west, the burn would run itself out in the canyon.

Closing his eyes, Hank surveyed the land in his mind. His property would be fine. He kept firebreaks plowed and all growth away from the buildings. If the fire reached the rim, he'd call and make sure his ranch hands moved any cattle. If it reached his house, the most he'd lose would be the far barn. Of course, the smoke would scare all the women he lived with to death. He'd make sure he called, giving them plenty of time to get out. They didn't even need to see the smoke getting closer. Aunt Pat and Aunt Fat would worry. At the speed they moved, he'd better call early. Claire would panic about her art collection, and Liz would probably explode in anger over why someone didn't do something about the smoke. The only calm one in his family was his mother. He wasn't sure she lived in reality most of the time, but he'd never seen her overreact. Maybe she'd gotten that all out of her system when his dad died. Since then, she'd been a rock.

Hank shook his head. Sometimes he thought fire was easier to deal with than all the women in his house, but right now, all he had time to think about was the fire.

The McAllen ranch wouldn't be so lucky if the fire came out of the canyon onto their land. Noah had been keeping an eye on the old place, but he was far more interested in horses than keeping breaks cut, and the couple he had living there didn't have time to do much. Alexandra's cabin on the rim would burn if the fire climbed out near her.

Then there was the old Truman place. A house built of sticks with old half-dead trees around. The orchard was irrigated, but if fire came, the trees would burn. If fire reached Jeremiah's land, it would destroy everything: the house, the orchard, the barns. If he managed to get fire trucks in before the fire reached Jeremiah, they could be trapped inside thanks to all the dead trees lining the only way out.

Logic told Hank to pray the fire came out on his land. McAllen's was unprotected and Truman's would burn, but if it hit his place, Hank would take a loss. He'd have his best chance to fight and win if he fought on home ground.

Hank was driving eighty when he passed Lone Oak Road. He almost smiled, remembering Tyler's confession. If the sheriff arrested every farmer or rancher who broke the speed limit, they'd all be in jail except Bob McNabb. Stella would never let him speed, not even when he'd been called in to assist the volunteers. Half the time when McNabb showed up on a call, Stella had packed him a lunch.

Turning off the road, Hank headed across open range vowing he'd fight and beat this one, no matter what it took.

An hour later Hank and all his men were in full gear watching the sun set. Smoke drifted up from the canyon, but nothing climbed. The men were starting to celebrate, thinking maybe this wasn't going to be so bad, just another story they'd have to tell.

Hank didn't say anything. He stood at the edge, a foot away from a hundred-foot drop into the canyon, and watched.

Brad Rister stood beside him. "It's not out, Chief. I can smell it burning."

Hank had a strong feeling he was right, even if Brad was more drunk than sober. He'd been a fireman for a year in Oklahoma City. He was the only man in the department who'd walked in the door trained. Hank had a feeling Brad would be moving on after his divorce was final. Right now Brad and his wife were in hell, trying to hurt each other as much as possible. Like most couples, they couldn't let the marriage die quietly; they both had to beat it to death. Word was Brad's wife had started dating again, which probably explained why Brad had doubled his drinking.

Hank would be sorry to see Brad go, even though the Oklahoman rarely trained and skipped most of the meetings. Sober, he was one of the best Hank had. Drunk, he was as helpful as a flat hose.

"There's enough juniper and mesquite in the canyon to burn for two days and no way we can get down to it to put it out." Brad fought not to slur his words.

"I know." Hank had climbed down these walls near his ranch. He knew that there were places ten feet deep with dried tumbleweeds. "We'll leave five men and both trucks where they are to keep watch. Why don't you ride along with me to check things out?" Hank would rather keep the drunk with him than leave him with the team. The last thing Hank needed was a drunk working a fire line. Maybe a drive across open range would sober him up.

Brad nodded. "Sure, I'll ride with you, Chief."

They both knew that the trucks were so far apart all the ground couldn't be covered. There was a good chance if the fire came, it would have a good hold on the grass before they would even see it.

Derwood called again to say he was heading in. "I can see the trucks," he shouted over the noise of the plane. "Looks like the smoke is concentrated right between them, but the way the wind is kicking up, it's hard to tell."

Hank motioned for Brad to get into the pickup. By the time he'd bumped across uneven ground for ten minutes, Brad was already complaining that he wished he'd stayed behind.

They reached the spot between the fire trucks. Neither truck was in sight, but Hank could see wisps of smoke coming from down in the canyon.

Brad jumped out and made it several feet before he threw up. When he walked back, he looked pale, but steady.

"Get the ropes." Hank nodded toward the back of his truck. "I'm going down to have a look."

Hank kicked off his gear, not listening to a word Brad was mumbling. The only way to find out how bad the fire was would be to rappel down the wall, and he couldn't do that in gear. He clipped his radio to a carabiner on his belt. If his cell didn't work in the canyon, maybe the police radio would.

While Brad tied one end of the rope to the winch on the back of the Dodge, Hank strapped on his harness. The canyon wasn't deep here, a hundred feet if he was lucky. He and Warren had made it down sliding on their butts many times, but if there was fire this time, Hank would need to get down and back fast. He knew he could get down, even in the shadows, but the ropes would be a great help when he turned to climb.

"You know how to work the winch to pull me up?" Hank checked the tie-on. "Slow speed or you'll drag me. Got it, Brad? Slow speed."

"I know. I'll remember." Brad looked like he might vomit again. "I'll be ready to bring you up as soon as you send the signal, but Hank, this is a bad idea. If the fire doesn't get to you, the smoke could. It's too dangerous."

Hank wanted to say, *Compared to what? To waiting?* If the fire was growing, there was still time to call in every agency they could. If it had played itself out, he could get a few men in good enough shape to rappel down, and with backpacks they could take down enough fire retardant to contain it. With the wind shear along the rim, a plane could never make a good drop of retardant to reach the fire.

Hank tugged on his gloves and began working his way down, trudging backward when he could, jumping from rock to rock, using the ropes like a vine in the jungle when he needed to and rappelling when he had to. He'd taken a few classes on how to do it safely, but like most, he hadn't practiced.

"I'm getting too old for this." He swore as the muscles in his legs burned.

At sixty feet down he saw fire beneath all the smoke.

Another twenty feet lower he could make out the blackened burn crawling across the canyon.

It was a full burn, building as it inched across sagebrush and buffalo grass. A monster growing, eating away the ground growth and belching dark smoke. Because of the wind, the smoke had blown down the canyon and not up. The danger was far greater than he'd feared.

There was no way to get closer to the fire except on horseback, and before men could saddle up, the fire would spread the width of the canyon. It was already climbing the walls in spots, spreading through the scrub trees and dead cottonwoods along the dried-up creek bed. Before long it would break free of its confinement of canyon walls.

Hank felt every muscle tighten, preparing to fight.

He couldn't send men down. Much too high a chance they'd end up trapped. They'd have no choice but to wait.

Hank let the ropes take his weight as he reached for his cell. The case clipped to his belt was empty. He grabbed the radio, trying to remember where he'd left the phone that never left his side.

As soon as Andy at dispatch picked up, Hank began rattling off orders. "Call in the parks department. They'll need to find a place in both directions of the fire where they can stop it in the canyon." He remembered a water crossing a few miles up where the canyon widened enough to get trucks in. To the east, the canyon narrowed. If the parks service could get a water dump from the base at Altus, that would stop the fire from crawling along.

"And, Andy . . ."

"Yes, Chief?"

"Call in all the help you can get from towns around. This is big and it *will* climb the walls." Hank stared down, swearing that the burn had grown even in those few seconds. "It'll probably break out of the canyon in more than one place. We're going to need more men than we've got now to control this one."

"I'll call." Andy's voice vibrated with excitement. "And don't worry, Chief, as soon as I can get off this desk, I'll be out there with you."

Hank could feel the heat now as he began to climb, pulling his weight up a few feet at a time. His hands were sweaty inside the gloves. His muscles strained. Smoke climbed with him, robbing him of oxygen.

He jerked the rope, the signal for Brad to start the winch, then waited.

Nothing.

Night had settled in and, with the smoke, Hank couldn't see the edge of the canyon wall clearly. He felt his way, climbing. Jerking the rope to signal. Climbing.

He had no idea if he was twenty feet from the ledge or forty. He tugged the rope hard, sending the message to Brad for the fifth time.

"Brad better be dead," he said with his teeth clenched, "or I'm going to kill him when I get out of here."

His shirt turned wet with sweat, but he couldn't stop. He tried yelling for Brad, but the wind whipped his call away, circling it down the canyon.

Then finally, the rope jerked and pulled. Hank relaxed for a moment as he started rising, than realized he was moving too fast. Brad must have pushed the winch full throttle. He wasn't climbing now, but bracing his legs, trying to swing away from the walls before the edges pounded him. He felt like a boxer who couldn't get his footing before another punch sent him spinning.

Hank cleared the top, scraping his knee before he could roll over on his back. He yelled as the rope dragged him across solid ground, with flying dirt and weeds scratching his arms and face.

Halfway between the ledge and the Dodge, he finally stopped.

"Damn it, Brad!" he yelled as he released his harness from the rope. "You trying to kill me?"

He closed his eyes, took a deep breath of fresh air, and looked into the stormy blue eyes of the sheriff. For once in her life, she looked like she was too angry to speak. She stood above him, fists on her hips, glaring at him as if it were all his fault for almost getting himself killed.

Over by Alex's cruiser Hank heard Trooper Davis shouting on the phone, "We found him. Damn fool almost got himself cooked."

Alex offered Hank a hand up. He clasped her arm while she grabbed his and tugged him to his feet. They were so close he could feel her brush his chest when she breathed, building anger like steam.

Before she started cussing he smiled and asked, "Worried about me?"

"Yes," she said without moving back. "If you die, there will be all kinds of forms to fill out. How could you have been so dumb to go down alone? Who did you think would winch you up, a jackrabbit? Another five minutes swinging above that fire, you would have been a marshmallow in full burn."

He didn't try to defend himself. It was almost worth all the scrapes and bruising he got to see how much she cared, even though she'd probably clobber him if he suggested that caring might be at the bottom of all her anger.

Hank spotted Brad coming out of the shadows. "Sorry, Chief, I had to throw up again."

Hank would have let Brad have it, but right now he had something else on his mind and far too close to his body. Alexandra.

Like a dozen times before, all she had to do was step away, but she didn't. Despite all her complaining, she was drawn to him.

He fought the urge to kiss her. She wanted him, needed him, just as dearly as he needed her. No matter what she said, she'd been worried about him.

"Right now, Alex, we've got a fire to fight, but when this is over," he whispered as Trooper Davis started toward them, "we've got unfinished business." He took a deep breath, loving the way she smelled. "And believe me, we will have time one day."

She didn't say a word, but her body brushing his was enough to make him hotter than the fire ever had.

Brad flipped on the bar of lights on top of the Dodge. Hank moved away from her and began folding up the ropes.

"Thanks for pulling me up," he said. "Remind me to teach you to use the slower speed."

She stared at Brad, figuring out where the problem must have been in Hank's plan. "How about I shoot one of your volunteers?"

"No need. He knows he's now an ex-volunteer." Hank tossed gear in the bed of the pickup. "How'd you know I was here?"

"Andy patched me through when the state parks service started asking questions. He told me about where he thought you were, and I headed this way while I talked." She looked at the rim of the canyon, glowing now as if dawn were just beginning to break. "What did you find?"

"It's growing, feeding off dried trees and brush. I'm guessing, but I think it'll break the rim before dawn, and then we'll have a full fight on our hands."

"Worst ever?"

He met her eyes. "Worst ever. You up for it?"

She nodded, and he realized he loved this wild, wonderful, brave woman.

Chapter 40

TYLER WRIGHT SAT IN THE SHERIFF'S OFFICE. He'd already tried the door. It was locked. At first he'd heard yelling and phones ringing, but then it grew quiet. The thought crossed his mind that everyone had left him behind, but he knew that would be too much to hope for.

He'd been worried for the first hour, eaten all the old candy in the sheriff's candy bowl the second hour, and finally slept a while in her chair with his feet on her desk. Which wasn't comfortable at all.

Tyler thought of trying to contact Katherine on Alex's computer, but doubted he could get logged on, and if he did he wasn't sure he wanted to leave a trace to Katherine on the sheriff's files. If he was in trouble, he might somehow pull Katherine in, and Tyler would face a firing squad before he'd tell them about his hazel-eyed friend. They had this private world no one else would ever know about.

He groaned at his own imagination. He had no idea why the law was keeping him, but he doubted he'd be shot for speeding. Hank had said they needed his help, but something didn't feel right about that. The sheriff, or rather that angry highway patrolman, wouldn't lock him up if they wanted his help. Davis had given him a look that said he'd already convicted him of something terrible and was just waiting around until some judge pronounced sentence.

Bored and nervous, Tyler began walking around the sheriff's office, examining everything. He discovered a closed vent over the door that when opened allowed him to hear conversations going on at the dispatch office across the hall.

He could hear the dispatcher calling in firemen for duty and giving directions to a meet-up spot a few miles north of the Matheson ranch.

Tyler moved a cell phone aside and un-folded a map sitting on the round table. He had no trouble finding the spot where the dispatcher was sending people.

The markings on the map interested him far more than the dispatcher's conver-sations. He pulled up a chair and tried to figure out what all the Xs and circles meant on the state map.

With his knowledge, it didn't take him long, and the meaning frightened him more than Trooper Davis ever could.

The Xs were burn sites . . . fires . . . each marked with a date. And—he held his breath—they were moving in a circle around Harmony.

The fires must have been set. Nature would never play such a game.

Another hour passed as Tyler read the details of every report as if it were the world's best mystery novel. He guessed the sheriff hadn't left it for any outsider's eyes, but Tyler considered it like magazines in a doctor's office. If it was there, he could read it.

Hard fear settled in his stomach. Whoever was setting the fires wasn't some kid
playing with matches. He reminded Tyler
of a hunter circling his prey. Two, maybe
three more fires and the circle would be
complete. What would the madman with
his weapon of fire do then?

Tyler knew the roads, even ones not
marked on any map. He could see the arsonist's pattern. Finally, he stood and moved
to stare out into the midnight sky. His eyes
burned from reading, but he still smiled. He
knew why they must have called him in.
He could help. He could show them the
back roads the man setting the fires would
have most likely taken. Maybe for them the
police could find a clue, like tire tracks or
maybe even footprints.

Tyler wished he'd watched more of
those detective shows and fewer dancing
shows.

Some of the fire points of origin were
close to roads, but others were well off even
the known unpaved roads. Whoever was
setting them knew the area well. Maybe
he'd grown up around here, or maybe he'd
studied detailed maps like only the police
and fire departments usually saw.

"Or maybe," Tyler said out loud, "he was like me. Collecting maps, studying roads, exploring."

Tyler didn't like the idea that any part of him could be like someone who would cause damage for no reason, but he felt he might be able to see inside a tiny part of the arsonist's mind and, in so doing, help in the capture of such a man.

The cell phone on the table began to vibrate. Tyler hesitated. He knew it was Hank's phone. He also knew the chief had forgotten it.

Slowly, he picked it up, deciding it was probably Hank on the line wondering where he'd left his phone. In all the excitement of the fire, he might not have had time to notice it was gone until now.

"Hello," Tyler answered.

"Uncle Hank?" came a small voice.

"No, dear, this is Tyler Wright." The caller had to be Saralynn. "Your uncle left his phone with me."

"Sir Knight," she whispered, sounding like she might cry. "I'm afraid."

Tyler forgot all about his problems. The little princess needed him. "What's frightened you, dear?" He glanced up at the clock and noticed it was almost two in the morning. Far too late for a four-year-old to be up.

"A man called and told my gram that we all have to leave our house by dawn. He said there may be a fire coming our way."

Tyler looked at the map. He wished he could lie and tell her everything was going to be all right, but if the wind was out of the north, it looked like the fire might just blow straight over the Matheson ranch.

"Is that true?" she whispered.

"It could be, child. But don't you worry, your mom and grandmother and aunts will get you out, and you will all be safe." Tyler knew Hank was out on the rim of the canyon right now with more than twenty men watching, waiting, ready. "If the fire does come, it will go around your house, but the smoke will make your eyes water and a princess's eyes should never water, so they'll take you somewhere to wait until everything is all right."

He heard a sniffle.

"Mom told me to go to bed, she'd come get me when it's time to leave, but I can't sleep. I can hear them all moving around the house." She sounded as if she might cry again. "Will you talk to me, Sir Knight? I don't want to be alone."

Tyler moved to a chair. "For as long as you like, Princess."

Suddenly Tyler wasn't tired and there was nowhere he wanted to go. He was right where he needed to be.

Chapter 41

ALEXANDRA WATCHED THE STATE TEAMS STORM her office just before dawn. Cars and vans full of them. The county offices of Harmony were beginning to sound like a crowd at the state fair.

Highway patrol cars to handle traffic if smoke from the fires blocked the roads.

The state parks service officers, whose only worry was state lands already on fire.

A high-powered arson specialist from federal named Major Cummings, who worked out of Austin. She'd flown into Amarillo, rented a car, and driven to Harmony just to make sure she'd be in place before dawn.

Alex couldn't even count the endless reporters asking questions and wanting to be allowed at the site to take pictures.

The main office was packed with people, and Alex knew these were nothing compared to the numbers at the site near the canyon. She tried to make room for all of them and offer office space and chairs for all federal and state people. The place was a working beehive. Irene had come in early to pass out cups of coffee and pencils provided by the chamber of commerce.

Andy, who'd spent the predawn hours watching for fire, was back in his chair at the phones. He jumped up from the dispatch desk and rushed toward her. Some men look good with a few days of stubble on their face. Andy Daily wasn't one of them. He also looked like he could use one of those washers he owned. Maybe he could find a big one and just climb in, washing clothes and body at the same time.

She backed into a corner, away from the others as Andy Daily reached her. She hoped for a little privacy, fearing what he was about to say. "You need to get some sleep," she said, knowing she'd need to pull all the part-time people in if she could get him to surrender his headset.

He leaned in, ignoring her comment. He was too excited to whisper. "Fire's climbed the walls in three places. It's into tall grass on the north side and short in two places on the south wall. We've got a full crisis on our hands. It's going to take a lot more than our fire department to handle this one."

Alex raised her eyes to the crowd, who all seemed to breathe in at the same time. For a second the room was silent. She saw a world of different emotions in their eyes. Some frightened. Some nervous. Some excited. For the firemen, it would be a fight. For the reporters, it would be a great story.

One woman—middle-aged, slightly over-weight, with intelligent hazel eyes—caught her gaze. Alex saw wisdom in those eyes and, more important, experience that had taught her not to overreact in times like these.

Alex nodded slightly, and the woman walked toward her. She'd been told that

Major Cummings, the military's top arson expert in the area, was good, but this lady hadn't made a grand entrance, she'd simply walked in and gone to work on one of the break room tables. If Alex had to trust someone, this one woman would be it.

"Can we talk in my office, Major?" Alex motioned toward her door.

The woman picked up her briefcase. She was letting Alex take the lead, not trying to run over her authority simply because she was older. Just by the way she followed a few steps behind told Alex that she was there to help.

Alex forgot she'd locked Tyler in hours ago. She'd unlocked the door and stepped in before she remembered.

The major walked past her as Alex looked everywhere for the undertaker. He seemed to have vanished. Trooper Davis couldn't have taken him to lockup. First, he didn't have a key to her office, and second, Davis was at the site. Tyler Wright didn't seem the type who could pick a lock, but then, he was gone.

"I'm here to help," Major Cummings announced. "I'll never leak information and

I'll never sugarcoat the truth. In return, all I ask is honesty and the opportunity to help when I can."

Alex accepted the woman's hand. She had bigger things to worry about than how Tyler got out of her office, plus she had a feeling that if he'd escaped, he'd probably gone home. "Thank you." Alex met the woman's honest stare. "I'll do the same, Major Cummings."

The major smiled. "Then let's go to work."

Alex quickly spread out Hank's marked map and showed her the area.

The major needed only a quick look to see the problem.

As Alex closed the open window, Major Cummings stuffed the map in her case and marched toward the door, "Call me Katherine, Sheriff, and I think it's time we head toward this fire."

"I'm Alex."

There was no more time for introductions. They had a fire to fight.

Chapter 42

HANK HADN'T SLEPT FOR TWENTY-FOUR HOURS, but he was pumped on coffee and adrenaline. The fire came over the edge of the canyon like a warrior charging into battle. Dry grass and wind were its allies as smoke breathed out a war cry.

He'd had word that other trucks from surrounding areas were coming in, but the fire came first. He hardly noticed the dawn as he fought through smoke and dust. His men, even those he feared would never stand in trouble, fought beside him. What they lacked in training, they made up for in spirit.

Hank yelled orders and the men moved in with every weapon they had.

And still, the fire spread. Twisting along the uneven edge of the canyon where they couldn't get water. Jumping in the wind. Flames three and four feet high in the tall grass. The heat made it seem like the hottest day of the year, and the smoke seeped through the equipment.

Half the team circled to the north to fight on the opposite rim, leaving Hank with less than half the men he needed. Trooper Davis kept yelling into the radio that more fire trucks were coming, but the fire was crawling sideways across the battle line, growing, raging, every minute.

By the time Hank saw the first truck bouncing across the field, he already needed two more. To his horror, vans from the TV stations nearby bumped along behind the fire truck.

"I thought I said no press!" Hank yelled at Davis.

Davis shrugged, as if he had no control over free press.

"Well, at least make them stay out of the way and far back." When this was over, Hank promised himself he would have a

very long, very private talk with Davis. The
trooper thought he knew everything, even
ordering the firemen around. In truth, he
couldn't handle his own job. He was a man
who talked a good story, but didn't walk it.

Davis gave a mock salute as Hank
cussed the man's incompetence. The highway patrolman directed the camera crew
over to Willie, the only one of the volunteers not black and sweaty.

Closing his eyes, Hank swore under his
breath, putting the pieces together. He'd
already guessed that the trooper and Willie were probably related, and now he knew
that Davis had brought the press in to take
Willie's picture.

Hank had made the boy stay back for
safety's sake. He had the least training and
judgment, but now it looked like he'd be the
hero on the news tonight. Hank couldn't
help but wonder if Davis hadn't planned it
that way to highlight his kin. In the past few
days he'd seen the two men talking several
times.

It didn't matter. Nothing mattered but
the fire.

As the sun rose, Hank ordered his men
to pull back a hundred yards and try again

to make a stand. With shovels on shoulders, they all moved back. They were on land owned by a corporation. It had never been farmed and probably not grazed for years. There had also been no fire breaks cut . . . ever.

While they waited for the fire to crawl toward them, they all gulped down water and rested aching muscles. Hank took inventory. They'd been fighting the fire for three hours. Two men were hurt. Three looked like they couldn't go much longer. The fire was burning hotter, moving faster than he'd ever seen grass fires move.

He glanced at Bob McNabb manning the radio and first-aid station. There was no need for him to yell the same questions he'd asked a dozen times. No need for Bob to report the fire still raging across the canyon. Bob just shook his head, and Hank nodded once in thanks.

As soon as he got reinforcements, he'd order his men to rest at least two hours. If he didn't, Hank knew he'd be dealing with more injuries than a few burns. The EMTs from the hospital were about half a mile back, working as hard as the firemen.

Alex pulled up behind the fire truck and

stepped out with a squatty woman at her side. They both marched right toward him.

Alex did a quick introduction of the major, then asked what they could do. He didn't miss the fact that Alexandra's gaze never left his face. She seemed to be reassuring herself that he was all right.

Hank described everything that had happened, but he noticed that Major Cummings was barely listening. She began walking the grass, bending now and then as if smelling invisible flowers.

"What's with her?" Hank asked, too tired to be polite.

"Federal government," Alex answered, as if that explained everything. "Where's this heading?"

"Unless the wind changes, right toward my ranch. The good news is we've got a great deal of open range to fight it first. No houses or herds to have to deal with. The bad news is we have open range. No roads, no breaks." He didn't sound upset. His mind had already thought every option through. He'd have to wait until the cards were dealt before he could play the hand.

Alex stared out at the black cloud on the ground crawling toward them. She

looked like she wanted to empty her Colt
into the wall of black smoke.

"One thing you don't have to worry about."
He fought the urge to touch her. "Looks like
it'll miss your place."

"What about your mother, the aunts—"

He didn't give her time to make the list of
women at his ranch. "They're all out, and
I've got the house protected. If it gets all the
way to me, I'll probably lose the old barn
my father built, but other than smoke damage, we'll survive. I knew the women would
panic if they saw the wall of smoke coming,
so I told them to get out before dawn.
They've been in town for over an hour."

"Your stock?"

"I've got men moving cattle onto your
land as we speak. Figured you wouldn't
mind." He grinned.

"They'll eat all my grass."

"At least you got grass." He would have
bet that she'd complain. He also bet she
wouldn't care if his cattle ate every blade of
her grass.

Alex reached out and almost touched
him. "You all right?"

"I'm fine. My biggest worry right now is
Jeremiah's place, just beyond mine." He

didn't say more. He couldn't. Hank might lose grassland for a season and fence posts, but Jeremiah stood to lose everything. The old man didn't have enough life left to rebuild.

"What can I do?" she asked, meaning every word.

"Keep Trooper Davis out of my hair. The guy gets on my nerves."

"Done."

The middle-aged major interrupted. "Gas," she announced from about five feet away. "Someone's seeded the grass here and there with gas. That's why it's flaring in spots. That's why it's moving so fast."

"But how?"

"I understand this land is owned by a company in Dallas. I assume no one patrols it." She didn't give Alex or Hank time to comment. "An arsonist would have had no problem crossing this land on a jeep or ATV, or even a pickup. He could have spread gas for a mile if he had barrels of it in the back of a truck. But he couldn't have crossed onto Matheson land," she said as she looked at Hank. "You have a working ranch, I understand. A stranger would be noticed." She made a face. "What I can't figure out is how he could get out here with a load of gasoline. Looks like someone would have noticed."

Hank had been so busy lately, he might not have noticed someone on *his* land, but the highway patrol had been watching the roads. "How'd you know all this?" he asked the major.

"I do my homework. You may have been up all night watching this fire, but I've been up learning all I could." She winked at him boldly. "If it matters, Mr. Matheson, I figured out the circle about three this morning. I'm glad to see that you did also. It's always good to know there is a logical man in charge."

"What do you think the gas means?" He found himself admiring the major. She might be short and built like an apartment refrigerator, but she had the most interesting eyes and a razor-sharp mind.

"I think"—she raised one eyebrow as if pleased to be asked—"that he's getting restless. He's tired of waiting for his big fire. If this one doesn't burn bright enough, I think he'll set another soon."

Hank agreed. "So, what do you know for sure, Major?"

"First, we know this was set. That's a matter for law enforcement. We let them do their job. Second, get your people back and let it burn. If one of your men is standing in a puddle of gasoline when the fire line reaches him, we could have a casualty. I'm thinking he wouldn't have had time to make more than one run spreading the gas. The chances he'd get caught were too great."

When Hank started to argue, she continued, "If we act fast and move back, we can form a break; the tanks can water it down before the fire line gets to it. Those folks in Dallas won't be happy that we let their land burn, but it's our best chance of stopping the fire."

"How far back?"

She pointed past his fence line. "Three, maybe four hundred yards that way."

Hank agreed. It was a hard course to take, but it might be their only chance.

Like an army of ants, they all began to move. Hank drove his truck, loaded down with men, to the fence. By the time the others reached his land, he'd pulled out enough fence poles to let them pass.

Alex banished the reporters to Lone Oak Road and Trooper Davis to the roadblock.

The highway patrolman looked like he might argue, but in the end he didn't. Two more volunteer fire departments joined the fight. There should have been a half dozen more by now, but Hank would take what he got.

For the first time in hours, Hank thought they might have a chance.

While they waited for trackers to plow a row and trucks to water the barrier down, Hank picked up the radio and asked Andy to patch him through to his mother. He needed to know she was safe. He didn't want her to know that they were fighting a fire on his land.

"Mom," he said when he heard her voice.

"Yes, dear," she answered. "Are you all right?"

"Fine, and you?"

"Pat, Fat, and I are at the bed-and-breakfast. We didn't get any sleep packing up last night, so we've checked in and are having breakfast before we take a morning nap. You're not going to believe what colors they've painted this place. I've already decided to suggest a better color scheme for a house this age."

"Good." Hank hated listening to his mother talk about colors. It crossed his mind that maybe she should have spent more time talking to his sister Claire, who only painted in black, white, and red.

She continued, oblivious to the fact that Hank hadn't commented. "Claire packed her paintings in the pickup and is going to drive them on to Fort Worth before something else threatens to harm them. Liz and Saralynn went over to Liz's friend's house who has a pool. They plan on swimming a few hours if it gets warm enough today and then joining us here."

Hank didn't like the idea of Saralynn swimming with Liz. His younger sister might be smart, but she'd never been able to keep a goldfish alive. If he didn't have his hands full, he'd go get the little princess right now. "Mom," he said. "Do me a favor and call Liz. Tell her not to let Saralynn in the water unless she's right there."

"All right, but you should give her some credit. She's not ten years old, she's twenty-seven."

"Promise," he insisted.

"All right. I promise. When I finish break-fast, I'll call."

"Good." He clicked the radio off, but he couldn't shake his anxiety.

Chapter 43

TYLER LET HIMSELF IN THE BASEMENT DOOR OF the funeral home, slipped out of his shoes, and rushed up the back stairs to his bedroom. He could hear Willamina in the kitchen making breakfast with CNN blaring away on the kitchen TV. His housekeeper had insisted on the TV ten years ago and, to Tyler's knowledge, she never watched anything but the news and *Oprah*.

He crossed to his bathroom and stripped off his bloody shirt. Crawling out the window in the sheriff's office hadn't been easy. Half-way through he'd gotten stuck and decided he'd probably be there until he lost ten pounds, but after finally wiggling out of his suit jacket and vest, he'd dropped to the rosebushes below the office window.

There, he'd been bloodied and unfortunately several of the rosebushes died in the battle for him to break free.

Like a thief in an old film, he darted through the darkened streets, constantly on the move and completely out of breath by the time he'd gone the two blocks to the funeral home.

Now he didn't bother with treating his wounds; he simply slipped on another white T-shirt and then pulled on an old sweatshirt he hadn't worn in years and a pair of even older tennis shoes. Sometime over the past twenty years he'd begun dressing the same way every day. Always a starched dress shirt. Always a suit or sports jacket if it was the weekend. Always polished shoes.

He glanced in the mirror and decided he looked like a pumpkin in his orange UT shirt, but he had no time to worry about it. He was on a quest.

Running back down the stairs, he slipped out the basement door and climbed into the old van they used for moving flowers from the home to the grave. The seats smelled like dusty potpourri and damp card-board, but Tyler hoped the van wouldn't be missed or noticed.

Saralynn called just as he reached the city limit sign. "Are you still coming, Sir Knight?" she whispered.

"I'm coming, Princess. Did you walk around the house one more time like I told you?" He'd hoped someone was still there packing and thought the kid was sleeping. He couldn't believe she was really alone.

"I did. I even called up to Momma's studio. I can't climb the stairs." She took a breath and continued, "No one is in the house but me. Momma told me to ride with Aunt Liz, but by the time I got out to her car she said it was too full and I'd have to ride with Momma and the aunts in the van. When I got all the way back to the garage, the van was gone."

He could hear her crying, and it broke his heart. He'd seen her walk using crutches a few times. Each step looked like it was slow and painful. The Matheson house was big, and she'd had to walk the length of it from the front steps to the back.

"They left me," she said between gulps for air. "They all forgot about me."

"No they didn't, Princess. You're the most important person of all. They just each thought that you were with someone else."

He heard her sobbing and wished he had more knowledge of kids. "I'm coming," he said. "I promise. I'm on my way." His foot shoved the gas pedal harder. "I'll be there soon. Can you get your bag of medicine ready?"

"I saw it on the counter. Someone must have packed it."

"Good. Get it and meet me at the front door."

"Can I call you back? Uncle Hank's phone number is the only one I remember. He got it special because of me. When I spell out my name on any phone, I get him. I can even leave off the last *N* and still get him."

"You bet you can call back. I'll keep your uncle Hank's phone in my hand until I get there." Tyler smiled at the interesting way Hank had taught her not only to spell her name, but to call him. "You get all your things together and then call me right back."

"What things?"

"Well . . ." He had no idea what little girls would think were important. "Things a princess should always have with her."

"Oh," she said. "I'll pack."

When she hung up, he closed the phone, hoping he'd be within sight of the ranch house by the time she collected her things.

He turned onto Lone Oak Road and saw the roadblock just past the Truman gate. To get to Saralynn, he'd have to pass Jeremiah's place and, from the number of cars, there was no way. After all, he'd escaped from a locked office. Somehow that couldn't be a plus. He was now a man on the run. The last thing he needed to happen was to be caught before he reached Saralynn.

Laughing to himself, he could hardly wait to e-mail Katherine tonight and tell her of his adventure. Of course, he'd have to leave out a few details.

Tyler pulled off the road and tried to think. He had no map with him, but he could see every back road in his mind. He'd even mentioned one to Hank yesterday.

Turning around, Tyler headed for a back road that would run into a trail that would lead to wagon ruts still marking a path where buffalo bones had been hauled off Matheson land a hundred years ago.

It was full daylight by the time he reached where the path would have been, and to his delight, he could see slight impressions in the earth now and then, marking the way. As he drove, he also saw something else. Smoke, moving like a long rolling cloud toward him. It was still miles away, but it looked to be on a direct path to the ranch house.

Tyler gunned the engine, not caring that he was probably sending the old van to the junk heap. He had to get to Saralynn.

The house was dark when he pulled up at the front door. Leaving the van running, he jumped out and bounded up the steps.

"Saralynn!" he yelled.

She was nowhere in sight.

He tried the door.

Locked.

Panic jolted through his entire body. He tried pounding on the door, then listening. Nothing. Out of his mind with worry and smelling the fire growing closer, he started around the house, stomping on flowers and knocking over pots as he tried every window, every door.

All were locked. How could five women leave the house, locking every door, and forget to take Saralynn?

He took a tumble in the mud where someone had left a garden hose dripping in what looked like a newly planted garden. Getting to his feet, he tugged off the orange shirt, now soaked and dirty, and kept circling the house.

"Saralynn!" He wouldn't leave, couldn't leave until he found her. He tripped again, watching only the windows and not his footing. A branch caught his shoulder and bloodied the skin as it ripped the cotton of his shirt.

He'd made a complete circle and started another when he felt the phone in his pocket shaking.

"Saralynn!" He tried to sound calm. "I'm here."

"Sir Knight," she said. "I can't carry my things and walk with the crutches. Will you help me?"

"Where are you?" He could smell the fire now and knew it was getting closer. They had no time to waste. If she'd been another child, he would have yelled for her to run, but his little princess could barely walk and, if she hurried, she might fall and hurt herself.

"I'm in my bedroom next to the kitchen."

Tyler looked over at what looked like it might be a kitchen door. A few feet away, on a bench, he saw the gardening tools. Without hesitation, he committed a crime. He grabbed the hoe, raised it like a bat, and smashed the window in the door.

A moment later, he was in and moving toward the first room off the kitchen. "Princess?" he yelled.

He opened the door to the laundry room and almost swore aloud. "Princess," he called again as he moved to another doorway

"Yes," she answered just as he opened the next door.

She was sitting on her bed, her toys all around her. Relief washed over him.

She smiled up at him. "You are a mess, Sir Knight."

He caught a glimpse of himself in her dresser mirror—his shirt bloody in spots, mud on his face and hands, and not even a hat to cover hair he didn't remember combing since yesterday. "I've been fighting my share of dragons today."

Taking a step toward her, he bowed as politely as he knew how. "Are you ready to go, Princess?"

She stuffed the toys into what looked like a laundry bag. "I'm ready."

Tyler strapped her medical bag over one shoulder and a bag of toys over the other, then lifted her up as carefully as he'd seen Hank do in the diner.

She put her thin little arms around his neck and held on tightly as he moved though the house to the front door. He didn't want her to see the broken glass or the smoke moving toward the back of her home.

"I'm very tired," she whispered and rested her cheek against his shoulder.

"You sleep now, little one; I'll get you to town. It shouldn't be hard to find your aunt's sports car or your grandmother's old van. In no time you'll be tucked into a blanket and down for a morning nap."

"Okay." She sounded almost asleep.

Tyler smiled. He'd gotten her in time.

At the front door, he turned the knob and stepped out into chaos.

Chapter 44

ALEX HEARD THE REPORT OF A BREAK-IN AT THE Matheson home on her radio. Hank was one of the few ranchers who'd installed alarms, to satisfy the fears of the women in his household. Hank's house wasn't anything fancy, but between his mother's pots and his sister's art, someone might have decided to take advantage of the fire to do a little looting.

Katherine caught her attention. "Go," she'd said. "Check out that alarm. There's not much you can do here."

Alex nodded and climbed into her car. She had to cross over open ground to get to the road and then go back almost to Lone Oak Road to enter the Matheson ranch entrance.

It took her five minutes and, by the time she pulled up, Trooper Davis was already there, his gun pulled and waiting.

"He's in there," Davis snapped. "He left his van running so he could make a fast getaway. Let me handle this, McAllen."

Just then, the door opened and a mud-and-blood-covered man pushed his way out. He had bags on both shoulders and a child in his arms.

Saralynn!

Alex started to move, but Davis shoved her back with one hand as he yelled. "Take another step and you're dead, Wright."

Tyler Wright? She hadn't even recognized him. This was impossible. Some kind of sick dream. She'd never seen Tyler with even a smudge on his suit, and why would he be taking Saralynn?

Alex glanced at the van. It was the one usually parked at the back of the funeral home.

"Put the kid down and step away from the door," Davis ordered.

"No," Tyler answered. "I'm not putting her down."

Davis raised his service weapon at Tyler's head.

Alex reacted. No matter what it looked like, Hank's words came back to her. *Tyler isn't guilty.*

"Hold your fire, Davis!" she ordered as she stepped out in front of the trooper and moved toward Hank's friend. If Hank believed in the man so completely, she could believe in him a little.

"What's going on here, Tyler?" Alex snapped.

He looked at her with fear in his eyes.

"Get out of the way, McAllen. You're blocking my shot!" Davis yelled. "There's only one thing to do with a pervert who kidnaps a child."

Alex didn't move, and she heard Davis mumble "Bitch" under his breath.

Tyler lowered his head slightly and spoke softly. "They accidentally left Saralynn, and I had to break out of your office to come get her. I'll replace the roses I fell on and the window I broke here, but I'm not putting her on the hard ground."

Alex looked down at the little girl. "Are you all right, honey?"

"I'm a princess," she whispered in a sleepy little voice, "and Sir Knight came to rescue me."

Alex smiled at Tyler. "You've had a rough time of it, even for a knight."

He managed a smile. "Just part of the job."

Alex extended her arms and lifted Saralynn. "How about you ride with me? There's a blanket in my car and I'll drive you around until we find your grandmother."

When she stepped away from the porch, Trooper Davis slammed Tyler Wright to the ground. His head made a thud like a melon as it hit the stones steps. Alex twisted to block Saralynn's view as Davis jerked Tyler's hands behind him and began reading him his rights.

"That was not necessary, Davis," Alex said.

He smiled as he pulled Tyler to his feet. "Oh, yeah, you know right from wrong, don't you, Sheriff? Sleeping your way into the job teach you all you needed to know about being a cop?"

Alex headed toward her car. She'd deal

with Davis as soon as she'd made sure
Saralynn was safe. He'd had something
against her from the day she'd been sworn
in, and now hatred was boiling to the surface. Davis wasn't mad about the crime he
thought Tyler had committed or frustrated
about the fires. He was furious at her. She
could hear it in his words, feel it in his
stares. Maybe it had always been there,
boiling deep inside, but she knew without
doubt that he wished it had been her head
that hit the walk.

Hank's Dodge came flying across the
pasture at a speed that looked as if he were
about to become airborne. He slammed on
his brakes just in time to slide into the flower
beds. A moment later he was out of the car.

"We caught the burglar!" Davis yelled
with pride. "Making off with two bags of
plunder and your niece."

Hank stormed up the path and stopped
in front of Alex. He placed his dirty, smoke-
covered hand on the back of Saralynn's
head. "Are you all right?"

She nodded. "Sir Knight came for me
when I called your phone."

That seemed to be all Hank needed to
know. He moved toward Davis as Alex

hurried Saralynn to the car. She had no idea what was about to happen, but she guessed the language wouldn't be for children. Flipping on the radio, she made the little girl promise to stay in the car for a few minutes.

Saralynn leaned against the armrest, looking too tired to answer.

Alex covered her with a jacket and closed the door, then noticed Major Cummings sitting in Hank's Dodge. As always, the woman seemed to be studying everything around her.

Alex marched back to the men. Whatever Trooper Davis's problem, they'd deal with it here and now. Whether he hated her being a woman in what most thought of as a man's job, or loathed the whole county, she knew she could ignore his attitude no longer.

Hank was nose to nose with Davis, demanding he take the handcuffs off Tyler Wright.

Tyler stood, feet wide apart, head down as if it was taking all his effort to keep from falling over. Blood dripped from somewhere on his forehead into a puddle between his feet.

"So you want me to just let him go after he tried to steal you blind and do God knows what with your niece?" Davis looked angry enough to shoot Hank for getting in the way. "You're about as brain-dead as this sheriff who slept her way to—"

Hank's fists slammed into Davis so hard the man toppled backward, almost taking Tyler with him.

"That's it!" Davis said as soon as he could get to one knee. "I'm arresting you for assaulting an officer of the law. Turn around, Matheson, and lock your hands behind your head."

Hank didn't move except to harden his hand into a fist. "Get off my land," he said in a low, angry tone.

Alex knew she had to do something. "Wait!" She pushed her way between the two men. "This is ridiculous."

Davis turned on her, but his words were for Hank. "I can't believe anyone in this town even speaks to this woman, especially you. Don't you know she's the reason your best friend died? I should know, I worked with both Warren and his partner. I heard him talk about you, and after Warren died, I heard his partner talk about what he'd done that night with Alex while her brother was out on a back road getting killed."

Hank pulled back as if he'd been slapped. "You're insane."

Davis smiled, sensing that his words hurt more than any punch could have. "Am I? Why don't you ask her what she was doing when her brother was shot? Or better yet, who she was with. If she hadn't begged Warren's partner to stay behind and play, Warren would have had backup that night. He wouldn't have been shot."

Davis pulled Tyler forward, no longer interested in dealing with the sheriff or the fire chief. He knew his words had wounded them both. "I've waited three years to file a formal complaint against you, Sheriff." He said the last word as if it tasted dirty in his mouth. "I'll have your badge, McAllen, and there'll be an arrest warrant waiting for you, Matheson, when you finish with this fire. I wouldn't be surprised if the folks in Harmony don't run you both out of town."

Pushing Tyler down two steps, Trooper Davis froze as the major stepped forward and dumped the bag of toys out on the ground. "Interesting things for a man to steal," she said in her calm way. "Toys and a small bag of medicine."

Alex watched confusion cloud Davis's face. For the first time, he seemed to question his logic.

"You're arresting a man for saving a child's life." Major Cummings straightened to all of five feet two. "If you don't remove those handcuffs, I'll see that you not only are fired, but are also sued for every dime you have in retirement."

Alex swore the major smiled before she gave Davis his only out. "Now, Trooper, I suggest you get back to the roadblock and stay there. Sheriff McAllen will handle everything here without your assistance."

Davis growled. He could fight one of them, maybe two, but apparently they had decided to gang up on him. He jerked the handcuffs off Tyler. "You're right. We've got bigger problems than petty theft to deal with."

He was gone before Alex could think of anything to say. She'd always thought she was a good sheriff, able to handle anything, but she'd just witnessed a master at work. She had a feeling Katherine Cummings could stand down an army and win.

Major Cummings picked up the toys as Hank helped Tyler to the cruiser. When she finished her simple task, she said as calmly as a den mother, "Now, we get back to the crisis at hand. Sheriff, if you'll take that poor man to the hospital, then drop the child off somewhere safe, I'll go back to the fire with the chief and keep you posted."

"Chief," the major said to Hank, "we've got a fire to put out. Set all else aside."

He nodded once and stormed back to his truck without looking at Alex.

Katherine hurried to climb in before he drove back to the cloud of smoke at the same speed at which he'd driven home only minutes before.

Chapter 45

REAGAN WOKE TO SOMEONE POUNDING ON THE front door. She slipped on her jeans, tucked in the T-shirt she'd been sleeping in, and ran down the stairs.

Uncle Jeremiah was already there and fully dressed.

Noah stood on the porch, looking only slightly better than he had the day before. He still had bandages and bruises every-where.

"This ain't the hospital, son," Jeremiah said. "I think you came to the wrong place."

Reagan moved around her uncle, who seemed to think at eighty-six he should start his comedy career. "What is it, Preacher? Noah wouldn't be here if it weren't something very important."

"The fire is spreading this way," he said. "I came to warn you. You need to get out."

"I'm not leaving my land," Jeremiah said, and turned back toward the kitchen.

"That's why I'm here," Noah said. "I knew you wouldn't listen to anyone."

Jeremiah turned back. "And you thought I'd listen to you, kid?"

Noah shook his head. "No. I came to get Rea out. I can't stop you from staying, but she needs to be somewhere safe."

She looked from Noah to Jeremiah. "I'm staying with my uncle."

"No, you're not," said both men at the same time.

"I'm not leaving this land." She widened her stance, as though she were willing to fight them both. "I stay and fight. Tell me what to do."

Jeremiah almost smiled. "That's right. Trumans stay and fight, no matter what comes." He'd never tried to tell her what to do and he wouldn't start now.

Noah took a long breath. "Then it's

settled. When the fires come, I'll be standing right here beside the two most stubborn people in the world."

Jeremiah shook his head. "We're not much of an army. An old man, a busted-up kid, and a girl. If I was the fire, I'd be real scared about now." He reached for his hat and stepped around Noah.

"Where are you going?" Reagan finally found her voice.

"I'm going to the orchard and turn on the water. I saw the smoke at dawn and got both windmills pumping. If the fire makes it this far, it'll try to burn down the orchard first. The irrigation system will have the ground good and wet in a few hours and if the fire comes too close, I'll pull the water tank down and flood the place for a hundred yards around."

They watched the old man climb into his little cart. The old dog hopped into the passenger seat and they started off down the path to the orchard.

Reagan looked at Noah. "What do we do, Preacher? There's got to be ways we can help besides just waiting."

"Turn on the water hoses. Wet down

everything you can." Noah stared at her. "Rea, if fire comes, it'll hit those old evergreens and tall brush between here and the road. If we stay too long, we may not be able to get out."

"I'm staying," she said. "What do we do next?"

He shook his head. "I don't know much. I only had a few days of training, and most of it was on when to get out."

They moved outside. "I guess we round up buckets," he said, "anything that will hold water, and old blankets. If we place them around the house and barn, maybe we can fight back when the grass catches."

Reagan looked around. "What about the trees?" The house was surrounded. Old elms dry from winter, brown vines of all kinds twisting around every pole and pipe, bushes years past needing to be trimmed. "If one of the trees falls on the house, it'll burn. With the trees blocking us in, not even the fire truck can get to us."

Noah stared at the farm, not seeing the peace of now, but the horror that might come. "We got to make a wider circle. Not just the house, but all these trees around here."

She looked at the hundred-year-old elms circling the house with sheds and barns underneath them. Uncle Jeremiah hadn't hauled off a piece of wood in thirty years. Even the new chicken coop had been built in front of the old one. "What do we do?" she whispered, realizing she was standing in the center of what had the makings of a huge bonfire.

"I'm in no shape to hoe and we don't have a tractor. I'm still thinking we leave."

"We do have a tractor, several. Can you drive one?"

He nodded. "Easier than I can hoe or fight grass fires."

She helped him back into his truck and they drove behind the house, where Jeremiah kept his prized collection hidden away in a barn. Reagan didn't have time to think about how the old man was going to react. "The keys are in the few that take keys. Pick which one you think will do the job and I'll help you guide it through the doors."

Noah moved around them. "These are beautiful."

"Pick one!"

Minutes later, they were turning over dirt in a wide row around the barn and house.

Reagan rode with him, helping him with the gears as he drove one-handed and held his side with the other. If he was in pain, he never commented on it.

One by one they circled the groupings of trees that had been planted by Trumans years ago. The dirt row they made scarred the earth. Reagan fought back tears, realizing that tomorrow morning, if there was a tomorrow morning at this place, Uncle Jeremiah wouldn't be able to look out at this land and see it wild and untamed as his grandfather had. But, she reasoned, he'd have a porch to sit on.

When the grounds around the house had five feet of dirt around it, Noah used another tractor to dig a trench and Reagan began filling it with water. The place was starting to look like a fortress surrounded by a tiny moat.

"Should we go check on Uncle Jeremiah?" She could see the line of trees that ran along the boundary of Truman land and Matheson land. He might not care about anything but the orchard, but Reagan loved it all. Every inch. "Do you think he's all right?"

Noah shook his head. "He's where he wants to be. I don't think anything has ever mattered to him besides that orchard. He's got the cart. If fire takes the trees, he'll make it back here."

Chapter 46

HANK FELT NOTHING BUT THE DULL ACHE OF numbness as he worked. He told himself to keep his thoughts on the fire and what to do next and not let any emotions about anything else surface.

His land was burning as he watched. His niece could have died if she'd gone much longer without her medicine. Tyler almost got killed trying to save her, and at some point Trooper Davis would probably return the punch Hank had given him, plus some, even if he didn't carry through on arresting Hank for assaulting an officer of the law.

Hank couldn't, wouldn't think of any of that. He had a fire to fight. He planned to stay on point until he collapsed with exhaustion and they had to carry him off. Maybe then, he could sleep and forget the ugly things Davis had said about Alex. Maybe he could get the hurt in her eyes out of his mind.

As Hank worked, the memories of his best friend came back. He could not remember a time when he hadn't known Warren McAllen. They must have been in the church nursery together, probably fighting over the same toy. Hank remembered the summers spent riding horses and swimming. And then the college days when they roomed together and fought over almost every girl either of them dated. The hours they'd spent talking about their dreams and the problems at home. Warren had been the only person he'd ever totally trusted. Hank's father was dead; his mother was always preoccupied with her work. Warren's parents fought, and his dad spent most of his life on the road. As boys, they'd had each other to depend on. As men, neither ever doubted the other would be there when needed. Sometimes Hank swore he

could still see Warren standing in his doorway holding two longnecks and asking if
Hank had time to talk. Problems with work,
or women, or family were shared, if not
solved.

He'd never had a better friend than Warren. Letting him go was the hardest thing
Hank had ever had to do. If he could have
traded his life for Warren's that night on
the bloody road, he would have.

Don't think, Hank almost screamed. *Just
fight the fire. Don't think.*

He was barely aware of a hand patting
him on the arm.

"Hank," Bob McNabb yelled over all the
noise. "The major wants to see you."

Hank nodded and moved back away
from the fire. He felt stiff, as if he'd turned
into a tin man from the hours spent in the
heat. He hurt in so many places they'd all
blended together in a dull throbbing he
barely noticed.

He grabbed a bottle of water and moved
to where she'd set up a table out of everyone's way.

Major Katherine Cummings looked up
from a chart she'd been studying. "Chief,"
she said.

"Major," he answered. "Don't try telling me to stop."

She smiled. "I won't waste my time. I just wanted to tell you that it looks like we're finally winning. Unless the wind kicks up before three, we may have this fire under control by then. I've been in touch with the National Weather Bureau, and they predict a relatively calm day with a slight chance of rain. That may be the break we need."

Hank tried to relax the knots in his shoulders. "How much of my place will we lose by then?"

"Half the grass and fences. One barn. All the trees along the breaks to the north. But we saved the house and grounds, thanks to your foresight."

"Half," he said, thinking that he was barely keeping the place going when he had all his land. He'd have to buy feed to cover the grass he lost. With the price of cattle, he'd be lucky if he could hold out the winter.

Any other time the news would have buckled his legs, but now it hardly registered.

"You've been up and fighting thirty hours, Hank," she said.

JODI THOMAS

He didn't want to be told to quit. That word had never worked for him. "How's Tyler Wright?"

"Tyler?"

"The man who saved Saralynn. Alex should have reported in by now. Is he all right?"

Katherine frowned. "I haven't heard."

"You know him?" Hank asked.

"No." She hesitated, as if trying to put a puzzle together but the pieces wouldn't fit. "I know a different Tyler. A shy gentleman."

She looked down, and he was surprised to see her cheeks reddening as if she'd said more than she'd intended.

Hank shrugged. "Beneath all that mud and blood was a knight, Major Cummings. A true knight. He very well may have saved my niece's life."

"If you say so," she answered. "All I saw was the mud and blood and . . ." She smiled and added, "The way your niece held on to that filthy man's neck. I knew the minute I looked at her that she was not being kidnapped."

Two more trucks from counties fifty miles away pulled up, and men moved in to relieve exhausted fighters.

"I can take over here for one hour. You've already sent the original teams home to rest." She glanced at his house in the distance. "Go take a shower and eat something; you'll feel better. We're holding the line here."

Hank had finally reached the point where he was too tired to argue. She was right; with the new men, she could hold the line. He tossed his gloves in the back of his truck and drove across dried grass toward home.

Five minutes later, he climbed the outside stairs to his rooms, stripping off clothes as he climbed. By the time he reached his bathroom, all he had left to pull off was his jeans, and then without hesitating, he stepped into a cool shower.

The steady stream of water had washed away all thought when he heard someone call his name. For a moment, he just stood beneath the water, unwilling to step out. Then he flipped the shower off and grabbed a towel as he opened the shower door.

Alex was standing at his bathroom door staring at him.

Hank didn't bother to cover up. She'd

seen all of him anyway. "What do you want?"

"The major said you wanted to know about Tyler."

Hank dried off, waiting for her to speak or leave. He didn't much care which. "What about him?"

"The hospital put three stitches along his hairline where Davis slammed him into the concrete, and then they doctored a dozen deep scratches that will heal without stitches. He's going to be fine."

"Good. I'm glad you got there in time to stop Davis. If I'd been alone he probably would have shot me." Hank couldn't believe he was talking to her as if nothing had happened. Maybe they were just both pretending Davis hadn't made the comment about it being her fault Warren died.

He pulled on his underwear, ending her peep show.

"Katherine deserves the credit for saving you. It was funny . . . all the way to the hospital, Saralynn slept and Tyler didn't say a word until we were checking in at the desk. At that point, he asked me what the hazel-eyed lady's name was. When I said

Katherine, he looked so sad, like something had just died."

"Did he know her?" Hank pulled on a pair of clean jeans and pushed Alex out of the way so he could grab a shirt from a drawer.

She followed. "I asked him that, and he said no."

That was it, they'd both run out of anything to say. He stood holding his shirt. She stood fighting back tears, her arms crossed as if holding the world at bay.

He swore and tossed his shirt on the bed. "Come here," he ordered.

"Why? So you can hit me? So you can tell me how much you hate me?"

"Come over here." Hank felt like yelling, but he kept his voice low. "I've been trying to get close to you for years, but this time, Alexandra, you're going to have to make a move in my direction."

She took a step, and he saw a touch of fear blended with uncertainty in her eyes. She'd always drawn off his strength, even when they wouldn't talk about it. Now, he needed to draw off her.

Like he knew she would, she stood so

close to him he could feel her breathe. The nearness of her made all the tension in his body slip away. When had it happened? When had he stopped being her rock and she had become his?

He slowly raised his hands and moved them along her arms, tightly folded across her chest. He took her wrists in his hands and pulled them until she gave way and her arms fell to her sides.

Then he wrapped his arms around her and drew her against him the way he'd always wanted to hold her.

She fought for a moment, stiffened as if to rebel, but she'd come to him. She'd crossed the room and he wasn't going to let her push away this time.

"Relax. I'm not going to hurt you and you know it." He kissed her hair. "Relax, baby."

She slowly melted against him, raising her arms to rest them on his shoulders. When she swayed against him, he released his hold and moved his hands to cup her face, forcing her to look at him, hating the tears he saw in her blue eyes.

"Let's get one thing straight right now, McAllen," he started, and felt her try to tug away. He didn't let go. This time he wasn't letting go.

"I don't give a damn what Davis said. I know you would never hurt your brother intentionally." He kissed her forehead. "And you should know that I'd know that."

He kissed her full on the mouth, hard and completely like he'd wanted to for years. He felt passion shatter in his arms and flood over them both.

When he broke the kiss, she whispered, "It was my fault . . . I should have . . ."

He kissed her until she gave up trying to talk, then whispered in her ear while she caught her breath. "I don't want to talk, baby. I just want to be with you."

She wrapped her arms around him so tight he could barely breathe as he lifted her up and walked toward the bed. "We've only got a little while. I don't need sleep or food. I just need to hold you."

And then his wild and strong Alex did something he'd never seen her do, not even when she was a child.

She cried and he held her tight.

Chapter 47

TYLER WRIGHT WAITED IN THE HOSPITAL ROOM for Willamina to bring him some clothes. He refused to walk out of the hospital looking like he'd been in a bar fight with a mud monster.

He also refused to stand up, knowing full well that the hospital gown he had on did not meet in the back. The nurse had come in twice to tell him that he could go, but he'd wait for his clothes.

He tried to piece together everything that had happened this morning from the time he escaped out of the sheriff's office. It all seemed like one of those late-night

movies people watch but can never remember the name of at dawn. He'd never
done anything wild in his life . . . until this
morning. His rap sheet was probably a full
page by now. Breaking and entering.
Speeding. Resisting arrest.

And in the mix of everything, he'd seen
a woman with hazel eyes. Alex said her
name was Katherine, but Tyler decided
he'd misunderstood. Maybe at that low
point in his life he just wanted his Katherine to be there. A woman he talked with on
the Internet would not simply appear in his
world at a low point. His Kate couldn't be
that Katherine.

The nurse brought him in a hanging
clothes bag and announced that the woman
who delivered them said she didn't have
time to wait, this was her shopping day. Tyler wasn't surprised. He'd bought Willamina
the little Saturn five years ago and she'd yet
to let him ride in it.

Tyler called one of the men who worked
for him to come over and pick him up, then
hurried to the bathroom to dress.

A few minutes later when he walked out
to the black Cadillac, he looked and felt
almost back to normal, even though he

hadn't had a proper bath and a huge Band-Aid covered his forehead.

He stopped off for two double-meat cheeseburgers and fries before going home and straight to his study. He pulled up his e-mails. None from Katherine.

He typed a hello to her and ate one of the burgers while he waited. He checked again. No answer. He ate the other burger and all the fries and tried one more time.

When she didn't respond, he climbed the stairs to his room, locked the door, turned off the phone, and went to bed.

Eight hours later, after he'd taken a bath and redressed, he came back downstairs. His supper was cold, but waiting for him. Every lock was locked. Every light out.

Tyler discovered something. The world hadn't fallen apart when he took himself off call for a day. It had functioned just fine without him. Even the flower van had looked like it had been brought back from Hank's ranch, washed, and put back in place at the back door.

After checking his e-mail and finding nothing, Tyler did something he'd never done at night. He went for a walk.

Chapter 48

H<small>ANK</small> <small>LEFT</small> A<small>LEXANDRA</small> <small>ASLEEP</small> <small>ON</small> <small>HIS</small> <small>BED</small> <small>AS</small> he slipped from his room and went back to the fire. An hour hadn't been long enough to hold her, but it was a start.

He could feel change in the air even before he reached the fire trucks. The wind was still. The air not quite so dry and smoky. It was over, he thought. Finally, it was over.

Most of the firemen were still working, but a few were standing back, watching the monster die.

Hank stepped up beside the major. "You were right."

"I usually am, about work anyway." She

smiled. "That's why they pay me the big
bucks. Are you ready to go back to work?"

"Yes." He pulled on his gloves and
winked at her. "The hour's rest did won-
ders."

She smiled as if she understood. "I
hoped it might. Now you're back, I'm moving to the sheriff's office. I've decided to
camp there until this is over." She looked
like she felt sorry for him. "This isn't over.
You know that, don't you, Hank? Our
troublesome arsonist will strike again.
We've got to be ready. Twenty years in
this business has taught me a few things.
One is, when he hits again it will be harder
and faster. My guess is he's getting frustrated, and that will make him careless.
Likely he's taking this personal. We killed
his plan and now he's out for revenge."

Hank wanted to say he didn't know if his
team could take a stronger hit, but he'd
worry about that when the time came. She'd
been right about everything so far. He
knew she was right about this, too. "Revenge on who?"

"Who knows. You, the sheriff, the town.
We stopped his beautiful burn and he's
probably mad. He'll use his weapon of

choice to hit back. Our job now is to guess where, and maybe when, if we can."

"I'll meet you at the office as soon as I know this fire is out."

"I'll be waiting."

Hank turned back to the battleground. Black earth seemed to be everywhere. Fire still sparked in patches, but teams were moving across the land, putting them out one by one. Willie Davis was like a pup who'd been kept penned during the hunt and now could run free. He led the charge across the hot spots, yelling and running circles around the tired men.

Hank worked with them for an hour, then returned to the fire truck. "How's the fire on the north rim?"

Bob poked his head around the door. "They've got it contained, but it burned a few thousand acres of beautiful natural grasslands."

Hank shook his head. "You have to be born in Texas to see miles of nothing but grass as beautiful."

"Good news is when we get rain, it'll grow back."

"When," Hank echoed. "It's been so long since this county has seen rain, we'll probably all go outside and just stand in it once it comes. I think the rubber on my windshield wipers has fossilized."

Bob laughed. "My Stella says it's coming, she can feel it. She says it's a few days off, but it's coming."

Hank leaned against the truck, needing to talk to someone. "When this fire is over, we need to get the trucks serviced and ready to roll as fast as possible."

"I figured that," Bob said. "The last few fires have looked set. I'd be willing to bet a dollar that when we climb down in the canyon we'll find this one was, too. I don't know much about firebugs, but I watch a lot of shows and it seems to me they're kind of like serial killers; they keep going until they're caught."

Nodding agreement, Hank turned south and stared at the orchard a few feet beyond his fence line. He could barely make out the old man standing in the shade of the trees, watching.

Hank raised his hand in greeting. Jeremiah didn't return the wave. Hank didn't know whether Jeremiah didn't see him or still held a grudge against all Mathesons. Grinning, he thought of how his aunt still called the old man Dimples when she mentioned him.

As Hank walked back to help with the cleanup, he saw the circle around Harmony in his mind's eye. It was close to complete. The only spot left between here and the first fire would be either old Truman's place or a run-down trailer park built in the cottonwoods along a dried-up creek bed. The aluminum homes were scattered to within sight of town. If fire started in the brush and trees around the creek bed, it would move fast, burning homes and wood until it hit town.

On a hot day, in hot clothes, Hank felt the chill. If the arsonist wanted to make a big fire, maybe one that would do more damage than the canyon burn, he'd hit Truman's place next. Truman's people had never been much for ranching or farming, but they'd planted trees. Evergreens from the road to within a hundred yards of the house, apple trees along the fence line, pine and oak in groupings around barns and storage buildings. And hundred-year-old elms around the house. Hank had no idea what all Jeremiah stored out on his land, but he surrounded it with trees. A big burn there could take the fire right into town in one direction and take out the rest of Hank's grass in the other direction.

It the arsonist hit Truman's place, it could turn into a nightmare.

The sky was midnight blue and free of smoke by the time he made it to the sheriff's office.

At first, it seemed everything was back to normal. Dallas Logan stood in front of the counter complaining about her streetlight. The smell of burned coffee drifted from the break room. Andy manned the calls and looked like he might have gotten a few hours' sleep.

Then Hank saw the changes. Major Cummings had put two desks together at a right angle in a corner and appeared to be working on two computer systems at once. A highway patrolman sat in Irene's office, looking like he was fresh out of school. Trooper Davis's replacement, probably.

Hank thought for the hundredth time how hard it must be for Alex to deal with these men who wore the same uniform as her brother, but she'd done it if for no other reason than it was part of her job. He wondered if she had any idea how proud Warren would be of her.

A few reporters were still hanging around, waiting for the wrap-up story. It would be on the news at ten, which he planned to miss.

Alex crossed the room to greet him. When he met her eyes, he saw something he'd never seen before: a peace in her stare. No anger or worry or frustration, only peace. She was in the middle of the worst crisis to hit Harmony on her watch, but inside she'd changed. Without Davis, Hank might never have known the guilt she carried. If she'd said something about it, he could have told her three years ago that no one, including Warren, would have ever blamed her.

"How long did you sleep?" he asked as they walked toward the coffeepot in the break room. His hand brushed over hers when they reached for cups. The need to touch her was an ache he feared he'd never cure.

"Too long." She smiled. "Your bed's comfortable to sleep on."

"So am I."

She tilted her cup up to hide her smile. "I might test that theory one day, but right now we have a major staring at us."

He glanced around. Sure enough,

Katherine Cummings was waiting at Alex's door with a load of printouts.

As they moved toward her, Andy Daily left the dispatcher desk and hurried across the room, his pockets jingling with change. "Doesn't it feel good to have it all over, Chief?"

"Yeah," Hank answered, slowing down to talk to Andy.

"That was really exciting." Andy almost danced with energy. "I wish I could have been out fighting the fire more, but I was needed in here. I heard we got coverage of the fire all the way down to the Dallas stations. I thought about driving down one night just to buy a paper or two with *Harmony Fires* on the cover. The fire really put us on the map."

Andy drove the oldest Toyota pickup Hank had ever seen. He was surprised the piece of junk, which usually had one or two of Andy's broken washers or dryers rattling about in it, could make it ten miles out of town. He'd give it no chance of making the trip to Dallas.

Hank motioned for Alex and the major to go on in. "Thanks for all your help, Andy. We couldn't have done it without you." In truth, Andy was far better at talking than working, now being an example, but Hank figured the guy needed a pat on the back. Volunteers ask for nothing. A thank-you seemed little reward.

"I never saw anything like that fire." Andy shook as if with real fear. "It was like doomsday riding in on a cloud of black smoke and we were no more than toothpicks standing against the wind."

"You're not going to become a poet on me, Andy, are you?"

"No." He seemed to realize he might have gotten carried away a little. "I better get back to work. I got another hour before my shift is over."

Hank raised his cup in salute and watched the lonely man take his chair at the dispatcher desk. Andy was the kind of guy everyone knew, but few would call him a friend. The kind who joined the campus cleanup team in college, not to help but so he'd have an almost-gang of friends to hang out with.

Hank stepped in Alex's office and noticed that the sheriff and the major already had their heads together, talking. It had been his experience that when two women do such a thing, it's never good for the only man in the room.

Before they could outline all their plans to keep watch, Hank's phone rang. He saw his sister Liz's number and wondered if it was too late to tell Tyler to keep the phone.

"Excuse me," he said as he stepped out and flipped his cell on.

"Hank," Liz said, without waiting to hear him say hello. "Mother and Claire are both mad at me. It wasn't my fault Saralynn got left behind. My car was already full; what was I supposed to do, unpack? There was plenty of room with Mom and the aunts. I had no idea they were planning to leave so early, and Claire is her mother, she should have put her in a car before she drove off with the stupid paintings."

"Liz." Hank cut her off. "I'm mad at you, too. In fact I'm furious. So add me to your don't-call list." He hung up, remembering how it had felt to answer the radio at the fire site and hear his mother say they couldn't find Saralynn.

He wasn't surprised when Liz hit redial immediately. Hank let it ring. Liz was the youngest. When they'd been growing up, they'd always stopped when she needed to, eaten where she would eat the food, gone on vacation where she wanted to go. She'd been running the family since she'd been born, with no thought of anyone but herself. It was no wonder her husband divorced her. Hank wanted to divorce her and he was blood.

He wondered if the family could get together and all vote her off the ranch.

"Stop plotting the murder of your sister and get back in here." Alex's voice and hand pulled him through the office door.

"You overheard."

"Liz didn't mean to leave Saralynn. It was an accident. She just wasn't thinking."

Hank shook his head. "She doesn't want to work, or go to school, or help out around the house, or do anything. I think she's campaigning to be the family pet. She wants us to do everything for her, including taking her to get trimmed and bathed for ticks. I've had enough. I'm thinking of calling that bum of a husband she left and demanding he take her back."

"For a man who lives with so many women, you don't understand much. She's just looking for a hero to save her. Her husband must have refused to do that."

"Well, we'd better look in lockup for her next match, because any free man will run as soon as he talks to Liz for ten minutes."

"You'll see. One of these days she'll find a man who has problems bigger than what she thinks hers are. He'll save her by having her worry more about him than herself."

"Maybe." Hank shook his head. "But he'd have to be on trial for murder, find out he had cancer and a brain tumor the same day he was struck by lightning, and bankrupted to top her daily list of problems."

Alex laughed and tugged him back to the round table. They began going over every theory they could reason out about what might happen next. Two hours later, Hank walked across the street to the fire station and crashed.

Just before he closed his eyes, he looked out the window and saw the sheriff's office light burning bright. Alex and the major were still working.

HIS PHONE WOKE HIM THE NEXT MORNING AT dawn. He rolled out of bed and picked it up, mumbling that if it was Liz he would personally sign her up for the Coast Guard. They were a thousand miles from any ocean. That should be far enough away for her to live.

"Uncle Hank?"

"Yes, dear," he answered, trying to sound awake.

"Gram says I have to eat breakfast with them here at the bed-and-breakfast, but if I do I'll be late to school."

"I'll be there in ten minutes."

When he walked out of the fire station to his truck, he noticed both the major's rental car and Alex's Jeep still parked in the same spots they'd been in last night. Either they'd worked all night, or they were early risers. As soon as he got Saralynn to school, he'd drop by with a dozen doughnuts and see if they'd made any progress.

Thank goodness Andy Daily's Toyota, with broken washers in the back, was gone. It always junked up the parking lot, plus if Andy was still there, he would eat half of any box of doughnuts Hank took in. The man had no life other than the fire-house and the desk in dispatch. Most of his meals were passed to him from the drive-up windows in town.

Saralynn was waiting for Hank when he pulled up at the B&B. His mother and aunts

might love sleeping in the old home deco-
rated in antiques and plastic flowers, but
one look told him Saralynn hated it.

"When can we go back home?" was her
first question.

"A few days." Hank didn't want to admit
that he felt safer with them in town. "I
thought you girls might like a little holiday."

"You're kidding, Uncle Hank. There's a
wall of old hats in that place, and last night
the aunts kept me up laughing as they
tried on every one, twice. Can I sleep with
you at the station?"

"I wish you could, Princess. We need
someone who can cook around there."

They pulled into the diner parking lot
and he lifted her out.

"Will Sir Knight be here?"

"I don't think so," he said as he scanned
the windows and saw Tyler, wearing a hat,
sitting alone at a booth. "Correction, he's
here."

Saralynn was all smiles. When they
reached Tyler's table she insisted on giving him a kiss. When his hat fell off, she
had to kiss the Band-Aid over his stitches.
She told Edith that she planned to be a
nurse whose kisses could cure.

After she finally settled into eating her breakfast, Hank asked Tyler, "How are you?"

Tyler smiled, but his eyes looked tired and sad. "I'm fine. Lost contact with a friend yesterday, and that hurt more than my stitches."

"Anyone I'd know?"

Tyler just shook his head. "Just someone I was corresponding with. It's nothing. Any clues on who's setting the fires? Besides me, of course."

"Davis was a fool. He wasted good time going after you. He disappeared after the roadblock broke up. Word is he was called down to Austin to do some explaining. Alex said if he goes after me for slugging him, you can go after him for false arrest."

"I wouldn't do that," Tyler said. "I just want to forget the whole thing."

"I figured that, but he doesn't know it."

Tyler nodded. "Alex understands what really happened. Is she the one who turned him in?"

Hank shook his head. "The major did, and it wouldn't surprise me if she has the ear of all the top people down at the capital. She's quite a lady."

"I'm sorry I didn't get a chance to meet

her." Tyler's eyes were sad again. "I would have liked to talk to her."

Hank tried to cheer him up. "Good news about Willie; our youngest firefighter is becoming a star. He's now conducting interviews on grass fires, and one of the stations wants him to come in to do a series of shorts on fire safety. The kid's eating it up. They say he's got a face the camera loves. Who knows, he may give up firefighting and join the news team." Hank didn't add that the kid might be better at it. Willie tried hard and had all the excitement and enthusiasm in the world, but he lacked judgment.

Conversation stopped when the food arrived. With half his plate empty, Tyler finally broke the silence. "I want to thank you for standing solid behind me. The sheriff told me you fought to stop Davis even before I knew he was after me."

"That's what friends do," Hank said simply. "Just like you dropping everything and rushing to save Saralynn."

Tyler smiled. "You're right. That's what friends do."

Chapter 49

TWO DAYS AFTER THE FIRES WERE OUT, NOAH showed back up on Truman land. Most of the bandages and bruising from his bull ride were gone, but his movements were still slow.

Reagan feared that when he came over Uncle Jeremiah planned to let him have it for driving one of his tractors and plowing up good grassland when the fire never reached them. The old man had been complaining about the scarred earth for two days. When she saw Noah climb out of his truck, she knew Jeremiah was about to cause a great deal of trouble. By the time he got finished yelling at Noah, it would probably be another fifty years before the McAllens and Trumans would speak to one another.

Her uncle moved to the porch, widened his stance, and prepared to yell at the only friend she had.

She knew she had to do something or the two would say things they could never take back. Bonds and battles in this town went on for lifetimes.

Reagan picked up the hot chocolate pie she'd just made and ran out the side door. Just as Noah stepped on the first step of the porch, she threw the pie, plate and all, at his face.

It smacked flat in the middle of his smile and slid down his shirt.

Both men were so stunned, neither could say a word.

Reagan saw her chance. "Get off Truman land, Preacher. We don't want you here. You plowed up good land and almost ruined a tractor that belongs in a museum. My uncle and I hate you for what you did. We hate you!"

Jeremiah was so stunned by her outrage, he felt sorry for Noah. "Now settle down, Reagan," he yelled, as if they weren't standing five feet apart. "The boy was just doing what he thought was right. The grass will grow back, and I can fix the tractor good as new. I think you're way out of line here, kid."

Noah used one long finger to push a slice of pie off his cheek and into his mouth. "Fiery, isn't she, Mr. Truman. I've got a theory that it's because of all that red hair. Somehow it clogs up her brain."

Jeremiah stared at her. "I've been complaining for two days. I guess she took up the cause. As for red hair, mine was red until the day most of it fell out. Then, I swear what was left turned white with mourning that same day."

Noah laughed and stepped on the porch. "You got a towel I can borrow"—he ate another bite—"or a plate I can scrape this onto so I can finish eating?"

Reagan didn't like being ignored. "I thought I told you to get off my land."

Noah sat down in the green rocker. "I didn't come to see you, Rea. I came to see your uncle."

Reagan turned to Jeremiah. "Are you going to let him stay?"

"Of course. In fact, boy, you're welcome to stay for supper."

Noah smiled without giving Rea a glance. "Might as well. I've already had dessert, though. To tell the truth, things are crazy around my house. Mom's cooking and Dad is fixing things. I saw her give him a list of chores this morning, and he smiled. Can you imagine that?"

"Kicked once too often in the head during his rodeo days would be my guess." Jeremiah sat down beside Noah. "Is he acting loco? Bumping into walls. Talking to himself. Sleeping more than normal."

"He and Mom both are. They've been acting so strange, so often, I can't sleep at night."

Jeremiah, who had no knowledge of relationships, nodded as if he understood.

Reagan slipped into the house and grinned. She was brilliant. The two men were talking.

She could hear them as she checked on supper. Noah said he'd stopped by to tell Jeremiah that he saw Andy Daily pull off Lone Oak Road at the opening to Truman land when he was driving past.

Reagan moved to the window.

Noah saw her, winked, then continued talking to Jeremiah, "I slowed to a stop just past your turnoff and waited a minute, then turned on the dirt road just because I thought it odd that a guy hauling old laundry machines would be heading your way. It's not like there's anything else along the turnoff to your place."

Jeremiah leaned forward in his chair. "Is odd. Never seen Andy Daily on my land. Know who he is, though. I nodded at him a few times in town. He's the fellow with those two laundry places. There was an article about him in the paper a few years back. Something about making his living a quarter at a time."

"That's him." Preacher leaned closer. "I think he may be dumping old broken washers and dryers in that brush between the trees at the turnoff. He was acting real strange. When I turned in a few hundred feet behind him, he drove into the ditch like he was trying to hide from me. He got so far off that dirt you call a road, he almost disappeared in the trees. If he'd been coming to see you, he would have moved on. If he'd accidentally turned onto your road, he would have turned around and waved."

Jeremiah hollered for Reagan to wait on dinner a while. By the time she got out of the house, Preacher and Jeremiah were in the cart and heading toward Lone Oak Road.

She'd told Jeremiah the trees needed work for weeks. Old evergreens with dead branches on the ground caught every tumbleweed that blew close. Even Noah had mentioned that it was a real fire hazard. Now Andy Daily thought he could dump his trash in the pile of dead wood and brown branches.

The old dog whined beside her.

"Hate being left behind, do you, boy? So do I."

On a whim, she walked to Noah's truck, found the keys still in the ignition, and hopped in. The old dog barked and jumped in the back. They made it to the edge of the trees when she heard shouting.

Reagan jumped out and saw Jeremiah standing beside the cart, yelling, "Get off my land! This ain't the city dump, you fool."

The roar of an engine being pushed to the limit sounded, and she spotted Daily's Toyota parked in a ditch halfway between the road and the clearing. The man driving gunned it again, trying to get up the embankment. Something sloshed out of the washing machines in his truck bed, splashing over the ground.

Jeremiah yelled again as he backed toward the cart.

Reagan felt her blood chill. She couldn't see Jeremiah's features clearly, but she knew something was horribly wrong.

Suddenly, the old Toyota rolled backward and then shot forward in an all-out effort to make it up the embankment. Over the noise, Andy Daily yelled something that sounded like a curse.

She heard the roar of the engine, then saw a washing machine tumble out the back as the truck almost reached the chalky dirt road. The front of the truck bucked like a bronco and rolled, crashing back into the ditch along with the load of washing machines. Whatever liquid he carried inside the machines splashed out around the truck.

The smell of gasoline flavored the dry, warm air.

One blink later, fire shot from the ground, engulfing the truck in a ball as bright as fireworks.

Jeremiah jumped into the cart and pulled forward, but smoke and flames shot across the road before he disappeared.

Reagan thought she heard a cry, like a wild bird, then only the sound of a raging fire sweeping up the dried trees.

She started toward them, but fire seemed to be swinging in the branches. She could no longer see the cart, and she knew she couldn't drive into the black smoke that blocked the road. She was trapped.

Crying so hard she could barely see, Reagan turned the truck around and raced for the house. She ran to the water and turned it on, knowing that she only had minutes before the flames would reach her. The fire would take the trees, crawl across the prairie grass, and be at the plowed ground before help could get here from town.

Pulling the cell phone she'd bought yesterday from her pocket, Reagan dialed, then froze. The road was on fire. No one would get to her.

She was alone. If fire jumped the barrier Noah had plowed, she would have to fight it alone.

"Noah," she cried. Oh God, where was

Noah? Had he been in the cart? He had to be still in the cart. He was hurt. He wouldn't have gotten out. Pushing tears away, she whispered, "He's in the cart with Jeremiah and they're on the other side of the ball of fire." They had to be. She wouldn't think of any other possibility.

She ran around trying to wet everything she could as the sound of the raging flames grew louder. Forcing herself not to look toward the road, she filled the buckets still scattered about the yard. She soaked all the blankets she could find as she tried to remember what else Noah had told her to do.

The fire crackled and roared. The air grew thick with smoke, making her eyes water. Or maybe she was still crying. She no longer knew or cared.

The air grew warmer and wind whipped heat, like the first breath from a hot oven, in her face.

She checked the trench where the garden hose was running. It would never be full in time. She ran to the water tank. With fumbling fingers, she tied a hoe to a long rope and swung it over the top of the tank.

One. Two. Three times. No luck. The

hoe clanked against the side of the tank and fell to the ground.

How could she pull the tank down if she couldn't get a handle on the top? Something Preacher had said one night at the rodeo echoed in her mind. *Failure is not an option.* She tried again and again. The heat of the fire now radiated through her clothes. Pulling one of Jeremiah's old bandannas from the clothesline, she wet it and wrapped it around her head. She picked up the hoe and tried again.

On the sixth try, the hoe caught on something and she pulled.

Nothing happened. She pulled so hard she was airborne, but her weight wouldn't take the tank down. It was old and rusty and used only to irrigate the garden and water the trees around. But it was still stronger than she was.

Reagan looked down the lane to the road. The trees were all on fire, shooting flames into the sky that looked miles high. She could feel the heat of it blistering her face already. The black cloud on the ground that Noah had described was crawling toward her like hungry fingers. He'd said that from a distance, you couldn't see the flames on grass, all you see is a black cloud smoking its way across the ground.

"NO!" she screamed. "You can't have my home! I'm not giving it up."

Reagan pulled the rope once more, then swore. "Hopeless," she mumbled just as she saw the dog, still sitting in the pickup as if he wanted out of this place. Reagan ran for Noah's truck. She tied the end of the rope to the bumper and jumped in. When she gunned the engine and threw it into gear, the truck shot straight into the chicken coop, sending boards and chickens flying. It also tumbled the tank behind her.

The tank tilted in slow motion for a few seconds, and then a waterfall flowed down. Water hit the ground like a tidal wave, flooding everything.

Reagan lowered her head against the steering wheel. If the water didn't work, she'd lost. She'd lost everything.

Chapter 50

HANK HEARD THE ALARM SOUND A MOMENT before he saw a ball of fire shoot into the air from a couple of miles away.

They'd gone over what to do a dozen times, and he'd prepared every one of his men to respond quickly. The trucks were headed toward the fire before the siren stopped screaming, and he was dressed in his gear and running.

When Hank jumped in his truck to follow, Alex climbed in the other side.

He hit eighty before he glanced over and asked, "Why not your cruiser?"

"This thing can go more places faster and I'm going with you. The major will take care of setting up roadblocks, and we've already started calling in surrounding help if needed."

"But—"

Before he could say more, she added, "Noah called in the alarm. He was screaming so loud I could have probably heard him if I'd opened the window of my office. I could also hear the fire. He hung up before I could tell him to get away."

"He knows to get back. I drilled that in his head the first day he came to train."

They didn't say another word as they raced down Lone Oak Road. Smoke thickened like fog, and Hank slowed as he moved toward the bright lights of the fire trucks flashing like beacons.

When he pulled up beside the trucks, he saw that the old trees lining the lane to the Truman place were all ablaze. His men were everywhere, letting the trees burn, but putting out any sparks that flew off and threatened the grass on the other side of the road.

Alex saw only the little cart Truman always

drove around his place and her brother standing beside it. She jumped from the truck and ran toward him.

Hugging him wildly, she heard him groan. "You're killing me, Alex. I'm going to have bruises on top of bruises."

She pulled away as Hank reached them. "What happened, Noah?"

"We caught Andy Daily dumping a truck-load of old washers in the ditch along Truman's lane. They must have been filled with gas or something, because when his truck turned over trying to get out of the ditch, flames shot up like fireworks."

He looked at his sister. "The old man and I started toward Daily, but there was no way we could get to him. Jeremiah must have known we wouldn't have time to turn the cart around. He raced through the smoke to the road. Those trees shot up like huge matches. I swear, there was nothing we could have done for Andy."

Hank yelled over his shoulder as he moved toward his men. "Andy wasn't toss-ing old junk, he was setting a fire. He's our arsonist."

Alex had figured that out, too. Early this morning Major Cummings had reported that several of the closest fire departments didn't get the emergency signal until hours after the canyon fire started. Andy Daily had manned the phones that morning. He hadn't made the calls, even though he'd told the other dispatcher he would.

Alex radioed the major, filling in details as she patted her little brother. When she clicked off, Alex looked at Noah.

"Where's Truman?"

"He's over there yelling that the men should forget about the trees and go in to get Rea. She's at the house. Every fireman here has already told him it's impossible."

"Will the fire reach her?"

He shook his head. "I don't think so. She's got a plan. Truman even said he told her a story about how his grandmother survived a prairie fire once by climbing in the root cellar and putting wet blankets over her. I just hope the old guy remembered to show Rea where the root cellar is."

Alex made Noah sit down, then checked in again with the major. In what seemed like minutes they heard other sirens coming in. This time the calls went in immediately.

Clifton Creek and Bailee were already sending men with police escorts.

She walked beside Hank when he passed. He went to his truck to get extra gloves. She didn't speak; she just watched him. She needed to be near him.

Then he looked up at her, and for one moment she knew he was remembering their time together. "When this is over . . ."

"I'll be waiting," she answered, and then he was gone to do what had to be done and she stepped back into the role of sheriff.

By the time the fire began to crawl from the trees to the grass, a hundred men and six fire trucks stood by to fight. In an hour, there was nothing but smoke and ashes.

Hank loaded Alex, Noah, and Jeremiah into his truck and drove past the orchard, still standing. He crossed onto his land and stopped long enough to cut fence before he pulled around the apple trees and headed down the path toward Jeremiah's house. No one said anything, but they all let out a long breath when they made out the shadow of the house in the distance.

"Better fix that fence before fall," Jeremiah grumbled. "I don't want your cattle crossing onto my land and eating apples."

"I'll do that," Hank promised as he bumped his way over a plowed row and splattered mud for twenty feet when he pulled into the yard.

"Looks like it flooded," Noah said. "Where'd all this water come from?"

"She downed the tank." Jeremiah grinned. "That niece of mine is a smart girl."

Reagan stepped out of the house just as they reached the steps, and she was smothered in hugs.

Everyone talked at once. No one was listening, but Hank didn't think it mattered. He could feel a weight rising off his shoulders. It was over.

Jeremiah invited them in for supper, a slightly burned pot roast, but Hank and Alex begged off, knowing they still had a great deal of work to do.

As he circled Noah's truck, half buried in what looked like the remains of a chicken coop, Hank saw the boy lean down to hold Reagan, and he noticed her pull away. A strange reaction from a friend, he thought, but they were just kids; they'd have years to figure it out. Hell, he was still working on it.

Alex must have noticed it, too, because

she slid across the seat until their bodies touched from knee to shoulder. "I'm not an easy person to get along with," she whispered, "and I suspect I won't be easy to love."

"You're not telling me a thing I don't already know. I've loved you for years and I can testify it's not easy."

She kissed his neck, almost making him drive off the path. "My place when this is over?" she whispered.

"It may be late, but I'll be there. And this time, baby, we're not rushing anything. I'm taking all the time I need to show you how I feel about you."

The fire this woman was starting in him was a slow burn that would take days to put out . . . maybe even a lifetime.

He didn't touch her when they got out on Lone Oak Road. He didn't dare. He wasn't sure he could let her walk away if he did.

Chapter 51

WHEN ALEX GOT BACK TO HER OFFICE, THE major was packing up. "We got him," Alex said.

"The fire got him," the major corrected. "I'd been watching him for two days. I couldn't put my finger on it, but something wasn't right. I even ran a background check and only came up with one fact: He was bankrupt. But that wasn't enough."

"Why do you think he did it?" Alex asked.

"We'll probably never know. I had my eye on Brad Rister first, thinking with the divorce and getting kicked off the fire department team, he had nothing to lose."

She shrugged, silently admitting her first hunch was wrong. "Hank called in to say Brad was out with the others fighting tonight, and from the looks of it he was sober. Willie Davis loved the excitement too much and went a little crazy during the fires, so I watched him, too. Once I met his uncle, Trooper Davis, I figured crazy ran in his family."

Alex smiled. "You read people so well, you should move to Harmony."

"I've got my twenty years in, I just might. But to be honest, I'm not a great judge of people when they're not suspects at the scene. I can't seem to tell the good ones from the bad ones when it comes to me. All my life I keep finding a prince that turns into a toad when I kiss him. Several years ago I gave up and decided to just do my job. Know of any knights in shining armor?"

"Nope, but I'll keep my eyes open." Alex liked the major. She helped Katherine load all her computers into her rental car. "Where next?"

"I have to go to Washington for hearings, and no one knows how long those will take. I'd far rather be out in the field working than talking about it. Maybe I'll take some time off when I get back to Texas."

"Good idea." Alex hugged her, hoping that if the arson specialist were ever again to come to town it would be for a different reason.

After the major left, Alex looked over at the fire station and noticed that the trucks were still out. Which meant Hank was still at the site, probably waiting for everything to cool down so they could retrieve Andy's body or what was left of it.

She remembered something Andy had said one night as he manned the emergency calls. He'd said, "Life without thrills and danger isn't worth living. It's oxygen in my blood. I have to have it or I'll die."

Alex wished he'd found another way to get those thrills. In the end, he probably didn't want to hurt anyone. He was just after the buzz.

She stretched, realizing it was Saturday night and all she wanted to do was go home. The air was still tonight, and she thought she could smell rain in the wind.

Climbing into her Jeep, she took the long way home, wanting to avoid the mess on Lone Oak Road. She drove slowly, watching big white clouds roll across the evening sky. The country was so beautiful, it took her breath away sometimes. The openness of it. The way you felt everything around you was untouched.

A half hour later, she was in the shower when she heard someone call her name. Grabbing a towel, she stepped out, and there was Hank standing in her doorway making no attempt not to look.

Chapter 52

MONDAY MORNING NOAH, STILL PATCHED AND bruised, came back to school.

Reagan tried to act like she hadn't missed him terribly. Everyone wanted to talk to him. They wanted to relive his accident at the rodeo and hear all about how he saved the old Truman place from fire.

Noah "Preacher" McAllen was surrounded, and he loved every minute of it. She could almost see him famous, fighting off reporters and girls. Some people are born to ride fame. Whether he liked it or not, Noah would follow in his father's footsteps. He'd be a legend one day. The only question in her mind was, would she still be his friend?

The only time all morning she thought he noticed her was once in history class when he looked over his shoulder and winked at her. Other than that, he was in a crowd, and Reagan hated crowds.

At lunch, she thought she'd have time to talk to him, but when he walked out without his usual sandwich in one hand and drink in the other, she knew he was just stopping by to say hello before joining his friends.

"Busy?" he asked, propping up one long leg on her bench.

"Not very," she answered, telling herself she didn't care one way or the other if he stayed.

"Have time to come along with me? I got a strange text message from my sister this morning. She wants me to pick up food she ordered at the grocery and drive it all the way out to her place."

"She sick?"

"I don't know. I think maybe so. No one's seen or heard from her since Saturday night. She told me to leave the bags on the porch and don't bother to knock."

"She must be really sick."

"That's what I'm afraid of. My folks took off for parts unknown yesterday. If Alex is dying, I'm all she's got."

Reagan stood. "I'll help."

Fifteen minutes later, they had picked up the groceries and were pulling up in front of Alex's cabin. They eyed the huge black Dodge parked beside her little house.

"Good," Noah said. "Hank's here to help. He'll drag her to the doctor if she's bad off."

Noah climbed out of the pickup. "You better wait here in case she's got something contagious."

Reagan nodded. The last thing she wanted was to get sick. She'd spent all day yesterday talking Uncle Jeremiah into making some improvements around the place. He'd even said he'd paint the house. She noticed the boxes of spring flowers on the sheriff's porch and decided she'd talk her uncle into flowers as well.

Noah carried the bags of groceries to the door and walked into the cabin without bothering to knock. Two minutes later, he stormed back to the pickup and got in. Banged his head against the steering wheel several times, putting swear words together in such a mixed-up order they made no sense.

Reagan panicked. "What's wrong? Is she dying? Oh, no, she's not dead already. Oh, God."

"No," Noah looked up at her. "She's fine. So is the fire chief. But me, I'm double scarred for life. First I see my parents in bed and now I walk in on my sister and Hank Matheson. I'll probably be in therapy for years." He hit his head one more time for good measure. "I swear, I'm living in a porno movie."

Reagan laughed. "Did you give them the food?"

"Yeah, but they didn't look too interested. Both of them yelled at me, then forgot I was there by the time I reached the door. My sister makes those funny little sounds my mother does, and that is way more information than I need to know."

He started the truck and backed out to the road.

Reagan talked about everything she could think of except Alex and Hank, but Noah remained silent until he reached the parking lot. When she climbed out, he stayed in the pickup. "Tell everyone I'm too tired or that my side is hurting. I'm heading home."

Reagan thought he looked pitiful, but she couldn't tell if he was sick, tired, or hurt from banging his head. "Preacher, I won't tell anyone."

"I know, Rea. You're the one person I know that I can trust with just about any secret that comes along."

He drove off before she could respond. She felt sorry for him. They were within six months of the same age, but sometimes she swore she was a hundred years older than him. Reagan had a feeling she always would be.

That night after supper, she did her homework, then tried to call Noah on her cell. There was no answer. She thought of calling Alex and telling her to check up on him— after all, she was his sister—but Reagan figured Noah would get mad if she did anything like that. He'd probably gone home and gone to bed in a quiet house.

Uncle Jeremiah came in from working on the tractor they'd used to plow up his grass- land before the fires. He claimed Noah must have poured dirt into the engine.

He stopped in the kitchen for a drink of

water and watched as she picked up her
books. "You ever consider all McAllens
could be nuts?"

Reagan was tired of him complaining to
her about Noah. "Nope. It never crossed
my mind." She thought of adding that she
knew so few men who seemed sane that it
was hard to gauge normal.

"Well, you should think about it some,
since you got one hanging around here all
the time."

Reagan was tired. She'd spent all morning worrying about Noah not speaking to
her and all afternoon thinking about how he
trusted her with his secrets. Worrying about
him could turn into a full-time job if she
didn't watch it. "All right, Uncle, I'll consider
whether all McAllens are nuts tomorrow."

He frowned. "Might want to do it sooner
than that. There's one tied up out in the
drive."

"What?" The old man was making no
sense.

"When I came in from the shed, he was
sitting in the bed of his pickup. He asked
me to tie him up tight, and since I owed
him a favor, I did."

"Thanks," she said as her uncle poured

out the rest of his water and put the glass back in the cabinet, a practice Reagan hated. "I'll go see what he wants."

She walked out the back door. It took a minute for her eyes to adjust to the darkness, and then she moved to Noah's truck and leaned over to look in the bed. "You want to tell me what you think you're doing?"

He tugged on the ropes. "The old man did a great job of tying me up."

"Preacher, tell me."

He stared up at the full moon and said, "I think I got us figured out."

"There *is* no *us*."

"I know, and I think I know why. You keep thinking I'm going to turn into a werewolf or something and attack you. Every time I get within a foot of you, you jump. Well, I'm tied up, I can't hurt you, and I'm staying here all night to prove I won't change."

"Look"—Reagan climbed up and sat on the side—"maybe I just don't like being touched. Not by anyone."

"You didn't seem to mind it after the fire when Alex hugged you, and Jeremiah, and even Hank. It was only when *I* tried that you stepped away. Rea, do you have any idea how that makes me feel?"

"Why don't you go hug on one of the cheerleaders? They're all rounded and soft and I don't think they'd mind a bit."

Noah pulled against his ropes. "I don't want to go hug on anyone, Rea. I just don't want you to be afraid of me. What do I have to do to convince you that I'm never going to hurt you?"

She smiled. "You know, Preacher, I think you're doing it right now. You mind if I hang around and make sure no werewolf shows up?"

He didn't move. She slipped into the bed of the truck and stretched out a few inches from him. Not touching, but closer than she usually got to him.

"This blanket smells like a horse," she complained.

"That's who I borrowed it from. Put your head on my shoulder and I'll be your pillow."

She hesitated, than rolled closer and lowered her head against his shoulder. "Doesn't smell much better," she whispered.

He ignored her comment.

They lay watching the stars for a while before he whispered, "Any chance you'd kiss me?"

"No," she answered. "But, I might

snuggle a little. It's getting cold and I guess if you're tied, you'll be safe enough."

"I hadn't noticed the cold," he answered as she moved against him. After a while, he added, "You know, Rea, we're almost hugging."

She didn't answer.

"Rea?" He pushed at her head with his jaw.

She shifted, moving closer and turning her face up.

"Rea? Are you asleep?"

When she didn't move, he leaned over and kissed her lightly on the mouth. Then he tugged one hand free of the rope and pulled his jacket over them both.

He put his hand back inside the loop and turned his face toward hers. "You know, I lied, I do want something. I want you next to me." He kissed the top of her head. "I wish I could tell you how much I love your hair. I think it's really something."

She didn't move as she felt his breathing slow, and then she spread her hand out lightly over his chest and felt his heart. He was proving he could be trusted, and in a few years she'd tell him how much that meant to her.

Chapter 53

Rain

REAGAN WAS ALMOST ASLEEP WHEN A PLOP OF water hit her arm. Then another and another. All falling from hundreds of feet to land and splattering into tiny beads.

At first, she tried to ignore the drops, but Noah jerked awake beside her.

"Untie me, Rea, it's raining." He kicked at his bindings.

She laughed and shouted above the thunder. "What do you care if you get wet? You won't shrink."

"I might. Haven't seen rain in so long, I don't know what will happen." He lay flat as she untied his arms. "We might both shrink. I'd end up your size and you'd be about leprechaun height."

Scrambling, she pulled the ropes free, and they jumped from the truck, laughing. The downpour hit just as they reached the house. Sheets of rain blocked out everything beyond the porch.

He wrapped his arm around her shoulders and they watched the heavens open as they breathed in the fresh smell of a spring rain.

When it slowed, he tugged her a bit closer and lowered until their noses almost touched. "You okay with this?"

She was shaking, but she nodded and he closed the distance between them with a light kiss. He let her go and stared down at her. "Still okay?"

"Yes." His kiss hadn't brought back the nightmares she thought it would.

"Friends?"

"Friends," she answered.

He jumped off the porch and ran for his truck. "See you tomorrow, Truman."

"See you tomorrow, McAllen."

* * *

A FEW MILES DOWN THE ROAD, HANK LIFTED Alex from the bed and walked out of the cabin and into the rain.

She came awake squealing, then laughing when she realized they were standing nude in a downpour.

"Want to dance?" he asked.

"In the rain?" She laughed.

"No, not just the rain, forever." He offered his hand as if they were on the dance floor at Buffalo's.

She accepted his hand and his proposal and they danced.

HOURS EAST OF HARMONY, THE RAIN POUNDED down on the roof of Quartz Mountain Lodge beside a lake in southwest Oklahoma. The bar was empty except for one man who'd been there for a long while, holding a glass of wine he hadn't tasted.

Lightning flashed now and then across the lake, but Tyler Wright didn't turn and watch nature's show. He was busy tonight waiting.

In his imagination, he pictured Major Katherine Cummings walking up to his table and asking, "Is this seat taken?"

He'd move his wine aside and stand.

"No," he'd say. "I was saving it in case you came." Then he'd stare into her hazel eyes and offer his hand just as he'd done the first rainy night they'd met. "I'm Tyler Wright. I'm a funeral director in a small town called Harmony. I'd be very happy if you could join me."

He imagined her responding, "I'm Katherine Cummings, but you can call me Kate."

"Kate," he'd say, as if the word were a cherished gift. "Please, Kate, call me Ty, if you like."

He'd pull out her chair and she'd smile, teasing him. "Thank you, Sir Knight."

He'd act surprised. "I thought I'd scared you off forever that day after seeing me all muddy and bloody."

He couldn't think what would happen next. Maybe he'd kiss her? Maybe he'd suggest they step into the restaurant and have dinner. Then maybe they would walk along the covered paths outside and watch the rain sparkle across the water . . .

The waitress passed by his table again. She no longer asked if he wanted to order dinner. She just looked at him as if she felt sorry for him. She didn't know how lucky he was.

He was waiting for someone. He was waiting for Kate.

The storm grew louder and the only other guest in the bar called it a night.

When the manager circled by to tell him they were closing, Tyler stood, leaving his wine untouched. He hardly noticed the rain as he walked across the parking lot to his Cadillac.

The first Monday of next month he'd be back, and he'd wait again.

Chapter 54

REAGAN TRUMAN CLICKED ON HER FLASHLIGHT and walked out of her bedroom. The storm had knocked the electricity out again. She giggled. This place was spooky when there were no lights. Hell, she thought, it was spooky even in broad daylight. At least the rain was washing away the burned smells.

The faces of dead Trumans in the pictures along the walls were watchful as she moved downstairs.

Reagan flashed her light on each as she passed. The beam of the flashlight caught on something peeping out just behind one of the frames. She stopped and tugged a large yellowed envelope free and continued on down the hallway to the kitchen.

Uncle Jeremiah was already there, making coffee before he headed out to watch the dawn. He'd had to light a fire in an old potbellied stove that had probably sat in the corner since the house was built.

"It's raining," Reagan announced. "We can't go outside."

"I noticed," he said.

She grabbed a warm Coke and crawled into her chair. "Whose turn is it to make breakfast? I can't even remember."

"Then it's yours," he answered and sat across from her.

She shoved the envelope toward him. "I found this."

He turned his flashlight toward it but didn't reach for the envelope.

Reagan noticed the calendar on the wall. Ugly black Xs crossed out each day of the month that had passed. "You're marking off the days until I leave, aren't you?" It was a statement, not a question.

"Everybody leaves. I reckon you will, too."

She'd had enough. She stood, collected the cereal bowls, milk, and two boxes of cereal, then returned to the table. Without looking at him, she set breakfast down and reached for the calendar.

He didn't say a word as she rolled it up and tossed it on the fire inside the old stove. "I'm not leaving."

He filled his bowl and said without emotion, "Then I guess I'll quit counting."

She considered kissing his cheek and telling him she loved him, but he didn't need to hear the words any more than she needed to say them. They both knew. She was finally home and she wasn't going anywhere.

Halfway through her breakfast, she asked, "What's in the envelope?"

Jeremiah flipped it over. "My mom used to collect bonds. Put them behind every picture in the house during the war."

"You never cashed them in?"

He frowned. "Figured I would if I ever needed them. I even cashed one or two in a few years ago, but didn't see much fun in it."

"What did you use the money for?" she asked. Knowing him, the cash was stuffed somewhere.

"Built the shop."

She thought about it through the rest of the meal, then stated simply, "When it stops raining, we're going into town and putting all your collections of bonds in a safe-deposit box." If he'd built the shop for his collection with one or two bonds, no telling what a handful would be worth.

To her surprise, he didn't argue.

She waited a minute and then added, "Any questions?"

He raised an eyebrow. "How big is the box?"

THEY SPENT THE DAY CLEANING UP THE DRIVE between the house and the main road. People Reagan didn't even know came to help.

That night she was so tired, she tumbled into bed, but she couldn't stop smiling.

For a moment she thought of all the money from the bonds might buy, and then she realized she had everything she'd ever needed or wanted right here, right now.

"Home," she whispered, liking the sound of the word. She was finally home.